MOMENT OF TRUTH

As Lang looked away for a second, the Ranger stepped in quick and swung the rifle butt across his jaw. Lang went sideways to the ground. The gun flew from his hand and landed at Adele's feet. She picked it up as the Ranger stood over Lang and stuck the tip of the rifle barrel down behind Lang's ear. Lang tried to raise his head. But Sam shoved it down with the rifle barrel.

"Game's over, Cisco," he said. "Lie still or I'll give you another one."

Looking sidelong through swirling eyes, Cisco saw the gun in Adele's hand. "Sh-shoot him, Adele," he managed to say.

Sam looked around and saw her gripping the gun tight, the barrel pointed loosely at him. He gave her a questioning look.

"Decide here and now, ma'am," he said firmly, stepping back from Lang lying on the ground, seeing the downed outlaw wasn't going to do anything for a while. "The gun's in your hand."

"Gun-smoked believability . . . a hard hand to beat."—Terry Johnson

HIGH WILD DESERT

Ralph Cotton

BERKLEY

New York

BERKLEY
An imprint of Penguin Random House LLC
penguinrandomhouse.com

ISBN: 9780451239778

Signet mass-market edition / April 2013
Berkley mass-market edition / May 2023

Printed in the United States of America
3 5 7 9 11 12 10 8 6 4

For Mary Lynn . . . of course

PART 1

Chapter 1

Painted Desert, Badlands Territory

Arizona Territory Ranger Sam Burrack stepped down from his saddle on the dusty street of Humbly and reined his bear-paw Appaloosa, Black Pot, to an iron hitch rail. Beside his dust-streaked stallion, he reined up a spindly-legged roan gelding carrying the body of Ernest Trulock tied down across its back. Next to the roan, he tied a black-maned bay. Its rider, Harvey "Cisco" Lang, stepped down and took an awkward stance, his hands cuffed in front of him, a third cuff at the end of a two-foot chain holding him fastened to his saddle horn.

"This is a hell of a rig you've invented here, Ranger," Lang said, shaking the chain to his cuffs. "Are you expecting to make any money on it?"

"I didn't invent it," Sam replied. "It came from a blacksmith at the Ranger outpost." Dismissing the matter, he said, "Where will I find Rastatler?"

Lang shrugged and looked all around the half-abandoned high desert town.

"Beats me," he said. Then he said, "What that blacksmith don't know won't hurt him, I don't reckon. Like as not, you could claim these cuffs

as your own invention, and by the time news of
it got back to him, you'd be a rich man."

The Ranger looked back and forth warily
along the dusty street. Along the hill line stretch-
ing north to south beyond town, he saw no rise
of trail dust, no sign of anybody fleeing.

"That wouldn't be honest," he replied.

"Honest . . . ? You got me there," said Lang, a
slight smile showing through his black, dust-
caked beard stubble. "Of course, if you're that
particular you could always give him a little
something to settle him up. See what I'm saying?"

"Yeah, I hear you, Cisco," Sam said quietly, his
eyes pulling back into Humbly, scanning the
rooflines, the doorways, the alleys. Lang hadn't
said three words all morning. Now that they
were in Humbly, where Lang had assured him
Sheldon Rastatler would be hiding out, the outlaw couldn't seem to shut himself up.

The Ranger drew his Winchester from its saddle boot and wiped dust off its butt. He stepped
over in front of Lang, unlocked the cuff from the
saddle horn, pulled Lang over and fastened the
third cuff to the iron hitch rail.

"Hell, Ranger," said Lang, "you didn't have to
do that. We've been getting along well. I'm not
going anywhere. Don't you trust me?"

Sam just looked at him.

"What I mean is," Lang said, "I'm not going to
try anything foolish. I've learned my lesson. All
I want to do is get my time done at Yuma and get
myself started in a new life. I'm what you'd call a
changed man—*rehabilitated*, if you will. Far as
I'm concerned, my days of outlawry and unto-
ward shenanigans are over and I'm—"

His words of contrition stopped short as a

voice called out from farther down the empty street.

"Ranger, it's me, Sheldon Rastatler," a man in weathered trail clothes and a riding duster called out from beneath the wide brim of a tall-crowned Stetson hat. "I know you're dogging me. I won't have it." As he spoke he stepped sideways slowly until he stood in the middle of the street.

"Shoot him, Shel! Kill him!" Lang shouted. "Get me freed up here, pard!"

"You brought him here, Cisco, you rotten cur," the outlaw shouted out in reply. "I ought to kill you first."

"I had no choice, Shel," Lang shouted. "He's beat me, pistol-whipped me, threatened to kill me, kill my horse!"

The Ranger poked him a sharp blow to the ribs with the tip of his Winchester.

"Shut up, Lang," Sam said. "I can't even hear what the man's trying to say."

Lang grunted and fell silent, his cuffed hands clutching his pained ribs.

"Poke him again, Ranger," said Rastatler from fifty feet away, his duster pulled back behind a big holstered Remington on his right side. "Shoot the fool in the head for all I care."

"You don't mean that, Sheldon," Lang called out in a strained voice. "We've been pals too many years."

"Oh, I mean it," said Rastatler. "Fact is, I always figured you'd jackpot me and ol' Trulock. I so much as told him so. Watch Cisco Lang like a hawk—don't turn your back on him, I always said. He wouldn't listen. Now look at him." He gave a nod toward the dust-covered body sprawled across the horse at the hitch rail.

"I didn't get him killed, Sheldon," said Lang. "It was his own stupidity that caused him to look around just because someone called out his name. What kind of fool looks around like that?"

As the two outlaws argued, Sam had stepped sidelong away from the horses and moved out to the middle of the street, his Winchester cocked and in his hands.

"It makes no difference to me," said Rastatler. "Soon as this law dog's lying dead on the ground, look for me to come over there and gut you with my spurs for siccing him on me, knowing my name's high up on his wanted list." He looked away from Lang, back to the Ranger.

"Let me make it clear before we start," the Ranger said. "Your name's not on my list at all. I came after the three of you because I was nearby when you robbed the mercantile in Farm Town Settlement."

"Not on the list?" said Rastatler. He sounded disappointed, taken aback.

"No," said the Ranger.

"Then why'd you kill Trulock?" Rastatler asked.

"He threw down on me," said the Ranger in a firm tone, "the same way you're about to do."

"And we never were on your list?" Rastatler said, seeming to have a hard time dealing with the matter. Being on the Ranger's list had become a dark and short-lived honor to many of the thieves, killers, lowlifes and swindlers in the Four Corners area of the territory badlands.

"I once rode with the Painted Gang," Rastatler said, as if that fact might boost his suddenly deflated image.

"Good for you," said the Ranger. "But so has

every other gunman who's wandered in this Painted Desert. Yuma Prison is full of the Painted Gang. Some have learned to live like civilized human beings, under their circumstances."

"Yeah?" said Rastatler. "How about Old Byron Tappet? Is he still wilder than a three-eyed—"

"My point is," Sam said, cutting his conversation short, "you can give yourself up, like your pard here."

"This rotten bucket of slop is no pard of mine, Ranger," said Rastatler.

At the hitch rail, Lang gave a flat smile and waved his cuffed hands.

"I'm saying you don't have to die here in Humbly," Sam said, trying to get him to forgo his anger at Lang and focus on the matter at hand.

"I'll go to hell before I give myself up," said Rastatler. "I ain't spending my life breaking rocks beside that son of a—" He grabbed the butt of the Remington and started to swing the gun up into play.

A shot from the Ranger's Winchester hit him dead center, lifted him backward off the ground and turned him up in a complete back flip, like some acrobatic performer. The outlaw hit the ground face-first and trembled for a second. Then his life seemed to drain down out of him into the arid dirt.

The Ranger walked forward, keeping an eye on the roofline, levering a fresh round into the rifle chamber.

"If I was you, I'd shoot him again," Lang called out from his spot at the hitch rail. "But that's just me, Ranger, *conscientious* to a fault—a trait you might consider mentioning to the prison board, on my behalf."

*I don't know how I'm going to put up with this
one all the way to Yuma,* Sam thought, walking a
few steps along the street of the dusty, near-
abandoned town. He stopped when he saw a
fresh familiar set of boot prints appear out of an
alleyway and circle around to the front door of a
small saloon. Fresh, because the wind and passing sagebrush had not yet swept away the dis-
tinct edges of the soles. Familiar, because he'd
seen this stride pattern in a clearing along his
trail only the day before.

Whoever wore these boots had a slight pigeon-
toed gate—bowlegged, no doubt, he told himself, knowing that to usually be the case. Rifle
ready, he stepped onto a dusty boardwalk. Making no attempt to quiet his footsteps on the rough
planks, he walked straight and steadily toward
a pair of weathered batwing doors. But instead
of walking inside, he quickly turned, pressed his
back to the wall beside the doors, reached out
and shoved them open with his rifle barrel.

From the saloon's dark interior, three pistol
shots roared; bullets tore through the doors in a
spray of splinters. Following the sound and the
flash of fire, the Ranger swung around to his left,
took quick aim above the hard-swinging door
and fired at the figure standing crouched in front
of the bar.

The bullet hit its target and hurled the gunman backward against the bar. The man's pistol
roared again, but this time only in reflex, his finger squeezing the trigger as he melted straight
down to the floor and fell face-forward.

"Jesus, Ranger!" Lang shouted from down the
street at the hitch rail. "Are you going to kill
everybody!"

Without answering, Sam gave him a hard stare and levered another round into his Winchester.

Only one set of boot prints . . . , he told himself, but for all he knew someone could have come in through the rear door.

"Anybody who wants to come out of there alive better answer up now," he called out, taking the same position against the wall beside the doors.

"The man you shot is dead," a woman's voice replied. "I'm the only one here alive."

"What are you doing in there?" Sam asked.

"I'm the owner of the Desert Inn," came her reply.

"Who is he?" Sam called out.

"He *was* Bertrim Moore, or so he said," the woman replied, sounding closer to the door. "Can I come out? There's blood all over everything in here. I'm getting the willies."

"Come on out," Sam said. But he stayed in place until she walked out the door and looked up and down the street, her hands raised chest high. "Where is he?" she murmured to herself.

"I'm here, ma'am," Sam said quietly behind her, not wanting to startle her.

The woman made a gasp of surprise and turned quickly. She looked him up and down.

"My goodness, Marshal!" she said. "I'm guessing you don't get caught unawares much."

"I try not to," Sam said. "It's Ranger, ma'am," he added, correcting her. "Arizona Territory Ranger Samuel Burrack." As he spoke, he raised his hand from his rifle long enough to touch his hat respectfully. "You can lower your arms," he added.

"Well, thank you, Ranger," the woman said. She folded her arms in front of her in a stately pose. "I'm Miss Adele . . . Adele Simpson. This is my place, such as it is these days." She gestured a nod toward the inside of the saloon.

Sam looked closely at her. She was a tall, strong-looking woman, busty, wearing a dust-streaked but clearly expensive-looking dress. Over the full-skirted dress she wore a baggy, battered denim miner's coat. A slouch hat hung from a rawhide string behind her shoulders. Beneath the ground-level hem of her dress, Sam saw the scuffed toes of what looked to be black English-style riding boots.

"Would you like to gather your prisoner and come inside, Ranger Burrack?" she asked, gesturing toward Lang, who stood grinning at the hitch rail. "Maybe the two of you will drag Moore out and bury him somewhere?"

"Yes, ma'am," Sam said. "We can do that, straightaway." He looked back and forth along the empty street, seeing a ball of sage roll and bounce out of sight on a passing gust of wind. "Is there a restaurant left here, and a livery?"

"There's a barn out back," she said. "Nobody's tending it, though. You'll find some hay, maybe some grain left."

"Good," said Sam. "What about a place to eat? After we bury the deceased, that is?"

The woman just looked at him as she unfolded her arms and placed one hand on her hip.

"I hear you, Ranger," she said in a flat tone. "I'll fire up the stove while you get the *deceased* underground." She looked down the street at Lang. "Maybe he can wash out some of the blood and guts when he's finished eating. I saw a couple of miners headed this way down the high trail a while ago. That could mean more miners on their way." She gave a tired smile. "I sure need the business."

"I'm sure he'll be happy to clean up for you, ma'am," Sam said, cradling his rifle in the crook of his arm.

"Moore's black barb is tied out back," the woman said. "Any objections to me keeping him?"

"No, ma'am," Sam said. "Better you keep him than for me to turn him loose. These wild herds up here can get real testy with newcomers."

"Thank you, Ranger," Miss Adele said. "Go get your prisoner. I'll kindle the stove." She stopped as if in afterthought. "Who is your prisoner anyway?"

"Harvey Lang, ma'am," said Sam. "Do you know him?"

"*Cisco* Lang, sure, I know him," she said, an unpleasant look coming to her face. "Running a saloon like the Desert Inn, I expect I know every worthless reptile who's ever trekked the high desert." She gave a shrug. "But that's all right, I'll kindle the stove anyway. Even a reptile has to eat."

Chapter 2

When the Ranger and Harvey Lang had finished digging three shallow graves in the hard ground of a weedy cemetery, they dragged Sheldon Rastatler's body over from the street and Bertrim Moore's body from the saloon and dropped Ernest Trulock's body down from his horse. Trulock's corpse had stiffened to the shape of a horseshoe, and Harvey Lang had to walk across it like a freshly unrolled rug to get it lying prone in its grave.

Once Trulock's body had been straightened, they laid the three bodies in their graves and filled the dirt in over them. When they were finished, Sam watched as Lang walked over to an older grave, placed his cuffed hands on an iron grave marker and started to rock it back and forth to loosen it.

"Stop it, Lang," the Ranger said firmly.

Lang looked around, his hands still on the grave marker.

"What?" he said. "I'm only getting it for Shel. I thought he ought to at least have a marker."

Sam recalled earlier how Lang had argued that they could roll all three bodies in and be done with it. Now he decided Rastatler needed a head marker?

"We'll make some markers out of wood after we eat," he said, trying to be patient.

"This one will do," Lang persisted.

"But it's not his. Leave it be," Sam said, starting to suspect there was a trick in Lang's insistence somewhere.

Lang still kept hold of the marker.

"Shel wouldn't mind that it wasn't his," he said. "Anyway, all it says is unknown, and the date."

Sam just stared at him.

"The date will be wrong," said Lang, "but Shel wouldn't mind that either. He never held firm to close record keeping."

Sam took a breath; he remained patient and watchful. This was how it was going to be dealing with Lang, he decided.

"What I'm saying is, you're stealing it, Lang. Can't you understand that?" he said.

Lang gave a shrug and a crooked grin.

"Sure I can," he said. "But this thing has been here over three years. Whoever's under it ain't going to miss it."

Sam shook his head.

"Turn it loose," he said. "If the man under it won't miss it being gone, Rastatler won't miss it either."

"Whatever you say, Ranger," Lang said, relenting and taking his hands from the grave marker. Sam watched him sidestep away from the older grave and walk back to the other side of Rastatler's fresh grave, where two shovels stood stuck in the dirt.

So that was it, Sam thought, watching without looking directly at Lang. It was going to be a long trek to Yuma; they might as well come to an understanding right here.

"You being a lawman," Lang said quietly, "maybe you should say something over him?"

The Ranger took off his pearl gray sombrero and held it at his side, his rifle in the same hand.

"I can do that," Sam replied.

Lang took off his flat-crowned frontiersman-style hat and held it in front of him.

Sam bowed his head slightly, yet stared straight at Lang across the small mounded grave.

"Our Father who art—" he started to say.

"Hold it, Ranger," said Lang, cutting him off in prayer.

"What's wrong?" Sam asked.

"Ain't you going to close your eyes, out of respect for the Almighty?" said Lang, looking aghast.

"Yes, of course I will," Sam said in an off-handed manner. "But you first."

"Okay . . . ," said Lang, "both of us at once."

"Let's go," Sam said. He watched as Lang shut his eyes. "Our Father, who art in heaven . . . ," he said. As he spoke he took a silent step across the fresh dirt.

With his eyes closed, Lang reached his cuffed hands sidelong for the shovel. But as he grabbed the shovel handle and opened his eyes, all he saw was the butt of the Ranger's Winchester reach out and strike him a hard, sharp punch across the bridge of his nose. The world flashed purple-red; he staggered backward a step and crumbled to the ground.

"You peeped," Sam said flatly.

Having started the prayer, he stepped back across the grave, bowed his head and finished the prayer, while Lang rolled back and forth half-conscious in the dirt. When Sam had finished and said amen over the graves, he set his sombrero back atop his head and drew the string up under his chin. As he stepped around the grave to where Lang struggled to get back on his feet, Adele Simpson came from the saloon's rear door carrying two mugs of coffee. She handed the Ranger one of the thick coffee mugs and looked down at Lang, who held a hand cupped to his nose.

"I saw that, Ranger," she said to Sam. "If I ask what it was about, are you going to tell me it's none of my business?"

"No, ma'am, I wouldn't," Sam replied. "That would be rude of me." With his coffee mug in hand and his Winchester cradled in his right arm, he reached his free hand down and helped Lang pull himself to his feet. "I was making sure my prisoner here understands that I'm not going to warn him every time I see he's about to pull a trick out of his sleeve." He stared into Lang's dazed eyes. "I'll just let him go on with it—shut him down when the time comes."

"You didn't have to break my damned nose," Lang said behind his cupped hand.

"You're right," Sam replied. "Next time I'll hit you in another spot." He took the second mug of coffee from the woman and held it out to Lang. "Think it over while you drink this, decide if you're going to last all the way to Yuma or not." After Lang accepted the mug, Sam let the rifle shift from the crook of his arm deftly back into his hand.

Lang untied a dusty blue bandana from around his neck and held it to his nose.

"You can't blame a man for trying at least *once*, Ranger," he said into the wadded bandana. "It's only human nature." He shrugged.

"Holding to that same line of thought," the Ranger said, "it's only human nature to shoot a snake before it strikes you. Wouldn't you agree?" He tipped the rifle just enough for the barrel to aim at Lang's face.

"Not entirely . . . ," Lang offered, his tone relenting, looking away, dusting the seat of his trousers with his free hand.

"Well . . . when you two get your differences settled," Adele Simpson said, "there's food on the table. I set a pan of water and a towel out back—wash up first." She turned back toward the rear door of the saloon.

"Obliged, ma'am," Sam said as she walked away.

Sam looked over at the grave where they'd buried Bertrim Moore.

"You're sure Bertrim Moore here wasn't sided with Rastatler?" he asked.

"Naw, Moore was a loner, Ranger. You ought to know that much about him," said Lang.

"I don't know a lot about him," Sam admitted. "I know he worked for some cattle associations—hired his gun out to big ranches and railroads. Last I heard, he fell on hard times, took to bounty hunting, and didn't even do well at that."

"Yeah, bounty," Lang said, lowering the bandana from his nose. "Then I expect that ought to tell you what he's doing here." He stared at the Ranger knowingly.

"There's no bounty reward on you or Sheldon Rastatler that I know of," Sam said.

"That's right, but a reward is a reward, no

matter where it comes from," Lang said with the same look on his face.

Sam stared at him. Lang sniffed his red swollen nose, rewadded the bandana and held it back to his face.

"All right, Cisco, start making sense, or stop talking altogether," Sam said.

"Okay, act like you don't know," Lang said.

"Know what?" Sam said in a clipped tone.

"About the reward," said Lang.

"What reward?" Sam said.

"Come on, Ranger, you know *what reward*," Lang said.

"I can hit you again," Sam warned.

"The reward on *you*, Ranger," Lang said quickly, seeing the serious look in the Ranger's eyes.

"On *me*?" Sam said. "What are you talking about, Cisco?"

A bemused expression spread across Lang's face as he lowered the bandana from his nose once again.

"Hey, you don't know, do you?" he said.

Sam stared coldly at him.

"There's a reward on you, Ranger," he said. "I just figured you knew about it and wasn't wanting to talk about it."

"You figured wrong, Cisco," Sam said quietly. "Whatever you know, spit it out."

At the rear door, they both saw Adele Simpson look out at them with a hand on her hip, a large serving spoon in her hand.

"There's Miss Adele," said Lang. "Want to talk about it while we eat?"

"No," Sam said. "Tell me about it on the way to the kitchen."

In a small kitchen inside the saloon, Sam sat across the table from Cisco Lang and ate in silence, keeping expressionless eyes on his prisoner as he pondered what Cisco had told him. When Adele stepped away from a small cookstove, she walked out front to check on the two crusty old miners she'd seen coming earlier. The two had wandered into the saloon and sat drinking at a corner table.

As soon as the woman left the kitchen, Sam swallowed a bite of flatbread and black beans and washed it down with a sip of coffee.

"How much is this reward, and how long have you known about it?" he asked Cisco Lang, determined to get more out of him than he had gotten on their way to the kitchen.

Spooning up a mouthful of beans, Lang ignored the cloth napkin beside his bowl and tapped his shirtsleeve to his lips.

"How much it is, I don't know. But it was near two months back I heard it," Lang said, still chewing, his red nose bent and swollen, his eyes starting to blacken like a raccoon's. "I heard it from a few different people like Toy Johnson and Randall Carnes, to name two. They seemed interested in collecting it. Said they wanted to get to it before word got out up and down the Western Frontier."

Sam considered Lang's words. The Western Frontier meant loosely anywhere from Texas to the western Canadian border.

"Those two are in jail down in Missouri, last I heard," Sam said, searching for any holes in Lang's story, lest this be the setup for another trick of some sort.

Lang shrugged and spooned more beans.

"Toy Johnson's *in* jail so much and manages to break out so often," he said, "it's hard for him to tell which side of the bars he wakes up on. But that's where I heard it."

Sam watched him eat as he took another sip of coffee.

"And you never mentioned it to me because you figured I already knew and didn't want to talk about it?" he said.

"Take it or leave it, Ranger," said Lang. He swallowed his food and added, "Can I be honest?"

"You can *try*," Sam said dryly.

"Ha, that's funny," Lang said with a sour expression. "The truth is, I would've bet a hundred dollars on a fellow named Oldham Coyle, if I'd thought he could find you." He paused, then added, "And if I had a hundred dollars, that is. The El Paso sporting man, Silas Horn, has set odds at three to one in Coyle's favor, should the two of you ever throw down."

"Oldham Coyle," Sam said. "Robs trains and payrolls? Sometimes goes by Joe North?"

"Joe, James, Jack or Jonas," said Lang. "He's partial to 'J' names, I take it."

"I know of him," Sam said. "But he's not wanted in my jurisdiction."

"But can he take you?" Lang asked. "That's the question."

Sam refused to speculate. "I'm not a gunman, I'm a lawman," he said. "I won't turn killing a man into a sporting event."

"I'm just telling you what I know, the way you said to," said Lang. "If Bert Moore is the first to come claiming the reward, I'd say the word has spread by now. You'll have to watch your backside night and day."

Sam just stared at him, not about to tell him that he already watched his back night and day.

"All this because I shot Hugh Fenderson's nephew, him in the midst of robbing a bank?" Sam said, shaking his head a little at the particulars of it.

"Fenderson is a timber and cattle baron, Ranger," said Lang. "He come up the hard way. Far as he's concerned, it's a smear on his family name if he lets this thing go. This reward is his way of showing the world he's too big to have a relative gunned down in the street, guilty or otherwise."

Sam considered it. He pushed his empty tin plate away and sipped his coffee.

"As big as Fenderson is, seems like he'd just send some of his own hired men after me," he said.

"Don't you suppose he *has*, Ranger?" said Lang. "But this way he can deny anything to do with it when he wants to, or brag about it in the right crowd when it suits him." He grinned above his coffee mug. "Ain't that how a *powerful wealthy man* does it?"

Sam nodded. Lang was right. It was different when a wealthy man wanted revenge. A man like Hugh Fenderson could afford to keep his own hands clean and pay for someone else to bloody theirs, all the while avoiding any blame.

All right, Sam thought, if this reward story was true, and he saw no reason yet to doubt it, he still had a list of names that had to be attended to; he still had a prisoner to deliver to Yuma. He raised the mug to his lips and finished his coffee.

He'd watch for more signs of a bounty being on his head on his way back down across the Painted Desert. If there were professional bounty men out to kill him for a reward, so be it.

By the time he turned in Lang at Yuma, he'd know for certain if the story was true. And the minute he decided it was true, he wouldn't wait around for a string of gunmen to call him out in the street, or shoot him in his sleep. No, he thought, feeling his hand draw tight around the thick coffee mug. If it came down to that, he'd ride straight to the source, drag Hugh Fenderson out from behind his big desk and shoot him dead, *powerful wealthy man* or not.

"Can I pour you some more coffee, Ranger?" Adele Simpson cut into his thoughts, walking back into the small kitchen from the empty saloon. As she spoke, she picked up the coffee-pot from atop the woodstove.

"No, ma'am. Obliged, though," Sam said, catching himself, realizing he'd taken his eyes off Lang for too long. Luckily, Lang hadn't realized it would have been a good opportunity to make a move on him. Sam's Winchester was leaning against the table beside him, but it would have been an awkward move, swinging the rifle into play, had Lang lunged suddenly across the table while he'd been concentrating on Fenderson and the reward on his head.

Pay attention, he chastised himself.

"What about me over here, Miss Adele?" Lang cut in. "Or do I not count for nothing?"

Without a word, Adele stepped around the table with the coffeepot and poured more coffee into Lang's cup. As she poured the coffee, Sam caught a look pass between the two. *What was that . . . ?* Then he watched Adele step back from the table and set the pot down on the stove.

"I'm afraid the miners have brought me some bad news," she said quietly, showing an air of reserve.

"Oh?" said Sam, still wondering about the look he'd seen her and Cisco Lang exchange.

"Yes," she said, folding her arms in front of her. "The last of the Shambeck mines northeast of here are shutting down. Those two miners made it a point to come tell me, on their way to New Delmar, looking for work."

The Ranger and Cisco Lang looked at her. She was clearly shaken and upset. Sam stood and pulled out a chair for her.

"Sit down here, ma'am," he said, guiding her. "Can I get *you* some coffee?"

"No, thank you, I'm fine," Adele said, sitting. "The fact is, the Shambeck mines were all that's allowed me to hold on here. Once they're gone, I'll have to shut the doors on the Desert Inn for good."

"I'm sorry, ma'am," the Ranger said, sitting back down and laying his rifle across his lap.

The woman only nodded.

"Thank you, Ranger," she said. "I have to admit there's a certain amount of relief—I've been expecting this for a while." She took a deep breath of resignation and said, "May I ride along with you, Ranger, as far as the New Delmar Rail Depot?"

Sam looked back and forth at Lang and her. He wasn't going to spend the next three nights wondering what was between these two.

"I'm going to say yes," the Ranger replied. "But before I do, I want to know what it is that keeps the two of you passing each other looks when you think I can't see it."

Lang stared blankly; Adele Simpson looked surprised. Sam had only noticed it happen once, but he played that one time as a hunch that it had happened before.

After a second of silence, the woman sighed.

"All right, Ranger," she said, "the truth is, Cisco and I used to be *close*, I suppose is the best way to put it."

Lang chuffed and looked away.

"I should have told you right off," she continued. "But there was no reason to mention it. I knew the two of you would ride away, and that would be the end of it." She paused, then said, "But if I'm riding with you to New Delmar, I understand you need to know who you're riding with."

There it was, Sam thought, looking back and forth between the two of them.

"Everything is over now?" he asked them both, wanting to see each of their reactions.

Lang chuffed again, shook his head and looked away. He mumbled something under his breath.

"Dead and buried," Adele said, "and none too soon." She started to say more, but Sam raised a hand, stopping her.

"Excuse me, ma'am. That's enough for me to know," he said. "We'll spend the night, give you time to get ready. We'll leave here come first light."

He looked back and forth again. What else could he do? he asked himself. He couldn't let the woman travel that long desert trail alone.

Chapter 3

———

New Delmar, the Painted Desert

A surge of red and silver-gray desert dust blew along rows of colored hills, strewn out to the distance like striped tepees. Winds whispered low and mournful through endless stands of spiral stone, past totemlike hoodoos. Flat plate-stones rested slantwise and haphazard atop them like hats on careless drunkards.

Five dust-covered horsemen rested their horses, having just climbed a winding game path. They looked back down at the broad canyon floor and the intersecting trails snaking throughout it. Purple-gray tumbleweeds rolled, bobbed and bounced along like herds of strange creatures stirred into chase. Above the canyon, overhead, the men watched red-streaked winds rise and rejoin as one. Once whole, the wind swirled and twisted and raced across blue cloudless skies.

"I hate this damnable place," said one of the riders, a Kansas gunman named Chic Reye.

"You hate every damned place that ain't Kansas," a gunman beside him named Karl Sieg put in. The three other gunmen looked at each other; one spit and ran a hand across his dry lips.

"I allow there's some truth to that," Chic Reye agreed, eyeing Sieg narrowly, swishing a canteen of tepid water around in his gloved hand.

Atop a recessed ledge, tucked back among more tall twisted rock—much of it broken trunks of ancient trees turned to stone—the horsemen fell silent for a moment, watching a long red spin of trail dust rise and spread away behind the oncoming stage.

One of the men, a dwarf named Deak "Little Deak" Holder, finally let out a short laugh.

"I don't know about the rest of yas," he said. "But it's hard for me to be this close to a moving stagecoach and not ride down there hell-for-leather and rob it."

"I know the feeling," said the leader, Dave Coyle. "But contain yourself for now, Little Deak. My brother, Oldham, will soon have us some robbing work lined up." He held the reins to two horses, his own under saddle and tack, and a bareback buckskin with black stockings and mane, wearing only a hackamore bridle.

"Don't worry about me. I'm good with all this," Little Deak said quickly. "I'm always one for the making of *light* conversation." He turned to the man seated on a bay beside him and said, "Ain't that right, Blind Simon?"

"Yeah, he's a huckleberry, this one," said the older, gray-bearded gunman, Blind Simon Goss. "Loves to converse," he added. Goss' eyes wandered aimlessly behind a pair of black-lens spectacles as he spoke. "Sometimes he carries on so much you sort of want to smack him backward."

The dwarf gave the blind man a surprised look, but then he grinned and shook his head.

His hand fidgeted with a length of rope he carried slung over his shoulder, a small loop tied in either end.

"Simon's only kidding about that," he said.

"No, I'm not," said Simon.

But the dwarf ignored him and grinned as he looked almost straight up at the others towering above him.

"The two of us have been riding together now the past six or seven months. If we didn't get along, I expect we'd have already killed each other."

"Let me ask you something, little fellow," said Chic Reye, sounding as if something had been on his mind for a while.

"It's *Deak*, not *little fellow*," the dwarf corrected him.

"Yeah, okay," said Chic, shrugging it off. "What the all-fired hell are you two doing out here anyway?"

"What are you asking, Reye?" said the dwarf, stiffening at the gunman's question. He kept both his small hands near the butt of a Colt double-action Thunderer in a holster strapped across his belly. The gun, though a shorter model, looked almost as long as Deak's arm.

"Take it easy, Chic," Sieg said beside him.

"No, I mean it," said Reye. "We've all wondered. I'm just the one coming up to ask. No offense," he said to Deak, "but you're not big enough to fart above a whisper, and your pard there is as blind as a damn cave bat. What are you doing riding this long-rider trail? Ain't there a circus or something somewhere—?"

"Watch your mouth, you *son of a bitch*," Blind Simon cut in, his right hand gripping a big Dance

Brothers revolver holstered on his waist. He dropped his horse's reins and stepped forward, stumbling a little over a small rock that his tapping stick failed to detect for him.

"Look at this," Chic Reye said in disgust. "Pull your hand up off that smoker, blind man, else I'll put a bullet in your hide."

"Let it go, Simon," Little Deak said. The dwarf stepped out in front of the blind man in order to stop him, but Simon plowed over him, almost falling himself.

"Everybody calm the hell down," shouted Dave Coyle. He stepped over beside Reye. "Why'd you have to go and say something like that, Chic? The man's blind, but Oldham said he's a damn good gunman."

Reye gave a short disbelieving laugh.

"Check what you just said, Dave," he chuckled. "Blind, but a damn good gunman? He can be one or the other, but he can't be both."

Before Dave Coyle could say any more, Simon stepped in closer, dropping his hand from his revolver but balling his fists at his sides.

"I'm not blind, damn it," he said, "leastwise not all the way. I can see shadows, images and the like."

"I call that *blind*," said Reye, "no matter whatever else you want to call it, if all you're seeing is *shadows and the like*."

"I'm not so blind that I can't draw this smoker and burn you down right there where you're standing," said Simon, moving in even closer, his face turning back and forth trying to single out the sound of Reye's voice in the strong constant purr of wind.

"Ah, hell, I ain't drawing on a blind man," Reye said, settling down a little. "Forget I said anything."

"I'm not forgetting nothing. Draw, damn you to hell," said Simon.

"I said no, I ain't drawing on a blind man," Reye said, ignoring the blind outlaw's cursing.

"I'll make you draw!" Blind Simon shouted. "I'll spit in your damned face." He let go a foamy string of spittle and wrapped his hand on his gun butt, ready to draw. "Now, what are you going to do about it, *coward*?"

"Oh no," Little Deak murmured.

The rest of the men fell silent as stone.

"Jesus, Simon," Dave Coyle cut in, "you just spit on my horse." Coyle's dusty bay gave a low grumbling chuff and swung its head away.

"See what I mean?" Reye murmured. He shook his head in disgust.

"Hell, Dave, I didn't mean to do that," Simon said. He raised his hand from his gun butt and reached out for the horse's muzzle. "Sorry there, horse," he said, missing the horse, mistaking Dave's face for the horse's muzzle.

Dave ducked his face away from Simon's reaching hand.

"Can you come get him, Little Deak?" he said. The men milled in place and looked away.

"Simon," said Reye with a tinge of remorse, "I don't know what the hell I was thinking, saying all that to you and the little fellow, about the circus and all."

"Where are you, Reye?" Simon asked, turning his head back and forth.

Reye sidestepped farther away from Simon before answering.

"I'm trying to apologize here, Simon, damn it," said Reye, "to both you and the little fellow."

"It's *Little Deak*," said Deak, correcting him again.

"All right, *Little Deak*, then," said Reye, relenting his sarcastic position.

Hearing Reye's voice, Simon turned to hone in on it. But Reye sidestepped even farther way without speaking.

"Stage is almost there," said Sieg, drawing their attention toward the rise of red bluish dust drawing closer on the trail below.

"All right, everybody mount up," said Dave Coyle. "Let's get down there first. My brother don't like being kept waiting."

The men turned to their dusty horses and stepped into their saddles. Little Deak grabbed the rope from his shoulder and flipped one looped end deftly up and over his saddle horn. He stepped up into the loop with his left foot, into his stirrup with his right. Chic Reye and Karl Sieg watched him swing his short leg over the saddle.

Beside Little Deak, Blind Simon adjusted himself atop his horse and shoved his walking stick down into his rifle boot beside his Spencer carbine.

"There's some things takes me a whole lot to get used to," Reye said sidelong to Sieg, eyeing the two. "Other things . . . it ain't ever going to happen at all." The two turned their horses along with the others and rode away.

At the stage depot on the valley floor, Oldham Coyle stood up from the space he'd cleared for himself on the rear luggage rack and shook thick red dust from the breast and sleeves of his duster. Rifle in hand, he lifted his hat from his head, slapped it against his thigh and put it back on. As the shotgun rider stepped down and helped four disheveled women passengers off the big Studebaker coach, Coyle reached into the luggage compartment, dragged out his saddle, shoved his rifle down into a saddle boot and shouldered the load. Dust billowed.

As if from out of nowhere, a hooded four-horse double buggy rolled up to the four women and stopped with a jolt. Coyle stood watching, his coated face and mustache appearing as if molded out of red-blue clay.

Assisting the women into the large, stylish rig, the shotgun rider shut the buggy door and turned to Coyle.

"Stranger," he said to Oldham Coyle, "we're mighty obliged to have you riding our tailgate. As much trouble as we've had with road agents of late, I can't seem to keep watch on everything at once."

"Don't mention it." Coyle smiled and touched his hat brim.

"I'm Wilson Tash. I didn't catch your name," the shotgun rider said, looking him up and down.

Coyle let his thumb fall over his rifle hammer as he looked back and forth between the women and Willie Tash.

"I'm North . . . Joe North," he said, seeing a weathered sign pointing north toward the main street of New Delmar. Oddly, he had used the name Joe North before. The fact that the sign had brought the alias back in his mind struck him as a good omen.

"Well, Mr. North," said Tash. "I want you to

tell the bartender at the Number Five to stand you a bottle of rye and see me for its value."

"Obliged, Willie Tash," said Coyle.

A light giggle came from the women in the buggy.

"Tell him to send you up for a tight go-round with Utah Della, and see me for the value, *cowboy*," said a willowy brunette with a lewd grin and a smeared black beauty dot above her lip.

"Oh, or with Lila too," said another woman, this one a hefty middle-aged blonde with lips the color of calf liver, lipstick mixed with red silt from riding eighteen miles along a string of red-layered buttes through a hard-pushing wind.

Beside the voluptuous blonde, a young woman giggled and batted her eyes.

"Or, don't forget Betty, cowboy," she said. "You can ride tailgate for me any time."

"Ladies, I am nothing but, *nothing but*, obliged," Coyle said, sweeping his hat from his head in a grand gesture and holding it to his chest as he made a slight bow. Then he pointed at each woman in turn. "Let's see . . . that's Della, Lila and Betty, and . . . ?" His finger moved toward the fourth woman, a small, fine-featured redhead who sat staring at him with a coy smile.

"Don't be wagging that finger 'less it's the best thing you've got, cowboy," she said. "I'll whisper my name in your ear when you come see me." Her eyes played up and down his dust-caked clothing, his face and hat. "Once you get some of this countryside scrubbed off yourself, that is."

"I can't wait." Coyle smiled.

"Well, gals," Willie Tash said almost sullenly, "you sure know how to pale a bottle of rye, I reckon." To Coyle he said, "But the bottle is there for you when you want it. It's no small thing, guarding a stagecoach when you got outlaws like we've got up here."

"Real killers, I hear," said Coyle, touching his hat brim again and looking off toward five bands of dust following his men down the last few hundred yards of trail into the old Delmar depot.

"Something awful," said Tash, shaking his head.

"Don't forget us, cowboy," said Lila from the buggy. "We're getting tired of humping these rock crackers."

"I'd have to be a straight-out fool to forget you, ma'am," Coyle said, turning away as he spoke.

At the head of the five riders, Dave Coyle slowed his horse down to a trot, then down to a walk the last few yards. When he reined the horse to a halt and turned it sidelong to his brother, Oldham stood up from leaning against a corral fence. The rest of the men sidled their horses in around Dave Coyle.

"Well . . . ?" Dave asked. "How did it go?"

"It went dry and dusty," said Oldham, his face still coated red-blue. "How else could it go?"

"I mean how'd it *all go*?" said Dave. "Did they believe your story, that your horse died on you?"

Oldham grinned as he walked forward, spread a frayed saddle blanket on the buckskin and pitched his saddle up over the horse's back.

"They believed it enough it got me on the stage," he said. "They're so skittish about outlaws, or *road agents* as they called them, I even rode guard on their tailgate most of the way here."

"Did they stop at the Englishman's mines?" Dave asked.

"Yep, they did, brother," said Oldham, drawing the cinch snug beneath the buckskin's belly. "What we heard is true, the John Bulls are sneaking their payroll money in by stagecoach right now. They rolled in, set off a strongbox and rolled on. Nobody seemed any the wiser for it. Except for me, that is." He grinned, his teeth looking pearly white against the red-blue dust caked on his face. He swung up into his saddle and sat atop his horse staring from one face to the other. "Boys, we're fixing to become well heeled."

"*Whooiee!*" said Dave. "It's high time I was struck by some solid good fortune."

"Here's the deal," said Oldham. "We ride in, do some drinking, get fed and bred. Tomorrow we ride out to the mines—collect the payroll money from the John Bulls."

The men smiled and nodded at each other. Little Deak bounced up and down in his saddle, his stubby legs sticking straight out on either side. Reye looked at him, then at Blind Simon, and his smile went flat as he turned and stared at Oldham with his wrists crossed on his saddle horn.

"Not to take on a dark attitude, Oldham, but I've gotta ask, how much of a cut do these two new men get?" He nodded at Little Deak Holder and Blind Simon.

"Come on, Chic, let it go," said Sieg, getting disgusted.

"Keep out of this," Reye warned Sieg. He stared at Oldham Coyle for an answer.

"An even split," said Oldham. "Why?" he asked, sensing something brewing.

"I don't think they deserve full shares, that's *why*," Reye said bluntly.

"Everybody gets a full share, Reye," Oldham said. "What's wrong with you anyway?"

"Pay him no mind, Oldham," said Sieg. "He's had a mad-on off and on, all day."

"*I said* keep out of it, Sieg," said Reye. "I still want to know what they're doing riding with us."

"All right, Chic, since you're questioning my judgment," said Oldham, stepping his horse closer, "let's see if I can make you understand. Last year, Simon Goss hid me out from a Colorado sheriff and a hanging posse at a place called Apostle Camp, up above Black Hawk. For that, I told him if he ever needed to make a run or two, let me know. So he did a while back. Now here he is. And I'm good for my word."

"I understand you're good for your word, Oldham," said Reye. "But the man can't see."

"We've been through all this," Blind Simon called out. He turned his head back and forth, singling out the sound of Reye's voice.

"He sees shadows and such," said Coyle. "More important, he makes up for what he can't see with his other senses. He's got the hearing of a watchdog."

"Yeah, what else?" said Reye, sounding dubious, unmoved.

Staring at Reye, Oldham called out over his shoulder to Blind Simon, "Point us out the best hot food in this town, Simon," he said.

The blind man sniffed the air quickly, then raised his arm and pointed a finger in the direction of the town sitting three hundred yards away.

"Any womenfolk?" Oldham asked.

Simon kept his arm raised but moved it slightly to his right, stopping at three different points.

"There, there and there," he said respectively. "No shortage of females here," he replied, "but you best like rose-lilac perfume. It smells like there's been a cosmetics drummer through town of late."

The men all looked impressed. Reye only stared, not giving in yet.

"What's that restaurant serving today?" Oldham asked Simon Goss.

"Rocky Mountain ram shank," Simon said confidently, "all you can eat."

"Stewed or baked—?" said Oldham.

"All right, Oldham, I get it," Reye cut in. "I'm just a son of a bitch sometimes."

"Sometimes?" said Sieg.

The men chuckled.

Reye paused, then looked at Little Deak and asked, "What about this one?"

Oldham grinned and said, "He's not carrying that Colt Thunderer as a belly ornament. It's there for a reason."

"Yeah?" said Reye. "Is he just fast, or is he any good?" he asked, looking at Little Deak through new eyes now that Oldham had vouched for him.

"Both," said Reye. "The best and fastest I've ever seen, and I've seen them all."

Little Deak just sat staring at Reye with a thin smile that implied that every word Oldham said was true.

"All right," said Reye. "I had a right to ask, didn't I?"

"You did," said Oldham. "Now you best put it away. I'm hungry. I don't want to have to stop and bury you before we eat." He turned his buckskin amid a low ripple of laughter from the other men and booted it toward the main street

of New Delmar. The town lay obscure in looming red dust. Dave and the others looked at Reye,
still grinning as they turned their horses and fell
in behind their leader.

"Damn it," Reye grumbled to himself. "A man
has every right to inquire on things pertinent to
his well-being."

Chapter 4

———

New Delmar, Badlands Territory

On the crowded dusty main street running through New Delmar, Oldham Coyle led his five horsemen at a walk, each of them weaving in and out of thick wagon, horse and foot traffic. They advanced like bold explorers arriving in some strange exotic land. Passing a long line of skinned and gutted carcasses, they saw a variety of wild and domestic animals alike, all hung so closely that should some wily butcher slip in the corpse of an unfortunate miner or teamster, no one would take note until time to chop and boil their purchase.

They guided their horses around a tight gathering of onlookers who watched a man jerk and tremor on his way to death in a puddle of dark mud made by the released contents of his bladder and bowels. To the side stood a large Belgium mare calmly chewing on the man's straw hat, having removed him from beneath it with a murderous kick to his breastplate when he'd slapped the ordinarily sedate animal on its unsuspecting rump.

"I always admire a place with a lot going on," Oldham Coyle said sidelong to his brother, Dave.

"As do I, brother," Dave Coyle said, looking all around at the horde of humanity.

Farther along the crowed street, they passed a fistfight under way inside a covered wagon. The wagon's tall ribs had been dislodged in the fierceness of the fray, and the ragged canvas now billowed wildly as arms, fists and feet batted rapidly back and forth behind it. Oldham stopped his horse for a moment and stared at the battle until a loud metallic gong resounded and the canvas fell in a slump.

"That's that," said Karl Sieg, sidling his horse up closer to the Coyle brothers. "Somebody got their bell rung."

A cheer went up from the gathered onlookers as a naked woman slipped out of the wagon's rear, an iron kettle in her bloody hand. She staggered in place facing the onlookers. Like some ancient warrior wreathed only in victory, she refused a blanket held out to her, turned and walked away as if to continue on some long arduous journey she'd predetermined.

"That's worth a dollar to see any day," said Chic Reye.

But before the woman had gone ten feet, the onlookers closed in around her like lava, and in their admiration raised her over their heads. Bloody, dirt-streaked, she flailed in misinterpreted protest, shouted, tossed, bobbed and rolled on their hands and fingertips, until she was transformed from warrior to some pale, slick creature plucked recently from the sea.

"Show's over," said Dave Coyle as the crowd swept their heroine away with them. He started to nudge his horse forward, but stopped.

Beside him, Oldham reached down in the

crowd and grabbed a man by the shoulder of his wool shirt.

"Say, pilgrim, where is that Number Five Saloon from here?" he asked.

The man started to get surly about being grabbed in such a way, but upon seeing the faces of the five men, their ample display of firearms, he cooled quickly.

"Yes, sir, she's straight ahead if these bummers and jakes will let you get to her." He pointed at a giant, freshly constructed and painted wooden beer mug being raised on ropes by men atop a roof facade. Across the middle of the giant frothed mug, bold black paint read NUMBER '5' SALOON.

"We'll get there," Oldham said, releasing the man's shirt, straightening it a little. "I know there's some fine-looking women there. How's the gambling?"

The man grinned.

"Like everything else here," he said, "it's hot and fast."

"How about at the other saloons?" Oldham asked. "I take it there's four more?"

"Used to be, not anymore," the man said. "Number Five is all that's left."

Chic Reye cut in with a smug look, "So much for three different places for women."

"Oh, there's *three* places for womenfolk, sure enough," said the man. "Aside from the Number Five, there's four doves out of Denver and a colorful young man who presses flowers, working on their own, sort of sharing a small tent back and forth. And there's a baker's wife and her sister doing all they can at a dollar a jump to take up any shortage."

"There you have it," Oldham said to Reye, "Simon never misses his call."

"What happened to the other saloons?" Dave asked the man.

"Two burned," the man said. "One just fell to the ground for no apparent reason—killed six men inside and a mule standing out front. Number Four's owner got hung, and everybody sort of ran through, took what they wanted and kept going." He shook his head in shame. "Picked it clean to the frame, stole the boards from the floor and the nails holding them down. I'll tell you what, the Pawnee could learn from this bunch."

"Is it always this busy here?" Dave asked.

"I've been here nigh on a month, I've seen no letup," the man said.

"Gold findings?" Oldham asked.

"Lots of promising color," the man said. "It's got your other hard-rock miners walking off, taking company shovels, picks, mules and whatnot with them. The John Bulls are importing the Cornish to take up the slack. God knows what they're promising."

"But no big finds yet?" Oldham asked.

"If there is, I didn't hear of it, and I never sleep," the man said. "You fellows prospecting, are you?" He eyed their rifles and sidearms.

"No, just passing through," said Oldham. "Figuring on some poker and some man's play before we leave."

"Well, here's a word of advice," the man said. "Any money you've got left you ought to pitch it up in the air real quick, save you getting your throat cut over it."

"Obliged for your advice," Oldham said. "We'll try to be careful." He touched his hat brim and nudged his big buckskin forward. Beside him, his brother, Dave, sidled up closer and saw the hungry look in his eyes as he stared in the direction of the saloon. As they drew nearer to the Number Five Saloon, they saw men with hammers beginning to nail the giant frothing mug sign in place.

"Brother, you're not really going to start gambling right off, are you?" he asked.

There was a hungry look in Oldham's eyes as he looked at his brother with a flat, stubborn expression.

"Do I tell you how to spend your money, Dave?" he said.

"No," Dave came back, "but you should, if I start wasting it gambling away like a fool."

"Don't call me a fool, brother," Oldham said. He calmed himself and gave a short, tense smile. "Anyway, lucky as I feel today, you can't really call it gambling—more like reaping rewards on a short-term investment."

"Jesus, Oldham," Dave said. "It's always the same four things with you. All you do is rob, gamble, lose and go to jail."

"Make it three from now on, brother," said Oldham. "You can mark going to jail off the list."

"That's damn good," said Dave. "Now if you can mark off gambling, we'd soon have enough money to buy ourselves a big fine spread somewhere."

"Look at me, brother Dave," said Oldham. "Do you really want to punch cattle for a living?"

"Hell yes, I want to punch cattle," said Dave. "Don't you? That used to be all we talked about, getting ourselves a spread, punching cattle—"

"I'm not punching cattle," Oldham said, cutting Dave short. "Cattle never done anything to me." He gave his brother a grin, then reached out and jerked his hat down tightly over his eyes. By the time Dave pulled his hat back up onto his forehead, Oldham had gigged his buckskin through an opening in the crowd.

"Asshole," Dave said, shaking his head.

The other four men edged up around him as Dave took his hat off, redented the crown and put it back on.

"Is he going to be all right, riding out tomorrow morning?" Reye asked.

"That's a hell of a thing to ask," said Dave Coyle, looking him up and down. "Sure he is."

"Did he say how we'll handle it?" Reye persisted.

"No, but he will soon enough," said Dave.

"We can't wait around," Reye cautioned him. "Those rock busters could get paid most any time now."

"He understands that," said Dave. "He's setting it all straight in his mind right now. He don't like doing something until he's played it all out."

The men just looked at him.

"What is there to play out?" Reye asked. "The money's there. He saw the strongbox. We ride in, shoot the place up, take the money and ride away. It doesn't take a big thinker and a box of pencils to figure it out. The five of us could do it—I could take *any* four men I know, ride out and rob that damn mine."

Dave just stared at him for a moment.

"He didn't mean nothing by it, Dave," Sieg said. "We're all a little edgy, wanting to rob something."

Dave Coyle ignored Karl Sieg; he continued to stare coldly at Chic Reye.

"I'll tell you what, Reye," he said. "You go inside the saloon and tell Oldham exactly what you've told me. If you manage to walk out alive, I'll ride out with you and we'll rob that damn mine on our own."

The men fell silent for a moment.

"You can't keep your mouth shut, can you, Chic?" said Sieg.

Reye looked back and forth in disgust.

"To hell with it," he said, nudging his horse on toward the saloon. "I'm going to get myself a bath, a woman and a bottle. We get ready to rob something, feel free to let me know."

It was late afternoon when Oldham Coyle watched the last of the four men he'd been playing with—a whiskey drummer in an orange plaid suit—pitch his cards onto the rough table and push his chair back. At Oldham's side stood the young red-haired dove he'd talked to earlier at the stagecoach. As promised, she had whispered her name in his ear—Anna Rose—in spite of the fact that he still wore trail dust, having only washed his face and hands in a pan of water out back before sitting down to play.

"That's it for me," the drummer said to Oldham. "You're too damn lucky, even for a sporting man like myself." He looked at the seven-over-tens full house Oldham had spread out on the table. "I know when I've been had."

Been had? Oldham just stared at the drummer. In the far corner a player piano rattled and banged away on its own. Drunken miners watched the piano in awe.

"What do you mean you've been had?" Oldham asked pointedly.

"Whoa, now, don't get your bark on, sir," the drummer said. "My apologies. I should have said I know when I've been bested."

"That does have a better sound to it," Oldham said, cooling quickly. He raked in the chips from the middle of the table with both hands and let out a breath behind a short black cigar.

Seeing the atmosphere lighten, the drummer wagged a finger good-naturedly.

"But rest assured you have not seen the last of me. Losing once only piques my interest. The next time we meet, be prepared for the trouncing of your life—pokerwise, that is, of course."

"Of course," said Oldham with a thin smile. "I look forward to it." He nodded and watched the man turn, walk down three wooden steps from the platform the table sat on and across the crowded floor. Once the man walked out the front door, Oldham picked up a small stack of chips and slid it to the house dealer seated across from him.

"For you, Ozzie," he said.

"Obliged, sir," the dealer said as two new players stepped up onto the platform and threw down cash on the table. "Are you cashing in, then?" the dealer asked Oldham.

"You bet he is, if he knows what's good for him," Anna Rose cut in, before Oldham could answer. "Cash in his chips and send the money up to my room." She sidled in and looped Oldham's left arm around her waist.

"You heard the lady," said Oldham. He gave a glance toward the chips on the table, made a quick mental guess and turned away. "But only

cash in half my chips. I'll cash the rest in later."
He looked at Anna Rose and said, "Sorry it took
me so long. Now show me that bathtub in your
room."

"Right this way, bathtub and feather bed,"
Anna Rose said. They started across a floor
crowded with gaming tables, drunks and dancing girls. But halfway across the room, on their
way toward a set of stairs reaching up to the
second-floor landing, two men in black suits
and hats stepped out of the crowd and blocked
their way.

Oldham's right hand went instinctively to his
holstered Colt.

"We're not the law, Oldham Coyle," said one
of the men. He wore a drooping mustache with a
fierce scar running through it, circling wide on
his right cheek and ending beneath his eyes.
Both men held their hands as if in a show of
peace.

Oldham caught himself, but stayed ready. At
the bar, he saw Sieg, Little Deak and Simon Goss.
Sieg and Little Deak stared in his direction.
Simon's dark spectacles revealed nothing.

"We're here with an offer for you, one you're
not going to want to turn down," said the second man. He was cleanly shaved, wearing yellow shoulder-length hair, and younger than his
partner.

"Give your gunmen a sign so we can talk,"
said the first man.

"Yeah," said the younger man, "if we wanted
you dead, you'd be dead already."

"You think?" Oldham was skeptical. But the
bearing of the men gave him pause, the one with
the scar seemingly familiar.

"Let's not weigh each other's nut sacks, Sonny," the older man said to his partner. To Oldham he said, "This is Sonny Rudabough. I'm Henry Teague. The man we work for wants to pay you to do him an important service."

"A job?" Oldham appeared almost offended.

"Can we talk, off the floor somewhere?" Teague asked. He gave Anna Rose a passing glance, then brought it around to Oldham.

Oldham recognized the name Henry Teague. He spoke sidelong to Anna Rose without taking his eyes off the two men.

"Anna Rose, why don't you gather the chips from that table yourself, count them and cash half of them in for us? I'll be right on up."

"Remember, room seven. I'll be waiting in my warm feather bed." Anna Rose gave him a smile and slipped way, back toward the poker table.

Teauge and Rudabough gave each other a look.

"If you can't trust doves, what's the world come to?" Oldham nodded toward a table in the far corner where a miner lay facedown on a crumpled hat. He looked at the crowded bar and gave Sieg, the dwarf and the blind man a sign that everything was all right. The three stayed at the bar drinking, but Deak and Sieg kept watch as Oldham and the two men weaved their way across the busy room.

At the table, Oldham lifted the drunk to his feet, placed his hat on his head, turned him and gave him a slight shove. The miner staggered forward into a large timber post and clung to it to keep from falling over. Sitting down, Sonny Rudabough gave Oldham a smirk.

"You got to be crazy, Coyle, trusting a whore with your money that way."

Oldham just stared at him.

"Sonny," said Teague, "why don't you go get us a bottle and some glasses?"

The young gunman seethed but did as he was told. He stood up and walked to the bar. When he was gone, Teague let out a breath and shook his head.

"You'll have to overlook him," he said. "He keeps a mad-on at the world. Never knows when to keep his mouth shut."

"I've got a man like him who rides with me," Oldham commented. "What's this job, and who's offering it?"

"You know Hugh Fenderson?" Teague asked.

"Know him, no," said Oldham. "Heard of him, yes, I expect everybody has." He paused, then said, "He wants me to work for him? I got the idea he wanted me dead a couple years back, wanted to pay three thousand dollars bounty to anybody who'd burn me down."

Teague gave a thin, tight smile.

"Yet here you are, still alive," he said, "in spite of some of the fastest guns out there trying to pour it on you. Mr. Fenderson found that admirable after a while. Said you killed so many of his gunmen he had to give the rest of them a raise in pay."

Oldham gave a shrug.

"He's willing to forgo any malice toward you," Teague said, "and put five thousand dollars in your hand if you'll kill an Arizona Ranger for him."

Five thousand dollars! Oldham just looked at him, remaining calm and stoic. "This Arizona Ranger is Sam Burrack, I'm going to guess," he said.

"It is," said Teague. "You interested?"

"Five thousand . . ." He let his words trail, giving the matter close consideration. Finally he said, "No, I pass. I'm on a big winning streak right now. I don't want to do anything to break it. Anyway, I'm a thief, not a hired killer. I don't want to get started at it."

"You know what I think, Coyle?" said Teague, taking on a stronger tone. "I think you'd better think about it a minute longer, and say yes. You don't want to disappoint Hugh Fenderson."

"I did think about it," said Oldham, catching a threat in the gunman's tone. "My answer is no." He stood up as Sonny Rudabough returned carrying three glasses and a bottle of rye. Sonny turned and watched Oldman walk away toward the stairs.

"What happened?" Rudabough said.

"He turned us down cold," said Teague. "Said he's on a winning streak and can't turn it loose."

"Damn it, now what?" Sonny flopped down on a chair.

"Simple enough," said Teague, "we bust up his winning streak for him. I think I've got this *hombre* figured out. He's here in New Delmar to rob something, and it's not hard to discern what."

"What?" Sonny asked with a dumb expression on his face. He pulled the cork from the bottle of rye.

"The big English mines are the only thing around here with lots of money," said Teague. "Coyle always goes for the big money." He narrowed his eyes, considering the possibilities.

"I can't see why I don't kill this damned lawman for us," Sonny said, "collect the money ourselves."

"You might just be doing that before this is over," Teague said.

"Yeah?" said Rudabough.

"Yeah," said Teague. "Meanwhile, Fenderson said hire Coyle, so that's what we're going to do. Pour us some whiskey. We need to make some plans for this gambling fool. I'll fix his lucky streak for him."

Chapter 5

———

Instead of going to the room where he knew Anna Rose lay waiting for him in her feather bed, Oldham walked to the dark, quiet end of a hallway and looked out a window onto an empty alley below. He took out chopped tobacco and paper and rolled himself a smoke. He didn't like it when things started moving too fast on him. Yesterday, he was on the desert floor wondering how he and his men would manage to ferret out the mine payroll and ride away with it. That much was done. Now the mine payroll was waiting for him.

Good luck? Damn right it was, he told himself, drawing deep on the cigarette. But that was only part of it. The last time he'd sat down to play poker, he'd lost everything—couldn't get a break. Today, he'd been the cock of the walk, the big winner. He had money piled up and waiting for him in the young dove's room. And that wasn't all he had waiting for him. He smiled to himself, imagining the warmth, the feel of her as he turned back the covers just enough to slip in beside her. *More good luck?*

Please . . . He chuffed at his question.

He realized Anna Rose was a dove, doing what a dove does for money. But he also knew that women like her could choose their clients. She could sleep with whom she wanted to and turn away the rest. Yet, with her pick of the room, she had waited all this time for him while he swilled rye and played poker. That wasn't just good luck, he told himself. That was falling into a golden jackpot. He grinned to himself, studying the dark alley below.

His luck had changed—not just changed, actually shot straight up like a Chinese skyrocket. He blew out a stream of smoke in exasperation. So what was that gnawing deep inside his belly? Why didn't he feel right about all this? What was missing?

Damn it, he hated this feeling.

He'd waited some time for his luck to turn around again, and now that it had done so, he felt as if something was missing. He'd seen himself win a thousand times like this only to lose again, because no matter how much his luck changed, it was never enough for him. He had to push it further, take in more, squeeze the luck until it turned bitter in his hands. Not this time, though. He had learned his lesson.

Jesus. What was it about losing that always left him feeling fuller than winning ever did? He drew deep on the cigarette and blew out a stream against the dusty windowpane. He didn't know the answer, but he did know that this time he wasn't about to push his luck.

"Look at you," he murmured, half in disgust, eyeing down the front of his dusty shirt, his trousers, his dirty boot toes. *This is crazy, too crazy to even think about,* he decided. *Settle yourself down, go to her room, slip into the bath, slip into her bed. Stop feeling like a fool—stop acting like a fool.*

He took three more puffs on the cigarette, stubbed it down onto the windowsill. *All right.* Anybody can be a good loser. They learn it from plenty of practice. Being a good winner requires something different, a whole other kind of light in your head, he thought. It's a different feel in your guts. It isn't hard to quit when you lose because you're forced to quit when there's nothing left.

But winning? He let out a long breath. *Damn!* Winning took more of something, though he wasn't sure what. Enough of this. He dismissed the matter, turned and walked straight to room seven, where Anna Rose told him she would be.

"Now you're starting to make sense," he said to himself under his breath. He turned the knob on the unlocked door, stepped inside and locked the door behind him.

Anna Rose was lying in a large feather bed. In the soft flicker of a candle lantern, Oldham watched her throw back a sheet, stand up naked from the bed and walk to him. Through the half-opened door to a smaller room, Oldham saw an ornate bathing tub. Steam curled up from a frothy head of hot, soapy water.

"Well, there you are," she said softly. "I was starting to feel neglected." She stopped close in front of him and tugged his dusty shirttail up from his trousers. On the nightstand beside the flickering candle lantern, Oldham saw his winnings neatly resting in four stacks.

"God forbid such a thing while I'm around," he said to her, his arms wrapping around her, feeling her skin warm and creamy against him.

She pressed her face into his chest.

"Take off your boots. I'll take off the rest," she

whispered, drawing circles on his chest lightly with her fingertip. "Let me get you lathered, rinsed and dried, all very slowly."

"I can hardly wait." Oldham smiled as she stepped back enough for him to pull off his dirty boots. She took his hand and led him into the other room, to the steaming bathtub. She unfastened his gun belt and set it aside. She loosened his trousers and started to pull them down. He smiled a little to himself, seeing a bottle of rye standing on a small table beside the tub.

Oh yes, you're on a streak, pard, and this is what winning's all about.

But before Anna Rose could lower his trousers, he put his hand on hers, stopping her.

"Wait," he said, "there's something I've got to do first."

She watched him fasten his trousers and walk around to the bottle of rye, pour himself a double shot in a glass and swirl it around.

"Drink up, there's plenty more," she said, and added, "I drink too." She smiled.

"Sorry," Oldham said, quickly upturning another clean glass and pouring rye into it for her. She noted a seriousness that had suddenly set in on his face. His hand quickened, almost shook a little as he poured the rye. His eyes grew remote, distant, as he turned and handed her the glass—something she never saw men do, especially with her standing naked in front of them.

"Is something wrong?" she asked, reaching a hand up, cupping his cheek.

"No, not at all," he said. But instead of responding to her advances, he sipped the rye, stopped, then tossed it back all at once. He turned away and poured himself another drink.

Yes, something was wrong. She'd seen men act this way before. She sipped her rye and observed for a moment while he drank in silence and stared down at the glass in his hand. Had she pushed him too much, too far at once? That was something a girl had to be careful not to do. Some of these men hadn't seen a woman in weeks, *months*. For many of them the drinking and gambling had to come first.

Some men had to first sate themselves with their other vices before they could handle a woman. This one had not struck her as being that way, but maybe she'd been wrong—she'd been wrong before.

She set her rye down and stepped closer.

"What do I have to do to get you between my knees, cowboy?" she asked softly. She reached for the waist of his trousers, but he stepped away, turned and walked toward the bed.

Okay, maybe he couldn't wait, she thought, so perhaps the hot bath would have to. She could go that way. It wasn't her first choice.

Oldham stopped and picked up two of the four stacks of cash from the nightstand beside the bed. Next to the cash were six stacks of chips. Yet he didn't even touch the chips. *Here it is,* she thought. She slumped and drew a patient breath.

"I've got something I have to do," Oldham said, his voice sounding changed, harried. He picked up his shirt and walked about the room gathering his clothes. "I won't be long, Anna Rose, but I've got to go do this."

"A gambler . . . ," she whispered under her breath.

Oldham offered a tormented smile.

"No, I mean it," he said, hurrying with his

clothes. "I won't be long." He nodded at the money and chips still lying on the nightstand. "Watch that for me. Take whatever you need, but wait for me."

"Whatever you say." She picked up a night-shirt and slipped into it. "I'll wait for you." She stopped and gave him a serious look. "It's going to cost you plenty, but I'll wait."

At the bar, Karl Sieg and Little Deak watched as Oldham walked back down the stairs and weaved his way across the crowded saloon to the gaming table he'd left not more than a half hour earlier. From the table in the rear corner, Teague and Sonny Rudabaugh saw him too. Teague sat holding his glass of rye, a cigar hanging between his fingers.

"Look at this, Sonny," he said. "I told you this dog hadn't gone off the hunt, didn't I?"

"Yep, you did," said Sonny with a thin smile.

"I'll be honest, though," said Teague. "I thought it would be longer than this. What kind of man leaves a pretty little dove like that one lying in bed alone?"

"Beats me," said Sonny, watching Oldham Coyle pull out an empty chair, sit down and flop a stack of cash onto the tabletop. "You want to do like you was saying, set him up to lose, maybe see about slipping some dope into his whiskey?"

Teague puffed his cigar, watching Coyle, considering it. Finally he let go a long stream of gray smoke and gave a thin smile.

"Naw," he said, "this guy won't need setting up. I'm betting he'll beat himself without our help."

"What about doping him?" Sonny asked. "You

know, just enough to keep him from being able to handle his play?"

"I don't think so," said Teague, watching. "There's some men you don't need to dope to make them lose. They go around carrying their own poison." He puffed on his cigar in satisfaction. "Some men you don't have to do nothing but stand back out of their way. Sooner or later, their nose hits the floor."

"All right, then, what do you want me to do, Henry?" Sonny asked, looking back and forth almost nervously.

"I just said nothing," said Teague. He reached out and filled both their glasses. "For the time being anyway. Let's just relax, have our rye and enjoy the show."

Across the floor at the bar, Little Deak and Karl Sieg stood watching the poker platform as the dealer, Ozwald White, slid six stacks of chips across the tabletop to Oldham. Little Deak sat on the edge of the bar top facing out across the crowded floor. Beside him stood Blind Simon, looking back and forth at the dark shadows interwoven with streaks of pale light moving around before him.

"This is what Dave told us to watch out for," Sieg said sidelong to the dwarf beside him. "I don't like being put on a spot like this. Oldham's the boss. We shouldn't be asked to report his carrying-ons to his brother."

"That's so," said Little Deak, "but we were asked. So let's get it done." He hopped down from the bar top and adjusted his Colt across his belly.

"Where we going?" Simon asked.

"Karl and I are going to find Dave," said Deak.

"What about me?" Simon asked.

"Wait here and keep an eye on things," Deak said.

"You're being funny, huh?" said Simon, his face still turned as if observing the crowded saloon.

"Sorry, Simon," said Deak. "Sometimes I forget."

"Be glad I don't forget sometimes," Simon said, "and wind up pissing in your ear."

"We could be a while, Simon," Deak said, letting the insult go. "But there's still plenty of rye in the bottle and money on the bar if you need it for more. Are you good?"

"Get out of here. I'm good," Simon said, his face still turned to the swirl of shadows and light in front of him.

Deak looked up at Sieg and nodded toward the door.

At the bar, even amid the din of the crowd, Simon listened to the sound of Deak's and Sieg's footsteps walk away and out the front door. He stood with his glass of rye in hand, his tapping stick leaning against the bar beside him. Now that he was alone, his position staring at the crowd from behind his dark spectacles soon drew attention from some of the faces in the crowded saloon. After a few minutes, three miners half circled him, prowling back and forth across the floor like nosy wolves, held hesitant only by the big Dance Brothers pistol holstered on Simon's hip.

Finally one of the miners gathered the courage to move in closer in spite of Simon's big gun. With his right hand rested on the handle of a large bowie knife standing in a fringed sheath on his belt, he stopped a few feet in front of the imposing blind man.

"Are you looking at me, mister?" he asked.

Blind Simon didn't answer. He judged the closeness of the man by the volume of his voice, by the whiskey and beer on his breath, by the smell of his clothes, the lingering odor of lye soap, kerosene and unearthed sandstone.

Three feet? Four . . . ? Yes, four, he decided.

"I said, are you looking at me, mister?" the miner repeated in a firmer tone.

"I expect I am at that," Simon said flatly.

"What did I do that strikes your attention?" the man asked gruffly.

"Nothing," Simon said. "Your face just offends me."

"Oh?"

The sound of steel drawn quickly from its rawhide leather sheath whispered in Simon's ears. With it came the sound of a gasp from much of the crowd, even as the player-piano rattled on in its far corner. In reflex, Simon's right hand snapped tight around the bone handle of his big Dance Brothers revolver.

"Let's do it," Simon growled fearlessly.

The young miner in front of him crouched. Simon saw the dim shadow lower in the backlight of the candle- and lantern-lit saloon. *A knifer?* He didn't care; he'd just pull iron and start shooting. Odds were at this distance he'd hit something.

"Hold it, Hawk," said a voice farther to Simon's right. "This sumbitch can't see a lick."

"What are you saying, fool?" the knife wielder

asked, tense, his brain and spleen a-boil on rye, anger and fear.

"I'm saying, he's blind, Hawk! Damn it, he can't see you. He can't see scat! Can you, mister?"

"I can see just fine," said Simon. Palm upturned, he flagged the knifer to him with his fingertips. "Are you coming on with that pigsticker, or you going to go whittle with it?"

"He sees me, Tinker," the knife wielder, Dale Hawkes, said to his comrade. He retightened his jaw and tensed for a lunge.

"No, he's blind!" Tinker called out. He gestured toward the long stick leaning against the bar. "Look, he uses that to move around with, keep from knocking his teeth out."

"Keep your mouth shut, fellow," Simon warned, half turning to the sound of the other man's voice, "or it'll be your teeth all over the wall."

The few onlookers drew back in a wider circle.

From the poker platform, playing at a fevered pitch, Oldham Coyle neither heard nor noticed the disturbance at the bar, nor did much of the crowded saloon, except for those nearby.

"Is that true, mister?" said Hawkes, easing up a little. "Are you blind?"

"Make your move and find out," Simon said, defiant to the last word. He heard a letup of tension in the man's voice. Guessing that the man had lowered the knife an inch, Simon let his hand slide slightly off the handle of his gun.

Hawkes gave Tinker an uncertain look, unable to determine if indeed this man was blind or just playing some strange killing game with him.

"How many fingers am I holding up?" Tinker asked quickly, raising his middle finger toward

Simon with a half-teasing grin. He bobbed the finger a little; laughter rippled.

Hearing the muffled laughter, Simon caught on and played a hunch. "Keep doing it, I'll clip it off for you."

Tinker's hand came down fast.

"Damn. Maybe he sees us after all," he said.

"This is crazy," said Hawkes, cooling, losing interest in spilling blood. "Lift your spectacles, mister," he said. "I want to see your eyes."

"Go to hell," said Simon. But Hawkes noted that whatever fury had been in this stranger's voice had dissipated. Seeing that Simon had let go of his gun handle, he sheathed his knife and ran a hand across his moist forehead. "If you're not blind, why do you carry that long stick around?"

"If you're not stupid, why do you keep running your mouth?" Simon shot back at him. These men were young and drunk, he decided— not that it made them any less dangerous. Just a little less cause for concern.

"That's it," Hawkes said in exasperation, "he's blind. I'm not fighting no blind man." He looked at his friend Tinker and another miner named Paul Rosen. "He *is* blind, right?" he said.

"*Jesus!* Yes, he's blind," Rosen said adamantly. "What's it going to take?"

Simon couldn't help giving a slight chuckle, seeing the trouble was at an end. On either side of the would-be combatants, what few onlookers the incident had gathered began to wander off.

"He thinks this is funny," said Tinker.

The three watched as Simon raised his spectacles enough for them to see his dull, dead eyes.

"Damn it, damn it, damn it!" said Hawkes. "I would never have lived this down."

"What's that?" Simon said. "Getting your ass whupped proper by a blind man?" As he spoke, his hand felt over beside him, picked up the bottle of rye and held it out at arm's length.

Hawkes shook his head and chuffed in submission.

"Hell, I guess so," Hawkes said. He stepped in to reach for the bottle. "Are we drinking with you now?"

"Yep," said Simon, turning the bottle loose to him. "See the poker game going on over there?" he asked.

"What about it?" asked Tinker, his hand reaching out for the bottle when Hawkes finished with it.

"Every now and then, I'd appreciate one of yas telling me what's going on over there. I'm waiting on a friend who's in that game."

Hawkes looked over at the poker table. He grinned.

"I just saw one of the saloon whores toss a bag of cocaine on the table," he said. "You might be in for a long wait."

"Damn it," Simon cursed under his breath.

PART 2

Chapter 6

For three days, the Ranger, his cuffed prisoner and Adele Simpson had traveled the high wind-whipped desert terrain. They had ridden their horses at an easy clip, Sam leading the late Earnest Trulock's spindly-legged roan on a short lead rope behind him. The roan carried Adele Simpson's travel bag and other personal items tied down on its back. Sam wasn't going to mention it yet, but the roan would never make it to New Delmar. The desert had a way of culling out the weak, and the horse's thin legs were not up to the challenge of the rocky, rugged terrain.

They'd followed trails meandering through swirling, colorful sandstone, through basins, arroyos and deep-cut canyons so sculpted by wind, water and time as to dizzy the eye. Tall, twisted rock formations flanked their passing like silent onlookers from some strange alien universe given to the study of smaller, more transient forms of frail humankind.

A few feet ahead, Lang stopped his horse and turned it around to face the Ranger as they ascended to a level spot on a trail circling a rocky slope beneath a tall, rugged butte.

"At least the wind has lain down some," he

said, his hands cuffed to his saddle horn, his wrists crossed.

"Keep moving, Cisco," Sam said firmly, stopping his horse and waiting until Lang turned and moved his horse out of his way. As the Ranger spoke, his rifle standing on his right thigh, he let the barrel lower and leveled it at the prisoner's chest. "That's twice I warned you not to stop in front of me like that. There won't be a third warning."

Ahead of Lang, the woman looked back over her shoulder but kept her horse moving forward. This was no place to have a horse lose its footing. Over eighty yards of loose silt and gravel lay slanting down through spiked rock and land-stuck boulders and spilled into what appeared to be a bottomless gully below.

Lang drew a deep breath and let it out in a show of submission. He backed his horse a step, turned it and nudged it back along the trail in front of the Ranger, who brought up the rear.

"I don't know what you're worried about, Ranger," Lang said over his shoulder. "I was just making conversation. Not everything I do is an attempt of some sort."

"Yes, it is," Sam said flatly. "Keep moving. The next time you stop and face down at me topping a trail, I'm putting a bullet in you. You'd better count on it."

Riding on, their horses at a walk, Lang called out to Adele, who rode fifteen feet in front of him.

"Miss Adele, why don't you speak up for me?" he said. "Tell the Ranger here that I'm not out to make a getaway, leastwise not if it would put you in harm's way."

"I don't speak for you, Cisco," Adele said. "I

don't know what you're capable of. I'm sure the Ranger sees clear enough what you are and what you're up to."

"I have to say," Lang chuckled, "you two are the most unsociable folks I've ridden with for a while." As he spoke he veered his horse slightly off the inside edge of the trail.

Testing . . . , Sam decided, watching the outlaw's every move, knowing Lang would take advantage of any little thing he let pass. He would push and test, and push a little harder each time until he'd carefully turned the situation into what he considered to be his favor. Then he would strike. It was coming, Sam reminded himself. He'd seen it too many times before while transporting a prisoner. If he let up for a second, Lang would make his move.

"Stay midtrail, Cisco," the Ranger called out to him.

They rode on.

When the trail had passed a long gully and slanted back down off the butte onto a rocky but level trail, the Ranger sidled off the trail into the shade of a towering rock. He stopped his horse and looked down at hoofprints on the ground. As the other two drew up around him, Sam gave Lang a warning look that held the outlaw back a few feet.

"Apache, Ranger?" Adele asked, stopping closer up, looking down as Sam pointed out the prints of horse hooves in the dirt.

"I believe so," Sam said, looking at the prints. "Chiricahua, most likely," he added. "On my way up from Nogales, I heard that seven White Mountain warriors rode off the San Carlos Reservation."

"Good of you to mention it, Ranger," Lang said with sarcasm.

Sam ignored him. He looked all around the upper edges of cliff and rock. "I expect they meant to lie low here and make for Mexico before winter, but the army got on them too quick. From the looks of these prints, they've been too harried to yank the shoes off their stolen horses yet."

"They still do that?" Lang asked, farther back, watching the Ranger.

"Some do, when they have the time," Sam said. "Others just let the shoes wear off. If they're riding the high desert, they don't like iron shoes on their horses. Say their ponies can't feel the ground as well among the rocks. These being stolen army horses, I don't know that it makes much difference."

"One thing's for sure," said Lang, looking all around with the Ranger. "They know we're here."

"Yep," Sam agreed, "and they wanted us to know they're here. Otherwise they wouldn't have left these prints, not when they could have skirted higher up above the trail and never been detected."

Lang just looked at him for a moment.

"Good thinking, Ranger," he said finally. "What do you figure they want from us?"

"Food, guns, horses," Sam said, "everything we've got. Everything they were short of leaving San Carlos."

Adele looked concerned. Lang ventured his horse a little closer and stopped beside her, seeing the Ranger give him a watchful stare.

"Don't worry, Miss Adele," Lang said, sounding sincere. "If they wanted a fight with us, we wouldn't have known it until they dropped down our shirts."

Adele looked to the Ranger as if for confirmation.

Sam gestured at the hoofprints on the ground, the horses having stepped out of the rocks for a few yards, then veered back up onto the hillside.

"There's a couple of good reasons they didn't drop down on us," he said. "Whatever guns and ammunition they have, they don't want to use just yet. And they know the army's close on their trail. They don't want gunfire giving up their position if they can keep from it."

"You're right," Lang said. "The message here is give up something, or have them try to take it all. It's as good an offer as you'll likely ever get from warriors on the move."

"But you're not giving them any guns?" Adele said to the Ranger.

"No, ma'am," Sam said. "That would only show them two things."

"That we're scared and we're stupid," Lang cut in with a trace of a smile. "Apache don't respect fear or stupidity."

"Let's unload the roan," Sam said. "I'm figuring by now they're tired of eating lizards and bunchgrass."

"Give them the horse, to eat?" Adele asked.

"Eat it or ride it, that'll be up to them," Sam said. "Had they not spotted us, by now they would have been ready to eat one of their own horses. But the Chiricahua don't like walking when they can ride, especially when they're put upon by soldiers. This horse will settle things for them."

"But—but can't we just give them some of our food?" Adele asked.

"They'd see that as an insult and come after us anyway," Lang said. "No, Adele, it's going to cost us a horse to get to New Delmar. This is how quick a small band of Apache can take over a trail."

"I'm sorry, ma'am," the Ranger said. "This horse wasn't going to last long anyway." He swung down from his saddle. "You've been out here long enough. You should be used to these kinds of trade matters."

Adele took a resolved breath.

"Yes, I understand," she said as Sam untied her few belongings from atop the roan.

She watched as Sam started to carry some of her items to load them up behind Lang's saddle.

"Leave it all lie, Ranger Burrack," she said.

Sam stopped and looked at her.

"Are you sure, ma'am?" he asked.

"I'm sure," she replied. "It's nothing I can't replace when I get to where I'm going. I still have some money I managed to save."

Lang sat looking along the upper edges of cliffs as Sam led the bareback roan into the trail and slipped the lead rope from around its muzzle.

"You know, Ranger, not to be a nuisance, but with Apache breathing down our necks, you might want to uncuff me here so I can be some help if need be."

"Keeping your mouth shut is about as much help as I want out of you, Cisco," Sam said. Holding his rifle, he slapped a gloved hand on the roan's rump and sent the horse off on a fast trot along the rock trail. Dust spun and billowed in the roan's wake.

"*Bon appétit*," Lang said quietly toward the

distant shelter of rocks as the horse galloped away.

Sam just gave him a hard stare.

"Everybody's got to eat." Lang shrugged. He turned to Adele and offered a thin smile, which she ignored. Lang slumped a little as if embarrassed by his actions. Then he turned back to the Ranger with a more serious look.

"You don't figure on following this same trail, do you?" he asked.

"No," Sam replied. "I spotted another trail up the side back below the butte, before we got around the gully. I figured it's a good place to duck out if we had to. We're heading back now while the horse still has their attention."

"We could watch for their fire, slip in and take them down," Lang said, "if you would trust me with a gun, that is."

"I won't, so forget it," Sam said flatly, stepping back over to his Appaloosa. "Anyway, they won't build a fire and cook it with the army on their tails. They'll butcher it to the bone and eat while they ride." He gave Lang a look that implied he should have known that himself, and swung up into his saddle.

"Yeah, yeah," Lang grumbled under his breath. But he straightened in his saddle and turned and rode off in front of the Ranger, realizing the lawman had been watching, thinking, planning ahead this whole trek. This was not a man to discount when it came to knowing the art of staying alive, he told himself, nudging his horse forward.

"Okay, Ranger," he whispered to himself, "you know your business, I'll give you that."

Three hours later, having swung up the steep,

treacherous canyon trail, making better time without the spindly-legged roan, the three led their horses along the last fifty yards of loose silt and jagged rock. Once over the edge onto a narrow stretch of flatland, Lang allowed himself to collapse to the ground. Clasping his sweat-stained hat in one of his cupped hands, he fanned himself.

"You do not travel easy, Ranger," he said. "I could lie here for an hour or—"

His words stopped short as Sam grabbed the third cuff hanging on the short chain between his wrists and gave a jerk.

"On your feet, Cisco," he said, pulling hard, forcing the outlaw to stand.

"Damn it, Ranger," said Lang. "All I'm doing is taking a rest here. That's a climb that could stagger a mountain goat."

Rifle in hand, Sam pulled Lang a step closer to the side of his horse, raised his cuffed hands and snapped the third cuff around his saddle horn.

"For God's sake, Ranger, be reasonable," Lang said.

"I will, someday," Sam said flatly. "Right now you can lean against your horse and rest."

"That makes no sense," Lang said. "What's to stop me from jumping up in the saddle and cutting out?"

Sam gestured toward the Winchester in his hand.

"Take a guess," he said.

Lang shook his head and looked to Adele as if seeking her sympathy. She only glanced away, poured a few drops of water from a canteen onto a wadded handkerchief and touched it to her lips.

The Ranger reached into his saddlebags, retrieved a telescope and stretched it out in his hands. As he started to look out past the walls of the canyon they had just scaled, two men in dusty army tunics sprang up from a low stand of brush less than thirty feet away.

"Don't shoot, Ranger Burrack!" one of the men shouted as Sam dropped his telescope and swung his Winchester around toward them. "We're scouts, U.S. Army," the young man added quickly. "Riding renegade detail for Captain Stroud."

Sam eased his rifle barrel down, but not by much, scrutinizing them closely. The one speaking wore a full uniform and a cavalry campaign hat. The other man was Apache, wearing an army tunic, but instead of trousers he wore a loincloth, a pair of knee-high moccasins and a battered forage cap, thick black hair hanging beneath it to his waist.

"Where's your horses?" Sam asked, wanting to make sure these weren't a couple of deserters in sore need of transportation.

Good move, Ranger, Lang told himself, watching, listening.

"We left them thirty yards back," said the soldier. "I can send him back for them." When Sam nodded, noting the corporal stripes on the young man's sleeves, the soldier turned to the Apache and gave him a nod. The stoic-faced scout trotted away.

"I'm Corporal Malory," the soldier said, facing Sam again. We saw dust rise off the canyon wall." He gave a guarded smile. "I doubted you were pronghorn out this time of day. We came to take a look." He nodded off toward the end of the canyon wall. "I recognized you straightaway. We were told you was up here somewhere. You know what we're doing here, I expect?"

Sam eased up a little when he saw the Apache appear from behind a stand of rock and come walking back, leading an army horse and a shorter desert barb.

"We fed them a horse," Sam said. "We made it up the canyon wall while they decided what to do with it—eat it raw would be my best speculation, until they get somewhere safe enough to build a fire and dry it."

"Wise move avoiding them, Ranger," the corporal said as the Apache scout stopped beside him with their horses. "They've armed themselves, waylaid a stagecoach out of Farm Town Settlement. Got themselves a shotgun, two rifles, three or four handguns. But they're in poor want for bullets."

Sam only nodded, not wanting to mention that he'd already figured as much.

The corporal walked closer to Adele and Cisco Lang, noting the handcuffs holding Lang to his saddle horn.

"Prisoner, huh?" he said, looking Lang up and down. "What did he do?"

"Yes, a prisoner," Sam replied. But he left the other question unanswered.

"What did he do?" the corporal asked again.

"I heard you the first time," Sam said coolly.

The corporal saw the Ranger's refusal to reply was deliberate. Catching on, he cleared his throat and looked back and forth, embarrassed.

"More of this badlands desert trash, I take it,"

he said, attempting to save face. "If you want my opinion, Ranger, you'd do well to walk him out and put a bullet in his head."

Lang glared at him; the Ranger just stared blankly. Adele looked away as if not hearing any of it.

"Thank you for your *opinion*, Corporal," Sam said in a stiff tone.

Lang noted the Apache scout's dark eyes showing a sharp flash of humor move across them.

"Well, then . . . ," the corporal said, collecting himself after an icy silence. "Is there anything else we can do for you, Ranger?"

"No," Sam said flatly. He continued his cold stare.

"In that case," said the corporal, "my scout and I will ride down and sweep this valley floor to its end and meet the rest of our detail while they surround these bad actors." He smiled haughtily and added, "I can assure you this trail will be safe by dark."

Sam said flatly, "I'm hoping we'll be in New Delmar before nightfall."

"I hope you will mention to the citizenry there that we are out here doing a striking job, protecting this frontier from these murdering red heathens."

Sam didn't reply, but he slid a look at the Apache scout and saw that his blank eyes had gone back to some dark, guarded place.

As the two men took their horses by their reins and stepped over the edge of the canyon wall, leading the animals beside them, Sam shoved his rifle down into its boot, picked up his telescope and raised it to his eye again.

"Don't feel like you had to protect my personal business from him," Lang said as Sam scanned a cloud of dust at the far end of the canyon floor.

"I didn't do it to protect your personal business," Sam said as he spotted the band of renegades riding along, each of them with his shirt off, the sleeves tied around his neck, all supporting bloody bundles of horse meat resting on their laps. "You're *my business* as long as you're my prisoner."

He scanned a thousand yards ahead of the renegades and saw the cavalry detail riding straight toward them. Without mentioning what was about to happen out there on the dusty desert floor, he shut the telescope between his gloved hands and turned to his stallion.

Within moments, the three had mounted and ridden on along the rim of the canyon in the direction of New Delmar. Ten minutes later they heard the cacophony of gunfire rumble up the canyon walls ahead of them and echo out across the high desert hills.

"There went Mexico," Lang said, and they rode on.

Chapter 7

When the trail along the canyon spilled onto the stretch of rock and flatlands, the Ranger noted the gunfire ahead of them had stopped. In its place, a thousand yards beyond the Ranger, Lang and Adele, lay a low cloud of red trail dust and gray-black gun smoke. Out of the looming smoke a thin rising stream of red dust swirled toward them through a wall of towering buttes and chimney rock. A short distance behind the stream of trail dust, another wider, thicker stream began to rise. Shots began to ring out again.

"Good heavens," said Adele Simpson, "what now?" She gave the Ranger a worried look.

"My guess is that one of the braves managed to get away," Sam replied. He nodded out toward the distant trail. "I'd say right now the army is in hot pursuit." He looked out for a moment toward the shooting, then said, "Come on, let's not get caught in their fire." He gestured to Adele and Lang ahead of him, motioning toward a stand of rock twenty yards to their right.

Sam slid Black Pot to a halt at the foot of a jagged steep rock and handed Adele his reins and his Winchester. Telescope in hand, he stepped out of his saddle onto the rock and climbed five feet up onto a narrow ledge. Standing tall against the high rock, he stretched his telescope out and leveled it in the direction of the oncoming gun-fire.

In the circle of the lens, he spotted a young Apache boy racing along the trail, riding the spindly-legged roan they had sacrificed, of all things.

"It looks like their stolen horses were in such poor shape," Sam said, "they kept the roan and slaughtered one of their others."

"No kidding?" Lang said from his saddle below.

Sam noted a detached sound to the outlaw's voice. He had already started to look down when he heard Adele cry out for his help. He saw Lang grab the rifle and try to wrench it free from her hands. She held on long enough for Sam to draw his big Colt and point it down toward Lang's head.

"Turn it loose, Cisco," he said with finality, his finger on the trigger, ready to pull it.

With his hands cuffed to the saddle horn, Lang had little leverage to get the rifle free from the woman and aim it up at the Ranger.

Lang froze, but held on to the Winchester, weighing his chances.

"I'll kill her, Ranger," Lang said, giving his best bluff.

"No, you won't," Sam said. "It's a fool's play. I didn't leave a bullet in the chamber. Think how many bullets I'll put in the top of your head before you lever a round up and get a shot off."

In the distance, gunshots still rang out along the trail. Lang gave it another second of thought.

"Damn it," he growled, letting go of the Win-chester. He stared with disgust at Adele. "You'd see me killed before you'd give me a gun and let me have a fighting chance?"

Adele jerked the rifle farther away from him as he slumped in his saddle.

"Anything you think I ever owed you, Cisco, you more than used up long ago," she said. "I wish I had thought quick enough to put a bullet in you myself." She heatedly swung the rifle around in her hands and and aimed it at Lang's chest.

Lang gave her a cool look.

"Go on, pull the trigger, Adele," he said. "You heard the Ranger. There's no bullet in the chamber."

Her hand tightened around the rifle. Sam saw where her anger was taking her.

"Adele, stop. Don't pull that trigger," he called down in a grave tone. "There *is* a bullet in the chamber. You don't want his death on your hands."

There is a bullet in the chamber? Lang stared up at the Ranger with a puzzled, outraged expression.

"You—you bluffed me, Ranger?" he said with an air of shocked disbelief.

"Maybe," Sam said, behind the pointed Colt.

"You did, you bluffed me," said Lang, as if stunned by the impossibility of it.

"Imagine that," Sam said. As he spoke, he stepped down the side of the rock, over into his saddle. Reaching over, he took the cocked rifle from Adele's hands, let the hammer down and laid it over his lap. He knew Lang was watching, wondering now whether or not he had been bluffing. Yet Sam did nothing to reveal himself. Lang was good at playing games, he decided. Let him figure it out for himself.

"Stick close to the rocks," he said, offering no more on the matter. "This chase won't last long."

As they advanced, the sound of gunfire in the near distance grew more intense, but only for less than two minutes. They rounded a turn in the trail, sticking close to the rocks flanking their right, and the shooting stopped all at once. A silent moment passed, followed by a single rifle shot as they moved into sight and saw two soldiers standing over the downed Apache youth lying lifeless on the ground.

"Look at this," said Lang, seeing the roan still racing along toward them.

As the frightened horse drew closer and swung around them off the trail, the Ranger raced in beside it, grabbed its bridle and slowed it to a halt.

"Whoa, boy," he said, sensing the roan give in, circle to a halt alongside him and the stallion. Feeling the firm hand checking it down and the safety of another of its kind beside it, the roan blew and snorted and shook itself out. "You come out of this better than I ever expected," Sam said. He turned with the roan and led it over to Lang and the woman.

"Well, look at you," Adele said to the winded roan. She reached over and patted its sweat-streaked head. Lang just sat watching, knowing that each mile they drew nearer to New Delmar, the lower his chances were of getting away.

Now the army, Sam thought.

A hundred yards ahead through a drift of trail dust, Sam saw the two soldiers standing over the downed Apache watch closely as he followed Lang and the woman forward at an easy gait, leading the roan beside him. As the three approached, Sam watched a buckboard roll forward from among the rest of the detail, who sat back twenty yards watching from their saddles. The buckboard slid to a stop a few feet from the Apache lying dead on the ground. The driver jumped down wearing a long tan riding duster and a black bowler hat.

By the time the Ranger and his companions halted a few feet from the two soldiers, the driver had set up a tripod and attached a large camera atop it, pointed toward the two soldiers and the dead Indian.

"Hold your people back there for a moment, Ranger," one of the soldiers called out to Sam in an air of importance. "We need to let this dust die down."

Sam, Adele and Lang looked at each other.

"A photo grafter," said Lang, "making tinplates of the Western Frontier—something they're doing for posterity."

"So I've heard," Sam said, watching intently.

"Posterity, my ass," said Lang. He spit with contempt. "Who the hell cares about any of this?"

They sat watching the man in the duster and bowler hat run back and forth, fussing over the way the soldiers stood, adjusting their positions with a discriminating eye. At length the man ran, picked up a rock and placed it under the dead Apache's head to elevate it a little. A moment later, after returning behind his camera, a flash of powder rose from a flash pan in his hand and the soldiers relaxed.

Sam nudged Black Pot forward when one of the soldiers waved him in.

"Thank you for your cooperation," said a young captain with dust-mantled shoulders and a dust-streaked beard. Beside him, a stout sergeant who had posed with his boot on the dead Apache's shoulder stepped over and reached out for the roan's bridle. But Sam pulled the roan away.

"The roan is ours," Sam said. "We gave it up to the renegades earlier."

"Then I suppose it wasn't yours after all, eh, Ranger?" said the sergeant.

Sam just looked at him, holding the roan back closer beside him.

"As you were, Sergeant Durbin," said the captain, reading the Ranger's face differently than his sergeant. "The Ranger says it's his, he's welcome to it." He looked up at Sam. "It's certainly not one of our army horses from San Carlos."

The sergeant stepped back with a nod to higher authority.

The photographer backed away from his camera and looked the roan up and down.

"It would be good to have a photo of the horse this warrior was riding," he said.

"What say you, Ranger?" the captain asked, being diplomatic.

"Certainly, Captain," said Sam. "It is the horse he was riding when you caught him." As he spoke and gave the roan over to the photographer, he looked down at the face of the dead Apache, a bullet hole through his forehead from close range. "I wouldn't call this young fellow a warrior, though," he offered.

"Indeed?" said the captain. "What, then, would you call him, Ranger? He and his bloody band have massacred four white settlers in as many days."

Sam looked down from his saddle into the

back of the buckboard at the blank faces of the other dead Apaches piled in side by side. A shirt stuffed with bloody horse meat still hung around one man's neck, tied by its sleeves.

"I understand, Captain," he said, realizing there was no use commenting any further on the issue.

"Good, then," said the captain. "As you can see, our job is nearly finished here, Ranger. As soon as my scouts report in, we'll be riding back to San Carlos. You and your party are welcome to ride with us as far as New Delmar."

"I had planned on being in New Delmar tonight," Sam said, pausing to consider the captain's offer.

"And so we will, Ranger," the captain said. "We'll have our evening meal first, then ride on tonight by the light of the moon. We'll arrive there in the morning, rested and fed."

Sam noticed the look of disappointment in Lang's eyes. Riding with the army gave him little hope to make a getaway.

"Obliged, Captain," Sam said. "I'd like to take you up on your offer. First, I need to ride back into the canyon and collect the lady's belongings we had to leave beside the trail."

"Nonsense, Ranger," said the captain. "I'll send some men to fetch the lady's belongings."

"We're most grateful, Captain," Sam said. "It would be good to relax some, have more than one set of eyes on my prisoner here."

"I'll post two guards around him, Ranger," the captain said. "You may doze in your saddle all the way to New Delmar—travel by compliments of the U.S. Army."

The Ranger gave Lang a thin smile, then turned back to the captain.

"Much obliged, Captain," he said.

"All ready here, Captain," the photographer called out, having the roan stand over the dead Apache, the sergeant holding its reins.

"If you'll excuse me, Ranger," the captain said with a smile. "History calls on us to declare ourselves."

Sam only nodded and backed his stallion out of their way.

Inside the Number Five Saloon, a gambler named Ace Myers shoved his chair back from the table and stood up into an angle of morning sunlight breaking through a dusty window. He looked down at Oldham Coyle, who was lying face-down on the battered tabletop, a few chips scattered around him. A half-empty bottle of rye stood at Coyle's elbow.

"None of my business, mister," the gambler said to Dave Coyle, who stood beside his sleeping brother, "but you ought to get him out of here while he's still wearing a shirt and britches. He hasn't won a hand since yesterday."

"You're right," Dave said. "It's none of your *damned* business." He took Oldham by his shoulder and shook him roughly. "Wake up, Oldham," he said in a loud voice close to his brother's ear. "It's all over."

Oldham stirred and lifted his head. A poker chip stuck to his cheek and followed him up. It fell as he swung his head back and forth and tried to focus his eyes, though an indentation of the chip showed on his face.

"What's over?" he asked in a groggy voice.

Myers stifled a laugh, already seeing that the least remark could set off trouble. He shrugged and folded a stack of dollars the dealer had given him for cashing in his chips. Handing the dealer a gold coin large enough to bring a smile to his tired face, he turned to leave.

"Wait!" said Oldham, seeing him go. "I'm still in." He raked his hands around desperately on the tabletop gathering his few remaining chips.

Ace Myers slowed a little and looked back over his shoulder, but noting the expression on Dave Coyle's face, he decided it best to keep walking. The dealer rose and stood back a step, watching.

"You're not in, Oldham, you're out," Dave said to his brother, shaking him harder. "Look at you. You've burned yourself up, all this rye, this damned Mexican powder." He swung a hand and slapped a small leather bag of cocaine off the table onto the floor. Powder billowed. "You've lost all your money."

"No! No, I haven't," Oldham said. "You're wrong! I've got more money upstairs." He rose and walked unsteadily across the floor.

The dealer looked at Dave and let out a breath.

"Go on, get out of here," Dave said, shoving the few remaining chips to him. Following his brother, he stopped halfway across the floor and watched Oldham stagger up the stairs, finally heading toward Anna Rose's room. Dave saw Little Deak, Blind Simon and Karl Sieg standing at the empty bar. They looked away from Dave as his eyes met theirs.

Next Dave noticed the stoic faces of Henry Teague and Sonny Rudabough. The two sat at the same table they'd occupied over the past three days, every time they'd come into the saloon to check on Oldham at the poker table.

"The hell are you two looking at?" Dave said in an angry voice.

Sonny Rudabough stared coldly at him; Henry Teague shook his head slowly.

"Nothing. We're here to see your brother, when he gets some free time for us, that is," Teague said smugly.

Before Dave could respond, Oldham came staggering back down the stairs, wild-eyed, his gun waving loose in his hands. He hung against the hand rails and looked back and forth.

"She's gone! So's my money!" he said.

"She's a whore, brother," Dave shouted up at him. "Of course she's gone. What did you expect?"

"She said she'd wait," Oldham called out, his voice week, shaky.

"Maybe she did wait for a while," said Dave. "But you've been gambling for three days and nights! You haven't eaten, haven't slept."

Three days and nights?

Oldham rubbed his beard-stubbled jaw in confusion.

"No whore waits that long for anybody," Dave said, "unless she's simpleminded. What'd you think, that you married her?"

At their table, Sonny Rudabough gave Teague a sly look.

Above them on the landing, Oldham slumped down onto his knees, gripping the handrail. He sobbed against his chest.

Dave gave a nod toward the bar. "Deak, you and Sieg give my brother a hand. Get him down from there."

As the two walked past Dave toward the stairs, Sieg spoke to him quietly under his breath.

"Where are we taking him?" he asked.

"Outside of town," said Dave. "We'll make camp and get ourselves shook out and sobered up some."

Deak and Sieg just looked at each other. The only one needing to sober up and shake himself out was their leader. But they kept quiet, crossed the floor and climbed the stairs.

While they gathered Oldham and pulled him to his feet, Dave Coyle walked over to the table where the two gunmen sat.

"I've seen you both snooping around here every time I come to check on my brother," he said.

"Snooping around?" Sonny Rudabough half rose from his chair, shooting an icy stare at Dave. Teague stopped him with a raised hand.

"The man's concerned about his brother, Sonny," he said. "Sit down and have some whiskey for breakfast." As Sonny relented and sank back down on his chair, Teague said to Dave, "I presented a business proposition to your brother the other day. I'm still waiting around for an answer."

"What kind of proposition?" Dave asked, hearing Deak and Sieg helping Oldham down the stairs.

"No offense," said Teague, "but it's between him and us. If he wants to tell you, that's his call."

"I'm getting him out of here and getting him some rest," Dave said.

"Good idea," Teague said. "I'm Henry Teague. This friendly young man is Sonny Rudabough. We'll be waiting. Tell him for me."

Dave nodded. As he and the others left the saloon with Oldham hanging between Sieg and himself, he saw a group of soldiers riding into sight at the far end of the busy street. A wagon loaded with loud, laughing, cheering miners rolled in at the other side of town. Behind the wagon, he saw other miners arriving, on mules, on horseback and on foot.

"Damn it, Oldham," he grumbled under his breath. "It's already payday for these square heads. We've missed our shot."

Chapter 8

Inside the New Delmar sheriff's office still under construction, the Ranger and Captain Leonard Stroud stood watching as the town sheriff chained a thick hundred-fifty-pound ball of solid iron to Cisco Lang's ankle. Cisco dragged the ball by its chain to the far side of the room. A chalk line on the floor showed where iron bars would soon stand.

"Stay behind the chalk line and we'll get along just fine, Cisco Lang," said the sheriff, Ed Rattler. Lang stopped beside a chair and sat down facing them. He gave the sheriff a cold stare.

"I always say it takes more than bars to make a good jail," said the sheriff. He smiled behind a thick coppery gray mustache. "It takes good attitude."

"I won't be forgetting this, *Rattling Ed*," Cisco called out in a threatening tone.

"It's *Sheriff Rattler* henceforth, Cisco," said the sheriff. "I wouldn't be threatening me if I were you. Dankett here would love to goose you with double loads of gravel rock and metal shavings." He turned to a grim-looking young man with a pale red-blotched face and eyes as sharp and cold as a viper. "Wouldn't you, Deputy Dankett?"

The grim young man, Clow Dankett, sat in a thick corduroy trail coat and a tall Montana-style high-crowned drover's hat, one knee crossed over the other, supporting a long-barreled shotgun. A leather shoulder strap drooped from the shotgun stock.

"Wouldn't I, though?" he said expressionless, leaning forward, his trigger finger tensed, ready to empty the shotgun into Lang at the slightest provocation.

"It is true," said the captain, his hands folded behind his back, clutching his yellow cavalry gloves. "'Iron bars do not a prison make.' Richard Lovelace, 1642," he quoted, smiling with satisfaction at his literary reference.

The Ranger and the sheriff looked at him askance.

"Captain," Lang said in disgust, "Loveless never said *iron bars*. He said, *Stone walls do not a prison make.*"

"Be that as it may," Captain Stroud said, his countenance undeterred, "in this case I suppose one could support the premise that an *iron ball* certainly does indeed."

Dankett gave Lang a hard cruel stare, as if in anticipation.

"At any rate, Ranger Burrack," said Captain Stroud, turning to Sam, "it has been my pleasure." He reached a hand out. "Good luck killing all of these waywards and miscreants."

Cisco Lang watched and listened.

"Obliged for your escort, Captain," Sam said, shaking the captain's strong, dry hand. He ignored the reference to the killing of waywards and miscreants and watched the captain turn and walk out the door.

As soon as the captain was gone, Sheriff Rattler stood facing Sam with his hands resting on his gun belt.

"What's the town council's excuse for your jail not being finished, Sheriff?" Sam asked.

"Officially, they're saying everybody's too busy to get it done, Ranger," said Rattler. "But that's malarkey. It's just low on their *give-a-damn* list. We're lucky it hasn't got Dankett or me killed. It's part of why Dankett stays drawn tight as a wire fence. He has to stay on his toes night and day, and it's getting to him." He leaned in close to Sam and whispered in secret, "He calls his shotgun *Big Lucy*."

"I'm all right," Dankett said, staring at Cisco as he spoke.

"Anyway, that's my worry, Ranger," said Rattler. "In case you don't know it, there's a five-thousand-dollar bounty on your head, Ranger Burrack. I hate to be the bearer of bad news. But I got a telegraph telling me all about it." As he spoke, he took out a wanted poster and unfolded it in his hands.

Five thousand? That was more than most murdering outlaws of high notoriety.

"I heard about it," Sam replied. He took the poster and looked at it closely, feeling a twinge in his guts, seeing his name and drawn likeness exhibited as if he were a criminal.

"Then I'm sorry I brought it up," said Rattler, noticing the look on the Ranger's face.

"That's all right," said the Ranger. He gave him a wry smile. "If someone's out to kill me, I appreciate somebody warning me ahead of time."

"That's the way I look at it," said Rattler, sounding a little relieved. "Note there's not a name as far as who's offering the reward is concerned," the sheriff said. "That shows the kind of coward they are."

"It's Hugh Fenderson," Sam said without hesitation, folding the wanted poster and handing it back to Rattler.

"Hugh Fenderson?" Rattler said, taken aback. "My goodness! He owns the rail spur that runs up here. Owns the beef that feeds both the army and the Apache in San Carlos! What the hell's wrong with him?"

"I shot his nephew, Mitchell Fenderson, during a bank robbery," the Ranger said.

"Kill him?" Rattler asked.

"No," said Sam, "he's in Yuma, getting himself rehabilitated with a pick and sledgehammer."

"Dang," said Rattler, scratching his chin. "You'd think a man of influence like Hugh Fenderson would just get his nephew sprung out of there instead of wasting time wanting to kill you."

"You would think so," Sam said. "Anyway, there it is. If he owns the rail spur here, I expect he owns other interests too?"

"Yep, I'm afraid he does," said the sheriff, "including the money it takes to finish building this jail. But I'm going to try not to let that influence me upholding the law."

Try not to, he'd said. The Ranger saw the look on Sheriff Rattler's face change. Before, he'd exhibited a sense of being in charge, but now his face showed something else, something less assured.

"I understand, Sheriff," Sam said. "I'll see to it my trouble doesn't rub off on you."

"Not that I'm going to allow you to be put in a

bad spot," he said. "Just that I might ought to step back away from this." He stopped and shook his lowered head, ashamed. "How come these rich sons a' bitches run every damned thing?" he said. "Their rules make their money, and their money makes their rules. That's all there is to it—all there's ever been to it."

"I understand your situation," the Ranger repeated. "As soon as I get a telegraph to Yuma and get myself and my prisoner fed, I'm headed out of your jurisdiction. You won't be seen with me. You'll have no hand in the game."

"To hell with Fenderson, you're coming to eat with me, Ranger," the sheriff said, reconsidering. "Since when does one lawman have to worry about being seen with another? We'll send some food over here for Dankett and this one."

"Sounds real good to me, Sheriff," Sam said. Under his breath he asked, "Is Cisco going to be okay with this man watching him?"

"He will be unless he starts acting ugly," Rattler said. "That's as fair as it gets, ain't it?"

"I suppose it is," Sam replied.

"Oh," said Rattler, "I also need to warn you there's already a couple of bad eggs blew in off the desert, asking around about you."

Sam looked at him.

"They call themselves the Derby Brothers," he said, "but that's not their name, and they are no kin that I can figure out." He gave a shrug. "Who knows why these knot-heads do what they do— idiots, is all I can come up with."

"They're still in town, these two?" Sam asked.

"They might be. That's why I bring it up," said

the sheriff. "I had no real cause to boot them out of there. I had no idea you was coming, else I would have made up a reason. I still can as far as that goes."

"No," Sam said. "If they're out to collect the bounty, it's best I know where they are."

"Like as not they're gone on by now," said Rattler, the two of them turning to the door. "Their kind don't stick long. They most likely have bounty of their own to worry about."

Rifles in hand, the two turned, walked out the door and followed a double line of walk planks along the edge of the crowed street. But before they had gone thirty yards, Sam saw Adele Simpson running toward them from the direction of the Number Five Saloon, recklessly forcing her way along the middle of the street through a tangle of wagon, buggy, horseback and foot traffic.

"Ranger! Go back!" she cried out, seeing Sam and the sheriff walking toward her.

"What the—?" Sheriff Rattler said, stopping, his hand darting to the gun holstered on his hip.

Sam ran forward, seeing the frightened look on Adele's face. When he reached her, she steadied herself against him, winded, struggling to catch her breath.

"Go back, Ranger Burrack!" she warned. "There's men back there waiting to kill you!"

"Easy, ma'am," Sam said, looking past her shoulder in the direction of the big wooden beer mug hanging overhead. "What are you talking about?"

"Two gunmen . . . in derby hats, Ranger," she said, gasping for breath. "They're in the alley . . . right before the saloon. They found out you're here. They're waiting for you."

Derby hats? The Derby Brothers . . .

Passing onlookers gazed at them curiously, seeing the badge on the Ranger's chest. Looking toward the Number Five, Sam saw the thick crowd begin to part. Wagons veered off to the side of the street, horses and buggies hastily turned off into alleys. Pedestrians disappeared quickly into shops and businesses.

"All right, Adele," Sam said. "Take it easy. Take a breath."

She settled herself a little and looked back over her shoulder in fear.

"Now, then, tell me what you can," Sam said in a calm, even tone of voice.

"I came back from the depot . . . to get some things before my train arrives this evening. The clerk at the mercantile store overheard these men talking outside the open window. They're waiting there for you."

"It looks like they're not waiting now," Sam said, noting the street traffic changing before their eyes.

"Ranger Sam Burrack!" a voice called out from beyond the stirring crowd.

The Ranger didn't reply.

"I—I had to warn you," Adele said. "I couldn't let you walk into an ambush."

"Ranger Burrack!" the same voice called out.

The Ranger still didn't reply.

"Here, let's get you off the street, ma'am," he said to Adele. Looking toward the sound of the voice, he guided her off to the side of the quickly vacating street.

"What—what are you going to do?" she asked, a fearful look in her eyes.

Sam didn't answer her. Instead he looked at

the two men walking toward him in the middle of the now-empty street, each with a battered derby hat cocked jauntily to the side atop his head.

"Ranger Sam Burrack," said the same man, spotting the Ranger and the woman. "You can run, but you can't hide." He grinned. "You best stop and face us. We're trouble that's not going away."

Sam ignored the two and led Adele over to the doorway of a shop, where a woman rushed out, took her hand and quickly led her inside.

The two men stopped twenty feet from Sam and stepped away from each other, putting ten feet between them.

Still standing to the side, Winchester hanging in his left hand, Sam eased his big Colt from his holster and leisurely cocked it, as if it were something he did every day at this same time. Letting the cocked Colt hang down at his side, he stepped out into the street.

"The Derby Brothers, I take it?" the Ranger said calmly.

"What tipped you off?" said the gunman on the right. He was still grinning, a big beefy man with a red face and watery whiskey-swollen eyes.

Sam just stared at him, ready to swing the big Colt up and start firing. This big one would be the one to knock down first, he told himself. The other one was strictly the big man's backup.

"Manning," the one to the left said, trying to talk quietly, "he's already drawn and pulled back."

"I see that, Earl," the big gunman, Manning Childe, whispered sidelong. He raised his voice for the Ranger to hear. "But it won't matter. I've got a rifleman on a rooftop, just over there." He gave a nod and got ready to draw as soon as the Ranger turned his eyes toward the roofline. But the Ranger didn't fall for it.

"You're lying, mister," Sam said without batting an eye.

Sheriff Rattler's voice called out from behind the Ranger, to his left by the walk planks.

"Anybody shows their face up there, Ranger, I'll stop their clock for them," he said. Sam heard the sound of the sheriff's rifle lever a round.

The big gunman took a deep breath; Sam saw he was ready to make his move in spite of his failed bluff. He might have something else he wanted to try, but Sam wasn't going to give him the chance.

"All right, Ranger," the gunman said. "In case you're wondering, this is all about the bounty that's—"

"I'm not," Sam said quietly, raising the big Colt, leveling it at the gunman's chest, causing him to cut his words short. Manning's face twisted and turned in confusion. He made a grab for his holstered gun, but it was too late.

The Ranger's first shot hit him dead center and sent him backward to the dirt in a red mist of blood. His derby hat appeared to hang suspended in the air for a second, then fell to the ground.

Seeing his partner go down without even getting a shot off, the other man threw his hands up as Sam swung the big Colt toward him.

"No! Wait!" he shouted.

But there was no hope. The Ranger had already

cocked, leveled and squeezed the trigger of the big Colt. It bucked in his hand beneath a streaming rise of gun smoke.

The gunman, Earl Hyde, flipped backward with the impact of the shot and landed facedown in the dirt beneath a gout of blood jetting up from the exit hole in his back.

The dying gunman raised his head from the dirt and looked up at the Ranger. Sam stepped forward, his smoking Colt extended for another shot should one be needed.

"I—I had quit," the man said in a weak, trembling voice.

"Should have quit sooner," the Ranger said. He uncocked the Colt and stood watching as the man's face bobbed, then fell back to the hard rocky dirt and relaxed there as if he were sleeping on a thick, soft pillow.

Sheriff Rattler ventured forward, followed by a gathering group of onlookers. Adele Simpson stepped out of the shop where she'd taken cover. But when the two walked closer to the Ranger, pistol shots rang out from the unfinished jail.

"Stay here," Sam said to Adele. The two lawmen turned and raced toward the sound of overlapping gunshots.

Out in front of the jail, Sam stood on one side of the door and Rattler on the other.

"Dankett!" Rattler called out through the thick door. "Are you all right in there?"

"I'm good, Sheriff," Dankett called back to him. "I thwarted a jailbreak."

Sam gave Rattler a curious look.

Rattler eased and let his pistol and rifle slump in his hands.

"It's okay, Ranger," he said, taking a breath. "I should have expected this. Everybody tries to break out of my jail. But they never make it."

Sam and Sheriff Rattler eased inside the unfinished building and saw the deputy still seated, his rifle across his lap, his Colt curling smoke in his right hand. On the wall across from him, Lang hung upside down, swinging back and forth by his ankle on the end of the chain holding him to the large ball of iron. The ball was out of sight, hanging out the open window where Lang had thrown it, not realizing the weight of it would overcome him.

The Ranger winced, already seeing what had happened.

"Get me down from here!" Lang shouted, terrified. Fresh bullet holes dotted the wall, flanking him on either side. Splinters clung to Lang's shirt and hair.

"Dankett," said Rattler, "what happened this time?"

"I closed my eyes just for a minute, Sheriff," the deputy said innocently. "He pitched his iron out and was going to escape. What else could I do? I only shot my six-gun at him, didn't really try to pin him to the wall."

"He's crazy, Sheriff!" Lang shouted. "Ranger, get me out of here! He tried to kill me!"

Sam looked at Rattler.

"It's not the first jailbreak Dankett has thwarted, Ranger," he said. "If he'd meant to kill him, he would have lifted that shotgun to his shoulder. Cisco would be dead." He leaned in close to Sam and whispered under his breath, "The deputy here takes some getting used to. But nobody ever tries to break out twice."

Sam holstered his Colt and let out a breath.

"I'm going to pass on eating right now, Sheriff," Sam said. "I'm going to take some food with us and get out of here before any more gunmen get their bark on and try to collect that reward."

Chapter 9

It was afternoon when the Ranger and Lang stepped down from their horses on the far side of New Delmar. The Ranger left Lang cuffed to his saddle horn while he set down a canvas sack of air-tights, hardtack and salt pork he'd bought at a mercantile store as they left town. When he had sorted out the supplies, he freed the third handcuff and nodded toward some brush and downed tree limbs lying nearby.

"See if you can gather us some firewood and kindling without turning rabbit on me," the Ranger said. "The quicker we get us a fire started, the quicker we can eat."

"You've got it all wrong, Ranger," said Lang. "I'm not trying anything else. That lunatic Dankett has put running out of my mind."

"That's good to hear, Cisco," said Sam, not believing it for a second. "Maybe there's hope for you rehabilitating yourself after all."

As Lang spoke he stepped over and picked up a stout three-foot tree limb and hefted it in his hands. On his way back to where the Ranger intended to build the fire, he gazed out at a rise of trail dust and the rider coming toward them from the direction of New Delmar.

"What's this?" he asked.

Instead of turning his back on Lang, the Ranger stepped to the side and positioned himself in a way that allowed him to look out at the rider without taking his eyes off his prisoner. Lang noted his maneuver and dropped the limb as if in defeat.

"That's wise thinking, Cisco," Sam said sidelong to him, studying the rider until he recognized Adele Simpson and the spindly-legged roan riding alongside her with her load of belongings on its back.

"Sorry, Ranger, force of habit," Lang said. He sighed and dusted his cuffed hands together. Turning, he looked out with the Ranger as Adele drew closer. "Wonder what she's doing here," he said. "Think she missed her train?"

Without answering Lang, Sam watched the woman ride closer and slow the black desert barb to a halt a few feet away. He stepped over and took the lead rope to the roan from her hand.

"Evening, ma'am," he said to Adele. He looked the roan over as he patted it with his gloved hand. "This horse strikes me as being grateful to be alive, after that close scrape with the Apache."

The roan nuzzled its sweaty jaw against the Ranger's hand and sawed its head up and down as if in agreement.

"Evening, Ranger," Adele replied. "May I ride on with you to Yuma?" she asked flatly.

Sam looked up at her, a little surprised, as he rubbed the roan's jaw. Lang stepped up beside him and watched and listened.

"The train didn't show up. It won't be here until sometime tomorrow," she said. "I got tired of being at the depot listening to all the talk about you and those two gunmen."

"The talk dies down after a while," Sam said.

"I don't care," said Adele, shaking her head, "I'm done with that place."

"Still," said the Ranger, "the train will be a lot faster and more comfortable, once it does get here."

"No, I'm not waiting for it another day, Ranger, talk or no talk," she said with determination. "Once I start moving I don't like to stop. May I ride with you?"

"There might be more men wanting to kill me, ma'am," Sam cautioned her. "Are you certain you want to—"

"I know what I'll be getting into, Ranger," she said, cutting him off. "May I ride with you or not?" She wasn't being impatient, just persistent.

Sam tipped his sombrero to her and reached up for the roan's lead rope.

"Ma'am, I'd be honored," he said.

Adele handed him the roan's rope and swung down from her saddle, refusing a cuffed hand from Cisco Lang as he stepped closer and took her horse's reins.

Lang shrugged her rejection off as she stepped past him and the Ranger and looked down at the canvas food bag and the unlit makings of a cook fire.

"Ma'am, you don't have to jump right in and cook for us," Sam said, seeing her start rolling up her dress sleeves.

"Oh yes, I do," Adele said. She gave him a short smile. "I always earn my keep."

Sam and Lang looked at each other.

"Well, then, yes, ma'am," Sam said. "I'm much obliged." He looked at Lang and said, "Give me her horse. You gather up more wood for the fire."

Taking the reins and the lead rope in hand, the Ranger turned to walk the horses away.

"Oh, and by the way, Ranger Burrack," the woman said as if in afterthought. "I liked it better the couple of times you called me Adele instead of ma'am."

"Yes, ma'am—I mean Adele," the Ranger said. As he walked away, he heard Cisco Lang over his shoulder.

"Does that go for me too, Adele?" he asked quietly. "I've always called you Adele." His voice softened. "Among other things, remember?"

"No, I don't remember," she said flatly. "The fact is, I don't remember anything about you. I started forgetting about you a long time ago."

The Ranger smiled to himself and shook his head, leading the two horses away, his rifle in hand. The black barb sauntered along, but the roan followed him eagerly as if in appreciation of any water, grain or other human kindness that might come its way.

"Don't worry," the Ranger said to the roan, liking the horse's spirit and attitude. "I never figured you'd make it this far. Since you did, we're not going to let anybody eat you."

He walked both horses into the shade of a large boulder where his stallion and Lang's horse stood watching, chewing grain he'd given them from a sack sitting on the ground just out of their reach. The Ranger untied Adele's personal belongings from the roan's back and stacked them over to the side, easy for the woman to get to should she need anything from them. As he started to turn, a leather travel case fell from atop a worn carpetbag and spilled open on the ground.

Sam looked down and saw a small ivory-handled hideaway pistol lying in the dirt. Stooping, he picked the pistol up and looked toward the campfire site to make sure he wasn't being watched. Unseen, he opened the pistol and let two bullets fall onto his palm. Then he closed the pistol, stuck it back inside the leather case, closed the case and placed it atop the carpetbag.

No harm done, he told himself. Maybe the gun meant nothing. Everybody he knew carried a gun. But for now she didn't need the weapon. When the time came that she would go off on her own, he'd give her back her bullets and send her on her way. Meanwhile, he wanted no hidden guns around him, not with a price on his head, not with a prisoner who used to be the woman's lover.

"Now, then, fellows," he said to the roan and the black barb as both horses probed their muzzles toward the feed sack, "let's get you some water and grain, get you settled in for the night."

In the purple, starlit night, Dave Coyle sat at the campfire with Chic Reye, Karl Sieg and Simon Goss, the four of them sipping coffee and passing around a bottle of rye. Off to the side, Little Deak Holder sat staring out across the flatlands, a rifle lying across his lap, a blanket wrapped around his shoulders.

"The good thing about the dwarf being on watch," Reye said quietly, "is if anybody rides in and sees him, they'll think he's a frog sitting there grabbing bugs."

The men gave a low chuckle at his words, which encouraged Reye to keep going.

"Or a land rat squatting to relieve itself," he said, feeling his whiskey.

"*Shhh!* What's that sound?" Dave Coyle said, growing attentive toward the darkness surrounding them.

The men fell silent and listened with him. Little Deak stood up with his rifle and looked all around. But when a gagging sound came from the direction of Oldham Coyle's blanket outside the circle of firelight, the dwarf slumped in disgust and sat back down.

"Sounds like your brother's woke up," Sieg said quietly to Dave Coyle.

Another gagging sound came from the same direction. This time it lasted longer, and was followed by what sounded like a blast of water splattering on the hard ground.

"Jesus," Reye said under his breath, "he must've swallowed a waterfall."

Dave stood up from the fire and dusted his trouser seat.

"I better go see about him," he said. "Sounds like he's awfully sick."

Blind Simon sniffed the air.

"I can tell you everything he's et the past three days."

Sieg and Reye grimaced a little as Dave walked away toward his hawking brother.

"That's all right, Simon," Sieg said quietly. "We don't need to know all that."

"Whatever he et, it was still alive and most likely running from the sound of it," Reye said with contempt, now that Dave had walked out of hearing range. "The thing is, we've gone from ready to ride, to thinking things out, to just a few hands of poker first. And now he's gone out of his mind, gambling, eating dope—"

"That's enough, Chic," Sieg warned Reye.

"Anybody can make a mistake now and then. Let's let it go at that."

"A mistake?" Reye chuffed and looked at Sieg in the glow of firelight. "His mistake just cost me a heap of money."

"It cost us all money, Chic," Sieg said. "But we'll get straightened out. The John Bull mines pay their men like that every month. We've still got it coming."

"You ever heard the saying a bird in the hand is worth two in the bush?" Reye asked over the sound of Oldham still spewing up sickness outside the firelight.

"No, I've never heard that," Sieg said with sarcasm. "Pray tell us what it means."

"What it means is," Simon cut in, "say . . . you're holding a bird right here in your hand." He cupped a big hand in front of him. "But over there in a bush there's two more just sitting, chirping their heads off—"

"He knows what it means, Simon," Little Deak called out over his shoulder.

"Oh," Blind Simon said. He fell silent.

Sieg and Reye looked at each other. Reye spit in disgust and folded his forearms across his knees. He stared into the fire shaking his head.

"Hoss, you are riding with the wrong bunch," he murmured to himself.

Outside the circle of firelight, the gagging finally stopped.

"Sounds like he's feeling better," said Sieg, handing the bottle of rye out to Reye.

"Amen for that," said Reye, taking the bottle and throwing back a drink. "I was getting sick myself, just listening to it."

Hearing the whiskey slosh in the bottle, Blind

Simon put his hand out and wiggled his fingers toward Chic Reye.

"You boys haven't cut me off, have you?"

"No, Simon," Reye said, still sounding disgusted at everything in general. "I'd never forget you." He leaned over, stuck the bottle into Simon's outreached hand and closed the blind man's fingers around it. "Any damn thing I've got, I want to make damn sure you get a part of."

Simon chuckled, ignoring Reye's tone of voice and manner, and threw back a swig of rye.

From outside the circle of firelight, the men heard Dave Coyle call out, "One of you pour some whiskey and water into a cup and bring it over."

"Whiskey and water?" Sieg said under his breath, making a sour face.

"I'm pretending I didn't hear him," Reye replied quietly.

"I'll get it to you, boss," Simon called out. He pushed himself to his feet, grabbing his tapping stick from the ground beside him. The open bottle of rye tipped sidelong in his hand. He stepped forward dangerously close to the fire.

"Like hell you will," said Reye, jumping to his feet, snatching the bottle from Simon's hand. Simon backed up a step and sat down with a half smile on his face.

Chic Reye snatched a tin cup and a canteen from the ground. When he'd poured some whiskey and water into the cup, he handed the bottle down to Sieg and walked away from the fire.

"Here you go, Dave," Reye said as he stepped over to a patch of brush where Dave was standing at Oldham's side. Oldham was bowed at the waist, holding on to a scrub pine with one hand, his other hand pressed hard to his stomach.

"Obliged, Chic," Dave Coyle said, taking the cup of watered whiskey. "He just needs a little something to settle his belly." He nodded toward the fire. "We'll be on over there in a minute."

Reye walked back to the fire. But when he arrived he saw two dark silhouettes walking into their camp from the other direction, leading their horses behind them.

"Deak! Watch your front!" he shouted, drawing his Colt from his holster and cocking it on the upswing.

Little Deak scrambled to his feet, his rifle raised and cocked. At the fire, Sieg and Blind Simon stood up quickly, their guns drawn and aimed.

"Easy, fellows," Henry Teague called out from the purple darkness as he and Sonny Rudabough approached the fire.

"Hold it right there, you sons a' bitches!" shouted Reye, bringing both men to halt. "You don't just walk into a camp unannounced like that, no howdy, hello the camp or nothing else."

"Hello the camp," Sonny Rudabough said in a flat tone.

"Howdy one and all," said Teague.

"Who the hell are you?" said Sieg.

"I'm Henry Teague. This is Sonny Rudabough," Teague said. "We were in the saloon. We're here to see Coyle. Can we come in?"

"They're from the Number Five all right," said Simon. "I can smell them."

"Watch your language, pard," Rudabough warned.

"He's blind," Sieg offered on Simon's behalf. "He smells things most of us don't."

"Yeah?" said Rudabough, "I shoot things most of us can't."

"Easy, Sonny," Teague said sidelong. To the men around the fire he said, "He didn't mean nothing. He's excitable." He paused, then repeated, "Can we come in?"

"Let them on in," Oldham Coyle said in a weak voice, he and Dave stepping in from the darkness, their guns also drawn and ready.

"Evening, Oldham," Teague said as he and Rudabough walked into the firelight, their horses' reins in hand. "I saw your luck wasn't running as good as you might have wanted it to be— thought you might have reconsidered the proposition we talked about the other day."

"You needn't be concerning yourselves with how my luck is running," Oldham said. A troubled, confused look crossed his face. "What proposition was it we talked about?"

Sieg and Reye shot each other a look.

Teague gave a patient smile, stepped in closer and looked down at the coffeepot.

"We talked about my boss, Hugh Fenderson, paying you five thousand dollars to kill Ranger Sam Burrack," he said. "You turned us down, remember?"

Five thousand dollars? Holy Moses!

Sieg and Reye looked at each other again.

Oldham appeared staggered by Teague's words.

"Five thousand dollars?" he said.

"Yep," said Teague. "Burrack rode into town today, taking a prisoner to Yuma—would've been a good time to kill him."

"He's already rode on?" Oldham asked, his head still full of cobwebs.

"That's right, but he'll be riding back tomorrow," he said confidently.

"How do you know he will?" asked Dave

Coyle, who'd been watching closely, listening with a suspicious look on his face.

"Let's just say we heard something bad happened that will cause him to ride back to New Delmar." He gave a crafty smile and nodded down at the coffeepot. "If you're still not interested, I won't waste your time. But if you've become interested, what say we talk with cups in our hands?"

"I'm interested. Seat yourselves," Oldham said, gesturing them to sit down around the fire. "I'll tell you right off, Sam Burrack is not going to be an easy kill."

"I beg to differ with you, Coyle," Teague said. "You think too little of yourself." He looked from face to face around the fire, then said, "Silas Horn out of El Paso puts the odds three to one your favor against the Ranger."

"Forget it, mister," Dave Coyle cut in. "We want no part of this." He turned to Oldham. "Can't you see this man is about to get you killed, brother?"

Oldham smiled and licked his lips and rubbed his palm on his gun butt.

"Shut up, Dave," he said as politely as possible. "Let the gentleman speak his piece."

Dave shuddered as he recognized in his brother's eyes the same hungry look he'd seen when they'd first arrived in New Delmar.

Chapter 10

In the first pale light of dawn, the Ranger placed a fresh pot of coffee to boil atop the low-burning fire. He walked to where the trail turned off the desert floor into the rocks toward his camp. Through a silver-gray shroud, he watched the black silhouette of rider and horse gallop toward him from the direction of New Delmar. The sound of the approaching horse's hooves sent two wispy creatures of the night darting away into the morning gloom.

The rider stopped fifty yards away, stepped down from his saddle and walked around examining the rocky trail. Climbing back into his saddle, the rider put the horse forward, slower now. Sam eased back into the cover of rock and waited until the rider was less than fifteen feet from him.

"Hello the trail," he said just loud enough to be heard, standing partially hidden behind the edge of a tall, broken stand of tent rock.

"Be-jeez!" the startled rider cried out, his horse half rearing, veering away from the Ranger's voice. As the horse touched down, the rider swung a long-barreled shotgun around toward the Ranger.

Seeing the trouble his voice had caused, Sam

stayed covered behind the stand of rock, hearing the rider settle the spooked animal.

"Whoa, horse, easy," the rider said. "Is that you, Ranger Burrack?" he asked toward the rocks. "*Be-jeez*," he repeated, "you could've said something, warn a person before hollering out like that."

Ranger?

Sam had been right, it was someone fanning his trail. He recognized Clow Dankett's voice, even though he'd only heard the deputy speak a few words in New Delmar.

"Yes, it's me," Sam said, also recognizing the big corduroy coat and high-crowned hat. "I'm sorry I spooked your horse, Deputy," he added, although spooking the animal a little had been exactly his intent. "You're looking for me?"

"Yes, I am," Dankett said, lowering the threatening shotgun. "I've been tracking you all night."

The Ranger looked all around, not seeing how it could have been hard to follow his trail.

"Well, Deputy, looks like you've found me," he said.

"I was sent to tell you you're needed back in town," Dankett said.

As Sam stepped the rest of the way out from behind the rock, Dankett slid down from his saddle and stretched his back, the shotgun hanging by its strap on his shoulder.

"Walk with me while we talk," Sam said. He gestured the horse toward his campfire hidden back in the rocks. "My prisoner still has some jackrabbit in him."

"I'll have Big Lucy clip one of his ankles for you, if you want me to turn her loose on him," Dankett offered.

"Obliged, but I'm good, Deputy," Sam said.

As they walked along toward the campfire, Dankett leading his horse, the Ranger looked him up and down.

"So, Deputy, why did Sheriff Rattler send you looking for me?" Sam asked.

"He didn't," Dankett said bluntly. "Sheriff Rattler won't be sending nobody nowhere from now on. He's been shot dead, Ranger. That's why I'm here."

Sam stopped and looked at him closer.

"What happened?" he asked.

Ahead of them, the campfire came into sight. From its edge, Adele and Cisco Lang looked around at the sound of the deputy's horse clopping along the stone path. Lang sat with his hands cuffed to the saddle he'd dragged over to the fire.

"Some ambushing weasel shot him dead," the deputy said, "right out back of our new jail."

"I'm sorry to hear that," Sam said.

"And I'm sorry to tell you," Dankett said. "Anyway, the town council thought it best to send me out to find you, since you happened to be nearby. They need you to oversee things until they get a new sheriff stuck behind a badge."

"What about you, Deputy?" the Ranger said, wanting the deputy's opinion on the matter. From what he'd seen of Dankett's wild, strange behavior, Sam had his own ideas of why the town would not want Dankett as acting sheriff.

"What about me?" said Dankett.

The Ranger drew a patient breath.

"Oh, you mean me be acting sheriff?" Dankett said, catching on.

"Yes, you acting as sheriff," the Ranger said, wishing he hadn't broached the subject.

"They won't have me, Ranger," Dankett said quietly, giving a slight shrug, "but they won't come out and say so." He paused, then said, "I think they're scared of what I might do if they tell me I can't be sheriff—probably wanting you to be the one who tells me."

"I'm sorry, Deputy," Sam said, sorting through the facts as the deputy gave them to him.

"Why?" said Dankett, beneath his wide hat brim. "It's not your fault that I don't get along with people, that I'm too quick-triggered, too ill-natured, too . . ." His words stalled as he searched for another description of himself.

"Unpredictable?" the Ranger offered.

Dankett cocked his head toward the Ranger.

"You saw that too?" he said, sounding dejected.

"No," said the Ranger. "I was just helping you find a word."

"Obliged," Dankett said. He fell silent for a moment, then looked back at Sam. "I am trustworthy, though, and if I give my word, I'll take a beating and die before I'll ever crawfish on it."

Sam just looked at him, somehow knowing he meant it.

"But I'll be honest, it took me longer to find you than it should have, knowing once I found you, my chance at being sheriff was over."

"That took character, Deputy," Sam said. "That tells me more than anything about the kind of sheriff you'd be."

"So, here I am, telling you and cutting myself out," Dankett said with a sigh. "Are you going back with me?"

"Part of being a Territorial Ranger is filling in when something like this happens," Sam said.

"I'm going back. I'll agree to be sheriff, but only if you'll agree to stay on as my deputy."

Dankett appeared stunned and just stared at him. "Are you feeling sorry for me, Ranger? Because I don't—"

"No," the Ranger said, cutting him short. "I'm going to need a deputy. You're already wearing the badge."

"I don't know what the council will say," Dankett warned.

"They'll say yes if they want us," Sam replied. "They'll say no if they don't. Are you with me?"

Dankett gave him a proud, thin smile.

"Dern right, I am," he said.

"I need to tell you, Deputy," Sam said. "There might be men showing up wanting to kill me. Is that going to be a problem?"

"Yes, for *them*, it will," said Dankett. He straightened his back, quickened his step, appearing to hold his head a little higher as they neared the campfire. "Is that coffee I smell?" he asked, sniffing toward the fire where Adele and Lang turned at the sound of Dankett's horse clopping along the hard stone path toward them.

"Yes, it is, and you're welcome to it," Sam said.

"Obliged," said Dankett, "but I'll have to drink it standing up. I told the town I'd ride right back with an answer straightaway. Miners and drovers all coming to town at once makes everybody nervous. They don't want the town unprotected a minute longer than it has to be. You with a prisoner and a horse loaded with the woman's belongings, I can be three hours ahead of you. I rode Pony Express before the rails set in."

"I understand," Sam said. "We'll get some hot coffee in you and get you back on the trail."

As they drew nearer to the campfire, Lang recognized Clow Dankett by his hat, his corduroy coat and long-barreled shotgun.

"Jesus, no!" he called out, jumping to his feet, his hands cuffed to his saddle horn.

"Howdy, Cisco," Dankett said, affably enough—but still not affably enough to suit Lang.

"Keep him away from me, Ranger!" Lang said, the cuffed saddle hanging to his knees and straining his wrists.

"Settle down, Cisco," Sam said as he and the deputy stopped a few feet back from the fire. "You best get used to Deputy Dankett being around. We're riding back to New Delmar."

Adele gave Sam a concerned look, but Sam noticed that her eyes slid past Lang's on their way to him.

"Is everything all right?" she asked.

"Sheriff Rattler is dead," Sam said. "I'm going to have to ride back and keep order until they get another lawman."

"Man!" said Lang. "Somebody killed Rattling Ed . . ."

"Don't call him that," Dankett warned, taking a step forward.

"Whoa, sorry!" said Lang, seeing the big shotgun rise an inch in Dankett's hands.

"Let me pour you some coffee, Deputy," said Adele, stepping quickly to divert Dankett away from Lang.

"Obliged to you, ma'am," Dankett said. "I'll drink it on my way back."

Sam stood watching, thinking. Riding back to New Delmar might be all it took to tip these two's hand—*if there's a hand to tip here,* he reminded himself.

Almost before the sound of the deputy's horse's hooves echoed off along the stone path and the distant canyon walls, Sam pitched his saddle up atop Black Pot's back. As he drew and fastened the cinch under the stallion's belly, he noted Adele rummaging through her belongings. Lang stood over to the side waiting, his saddle hanging from his cuffed hands.

"Ranger, when we get to New Delmar, you're not leaving that idiot guarding me, are you?" he asked. "He talks to his shotgun, you know."

"That depends," Sam said, ignoring the remark about the deputy talking to his shotgun. He offered no more on the matter, making Lang reach for anything he told him.

"Depends on what?" Lang asked.

"On how you behave yourself, Cisco," the Ranger said, finishing with Black Pot. "Seems to me the only trouble you had with Deputy Dankett was when you tried to escape."

"All right, I made a mistake," said Lang. "But that was a setup deal and you know it. He's got that chain measured just long enough to hit the ground without pulling a man out the window."

Sam smiled a little to himself, picturing Lang hanging from the end of the chain when the heavy ball yanked him upside down off his feet and left him swinging on the wall.

"He set all that up, yet you call him an idiot?" Sam said.

"Okay, maybe not an idiot," said Lang. "But he's a straight-up madman. You've got no right, leaving me with him."

"There's a prison wagon runs through once

every month or so," Sam said. "I can stick you on it, if that suits you better."

"Damn," said Lang, "you expect we'll be in New Delmar that long before they get a sheriff?"

"I don't know," said Sam, pulling his Winchester from his saddle boot and checking it. He stepped over and led Lang's horse back to where he stood. While he reached out and unlocked the cuff from Lang's saddle horn, he noted a tense look on Adele's face as she watched. She turned and flipped open the leather case sitting atop the carpetbag and felt around inside it.

"Saddle up, Cisco," he said as the freed saddle fell to the ground at Lang's feet.

Lang picked up the saddle with his cuffed hands and started to pitch it atop his horse.

Looking up from the leather case, Adele cried out, "Ranger, he's got a gun!"

Lang turned sidelong. He shoved the saddle into the Ranger's chest, knocking him back a step.

The Ranger pushed the saddle out of his way. He started to bring his rifle up, but he froze as he stared into the bore of the small pistol from the leather case. Lang held the gun cocked and pointed in his face.

"The trail ends here, Ranger," he said. "Get the key out, get these jail bracelets off me."

"Huh-uh, Cisco," Sam said. "I'm not cutting you loose. Now you lower the gun, or I'll bury this rifle butt in your face all over again."

"None of your tricks or bluffs this time, Ranger," said Lang. "I'm not going to New Delmar and I'm not going to jail."

"Ranger, I had nothing to do with this," Adele

blurted out. "I saw the gun wasn't there. I told you right off."

"Shut up, Adele," said Lang. "You could have had the decency to keep your mouth shut about the gun."

"I want no part of this, Cisco," Adele said.

As Lang looked away for a second, the Ranger stepped in quick and swung the rifle butt across his jaw. Lang went sideways to the ground. The gun flew from his hand and landed at Adele's feet. She picked it up as the Ranger stood over Lang and stuck the tip of the rifle barrel down behind his ear. Lang tried to raise his head. But Sam shoved it down with the rifle barrel.

"Game's over, Cisco," he said. "Lie still or I'll give you another one."

Looking sidelong through swirling eyes, Cisco saw the gun in Adele's hand. "Sh-shoot him, Adele," he managed to say.

Sam looked around and saw her gripping the gun tight, the barrel pointed loosely at him. He gave her a questioning look.

"Decide here and now, ma'am," he said firmly, stepping back from Lang lying on the ground, seeing the downed outlaw wasn't going to be able to do anything for a while. "The gun's in your hand."

A look passed across Adele's face; the Ranger saw it but wasn't able to read it before it was gone.

"No, Ranger, no!" she said, shaking her head wildly. She turned the gun in her hand and held it out to him butt first. "I'm not doing this. I told him all along I wasn't going to help him escape." She looked tearfully down at Cisco Lang. "I've done things I shouldn't have done, but I'm not going to kill somebody."

Sam took the gun from her hand, and wrapped her in his arm as she bowed forward against him, sobbing.

"Forgive me, Ranger," she said.

"It's all right, Adele," he said softly. "You made the right choice. You don't need to be forgiven . . . not by me anyway." As he spoke, he reached back and shoved the gun down behind his belt. He wasn't going to mention that he had unloaded it. No one would ever need to know, he told himself.

Chapter 11

At daylight, Blind Simon sat his turn at guard. Instead of using his eyes, he kept his nose and ears turned to the trail as the distant sound of hooves moved farther away through the morning gloom. Soon after Henry Teague and Sonny Rudabough had ridden out of their camp, Dave Coyle poured himself a cup of coffee. Little Deak, Karl Sieg and Chic Reye sat near the fire, watching as Dave placed his steaming cup aside and filled another cup for his brother. He carried it over to where Oldham sat on a blanket leaning against a rock, fifteen yards away.

"Where's this going to put us?" Sieg asked Reye quietly. "If he wants to go off after the Ranger?"

"Do I look like I know where it puts us?" Reye said, sounding a little irritated. He spit and stared across the camp watching as Dave approached his brother, who sat holding his big Colt in his right hand, twirling it deftly back and forth, his eyes dark and riveted before him on things unseen, engaged in deep serious contemplation.

At the edge of his blanket, Dave stooped down and set the steaming cup of coffee on the ground beside him.

"Drink this, Oldham. It'll make you feel better," Dave said.

"What are they talking about over there?" Oldham asked, the gun twirling, his eyes turning toward the men across the camp from them.

"They're probably talking about the same thing I'm thinking about, Oldham," Dave said. "We're all wondering if you're going to stop everything and go after the Ranger."

"There's nothing to *stop*, brother Dave," Oldham said. The gun ceased twirling suddenly and stood near the side of his face, pointed skyward. "I messed up everything for us. I had a good thing set up, but I lost my mind gambling, drinking and eating dope. That's the truth of it."

Dave Coyle shrugged, reached over and lowered his brother's gun hand. He sipped from his own cup of hot steaming coffee.

"Everybody makes mistakes," he said.

"No, they don't," said Oldham. "Not as bad as I do."

"But there's no point in letting it eat at you," Dave said. "Learn something from it this time. Pick yourself up and let's go on. Everybody's depending on you."

"And I've let them all down," Oldham said. "We're all broke because of me."

"We're not broke. Not all of us anyway," said Dave. "We could use some money, sure. But there's always next month, far as the mine payroll goes."

"And the five thousand dollars bounty would go a long ways holding us over until then," said Oldham. "We're all proud men here. We live up to our appetites."

"Here you go, Oldham," said Dave, shaking his head.

"Here I go *what*?" Oldham asked.

"You do this every time," said Dave.

"What, damn it?" said Oldham, getting heated. "What the hell do I do every time?"

"This right here," said Dave. "You start making up all the right reasons for doing whatever it is you're aching to do anyway."

"I don't make up the reasons," said Oldham. "The reasons are there. I just consider them and—"

"Can I say something?" said Dave, cutting him off.

Oldham just stared at him.

"Here it is, then," Dave said. "Money is not the real reason you want to kill the Ranger. You want to do it because some sporting man has put the odds in your favor."

"So what?" said Oldham with a crooked smile. "What's wrong with me being favored to win? Would it be better if everybody thought I was going to lose?"

"What's wrong is it clouds the picture, Oldham," Dave said. "It makes it all into some game. And it's not a game. It's a dirty, dangerous piece of work. We're not assassins, brother. We're highwaymen, long riders."

"We've killed men," said Oldham in defense.

"But not like this, never for pay," said Dave. "And never a man like this Ranger."

Oldham cocked his head slightly and gave Dave a curious look. "You don't think I can beat the Ranger in a straight-up match, do you?"

"Jesus, brother, listen to you," said Dave. "This is not *a match*, not some sort of sporting event.

That's what I'm trying to tell you. Even if you do kill the Ranger, what do you think happens then? Do you figure you'll get a bronze plaque? Do you figure Hugh Fenderson will take you for a ride in a Pullman car?"

"Go to hell, brother Dave," said Oldham.

"They'll hang you—no, wait," he said, catching himself. "They won't hang you. They won't even take you to trial. They'll kill you in the street before you've even collected the bounty money. Every lawman between here and hell will be out to kill you, for killing one of their own."

"Leave it alone, Dave," Oldham warned him.

But Dave would have none of it.

"See?" he said with sarcasm. "They're the law. That's why, as rich as Fenderson is, he won't step out in front of this and put his own ass on the line. He'll pay some stupid thug who'll do the bloody work for him." He paused, then said, "Stick to what we do, Oldham. Let's get clear away from here and go rob something."

Oldham took a deep breath, placating himself, and slipped his Colt into his holster. He reached over, picked up his cup of coffee and took a sip.

"There's times I could bend a gun barrel over your head, brother Dave," he said, almost sighing.

Dave gave a short, dark chuckle.

"Yeah?" he said. "There's times I could bend one over *your* head and straighten it across your jaw." He sipped his hot coffee and said, "So, are you going to put all this bounty nonsense out of your mind?"

"No," Oldham said firmly, staring off toward the fire and the men gathered a few yards from it. "I'm going to kill Burrack and collect that bounty."

"Damn it," said Dave. "Why is it the more I talk against doing something, the more determined you get on doing it?"

"That's just me, brother," Oldham said. "I'm molded that way, by bigger hands than these." He glanced down at the hot tin cup in his hands, then looked back over toward the men.

From across the camp, Chic Reye turned away from Oldham's gaze and sipped his coffee. Sieg sat to his left. A few feet away sat Little Deak Holder.

"Sounds like they're arguing right now," Reye said, more irritated than he'd been earlier. "I expect this will last most of the day. Meanwhile, we sit and wait like a band of drooling idiots ready to laugh if one of them farts."

"I see you woke up in a good mood," said Sieg. "That's always worth something."

"I can't help it if I'm not some mindless fool," Reye growled. "I know what I see, and if what I see makes me ill, I ain't withdrawn from speaking my mind on the matter. The Reyes are known all across Kansas for speaking their minds and letting the chips fall where they will."

"I can believe that," Sieg said dryly.

"What's that supposed to mean?" Reye asked in a surly tone.

"It means I have taken note over time that you're not one to mask either your attitudes or opinions."

"It's true, I will orate where necessary," Reye said, seemingly satisfied with Sieg's explanation.

"That's all I was saying," Sieg concluded.

Reye sat quietly for a moment, then spit in disgust, looking out at the spot where Blind Simon sat with his senses tuned to the trail toward New Delmar.

"I'll tell you something else," Reye said. "That right there goes straight through me."

"What?" said Sieg, both he and Little Deak Holder looking toward Blind Simon.

"Him," said Reye. "That blind son of a bitch pretending he can hear this, and smell that, and sense one thing and guess the other. It's all horse dribble, and I know it."

"My God!" said Sieg. "I thought we were through with all that."

"We're not through with nothing," said Reye standing, slinging grounds from his coffee cup. "I just overlooked it for a while."

"When a man is blind, his other senses step in and take up the slack," Deak ventured quietly. "Everybody knows that." He paused, then said in the same low tone, "You want to know what I think, pards? I think we—"

"Nobody wants to know what you think," Reye said coldly, cutting him off. "We'd be a damned sight better off if it wasn't for having you two freaks of nature with us."

"Shut up, Reye," said Sieg. To Deak he said, "Pay no attention to Chic, Deak. He's just a turd when he first wakes up."

"Damn it, Sieg," said Reye. "I'm tired of skirting around the matter. This one knows what he is. He was born like this because his pa only let off half a squirt instead of a full one—like jerking it out at the last second, but not fast enough. Left just enough goo to make a mess of things."

"Why, you rotten—!" Deak stood and spread his feet shoulder-width, both of his tiny hands near the butt of his belly gun.

"Oh, look, he's going to draw on me. Ain't that cute?" Reye said in a mocking tone.

"Both of you settle down," Sieg demanded, "before everything takes a bad turn here."

Reye ignored him.

"I heard Oldham talk about what a fast and deadly gunman you are, Half Squirt," he said to Little Deak, still goading him. "But I figure he was just saying that to make you feel welcome. The fact is, your hands ain't even big enough to draw a gun and fire it. If you did, the kick would knock you on your ass."

"Stop it, Chic, damn it!" Sieg said.

"Let's see you draw it, Half Squirt," said Reye. "We like a good laugh."

Little Deak's face turned cold and stonelike. His hands dropped to his sides.

"I'm not drawing it," he said.

"Yes, you will draw it, Half Squirt," Reye said down to him. "Else I'll burn you down where you stand." His hand went for the big revolver holstered on his hip.

Across the camp, both Coyle brothers dropped their coffee and jumped to their feet, seeing what was going on.

"Whoa! Stop!" Oldham shouted as the two ran forward.

But it was too late. They saw Reye's hand wrap around the butt of his bone-handled revolver; they saw Little Deak's right arm come up from his side and point up open-handed at Reye. But they didn't see the two-shot derringer slip out of Little Deak's coat sleeve into his small hand until fire streaked from the barrel and the bullet hit

Reye in the face like a hard-flying hornet. The shot made a sharp popping sound.

Reye's gun flew from his hand. He staggered backward a step and slapped his cheek with his left hand as if that might help. He struggled to stay on his feet.

"By thunder!" said Simon, springing to his feet. "Little Deak shot that sumbitch, didn't he?"

"He sure did," Sieg said, wincing at the sight of blood spewing from the hole in Reye's cheek.

"One more coming," Little Deak said matter-of-factly to the dazed, staggering gunman. He waddled forward, pointing the barrel straight out against Reye's navel.

"Holy!" said Dave Coyle, he and Oldham sliding to a halt as Deak fired again. This time the bullet punched into Reye's belly and jackknifed him at the waist. His arms went around his bleeding lower belly. He fell onto his side, thrashing in the dirt, his boots scraping, walking him in a circle on the ground.

"I knew he'd do it," Oldham said quietly to Dave. "I tried to tell him."

"Now for your *big surprise*," Little Deak said almost to himself, looking down at the writhing gunman. The smoking derringer slipped back up inside his coat sleeve. He drew the big Colt from across his belly and cocked it. Holding the big Colt with both hands, he leveled it down at the side of Reye's bloody head. The first derringer bullet had hit the gunman right beneath the ball of his cheekbone and come out in front of his right ear, leaving a ragged hole. Deak aimed the big Colt just beside the ragged bleeding exit hole and started to squeeze the trigger.

"Hold it, Deak," said Oldham with authority. "Don't kill him."

Deak kept the gun pointed as he turned his head and faced Oldham with a bemused expression.

"Why not?" he said, as if having trouble understanding Oldham's reasoning on the matter. "I've already cocked the gun," he added.

"Because I said not to," Oldham said firmly. "Uncock it, put it away."

"Can I mark him?" Little Deak asked with a thin, devilish grin. He reached down to unbutton his fly.

"You've marked him plenty," said Oldham. "Back away and leave him alone. Don't make me tell you again."

"Damn it. Please! Somebody help me here," Reye said in a strained, pain-filled voice. "The sneaking little son of a bitch *shot me*!" His voice sounded stiff and unreal from the bullet having sliced through his cheek. Blood ran freely down from both the small entrance and the larger exit holes.

"Shut up, Reye," said Oldham, he and his brother stepping in closer, looking down at their wounded comrade. "Or I'll let him finish the job. I warned you to leave this man alone. You had to keep running your mouth."

Little Deak stepped back, sliding the big Colt into his belly holster. The derringer smoke still curled up from the cuff of his coat sleeve.

Sieg and Dave Coyle helped Reye to his feet and guided him, bowed at the waist, to a rock.

"I need you to cut this bullet out of my guts, Oldham," Reye said, clearly in pain.

"You don't want me dipping my fingers around in your guts, Reye," Oldham said.

"Especially not this morning while he's still got rats dancing on his brains," Dave put in.

"Somebody's got to do it," Reye said pitifully.

"I'll do it," said Little Deak. Feeling much better for having avenged himself, he gave Reye a secretive wink and a smug grin.

"You little bastard!" Reye shouted. He tried to lunge forward at Deak, but Oldham grabbed him, stopped him and pressed him back down firmly onto the rock.

"Somebody get some water. Let's wash his face some," Oldham called out. "Jesus, Chic," he said to the wounded gunman, examining the ragged exit hole in front of his ear. "Can't you ever just keep your mouth shut? I told you Deak Holder is not a man to fool with."

"I didn't believe you, boss. I'm sorry," said Reye. "How bad is that anyway?"

"It's not *good*, that's for sure," said Oldham. "If you were anybody else, I'd be surprised you're able to talk."

"I ain't going to no doctor," Reye said.

"You can say that again," Dave cut in as Sieg handed him a canteen and a wadded bandana. "We're not going to New Delmar. We're headed in the opposite direction."

"Huh-uh," said Oldham. "He's got a bullet in his belly. Either we all ride in or one of us rides in and brings the doctor back. You decide, brother Dave."

"Damn it to hell," Dave said, kicking the ground. "Just when I thought we might get out of here." He rubbed his face in frustration and said, "All right, we'll send a rider. Get the doctor and get him right back here. We're not dallying around here any longer than we have to."

"Some things are meant to play themselves out, brother," Oldham said. "We've no choice but to roll with them." His hungry gambler's look came to his face.

"Yeah, right," Dave said. "I've heard enough of that malarkey to last me a lifetime."

"Who's going to ride to New Delmar, you or me, brother Dave?" Oldham asked.

"I'll go," Sieg put in.

"Huh-uh, it's going to be me or Dave," said Oldham.

"Hell, I'm going," Dave said. "There's no way in the world you're riding in there."

"There you have it, men," Oldham said. He gave his brother a slight grin. "Our problem has been well considered and reasonably solved."

Chapter 12

A few miles outside New Delmar, the Ranger, his prisoner and Adele turned their horses onto a short, wide path leading to a large shack out in front of Antioch Ore and Trade Alliance, a near-defunct mining company. As they rode up to an open well that drew its water from an underground stone tank, Sam stepped down from his saddle and looked around. A thin man came trotting out from the shack, glancing over his shoulder at another shanty farther back on the rocky hillside.

"Hello the camp," Sam called out as the man neared. "We'd appreciate watering our animals before riding on into New Delmar."

"Ranger, this is not a good place to water!" the man said with a worried look, having noticed the badge on Sam's chest before leaving the shack.

The Ranger looked at the drawn water contained behind a low stone wall, and at a mule standing under a ragged canvas overhang chewing on a muzzle-full of hay. A long pole hitched to the mule's back ran to a water wheel, which drew water from the earth in a series of clay pots and poured it into the open containment well.

"It looks like you've got plenty," the Ranger said. He turned and looked back at the nervous man as he picked up a gourd dipper, dipped up a swig, swished it around in his mouth and spit it out. "Tastes all right to me."

"I've got plenty, and it's good, Ranger," the man said. "You're welcome to it. But I've also got three drifters who blew in here last night drunk as hoot owls. All they talked about all night was killing you." He paused and looked the Ranger up and down. "If you be Ranger Sam Burrack, that is—and I take it you are."

"Yep, I am," the Ranger said. He raised the gourd to his lips and drank as he motioned Lang and the woman down from their saddles.

"That's what I thought," the man said. He nodded at the Ranger's dusty pearl gray sombrero. "I recognized your hat. I always heard you wear a sombrero." He smiled, squinting in the glare of sunlight. "I'm James Hilton. Pleased."

"Pleased," Sam replied. "You heard right, Mr. Hilton." He touched the brim of his sombrero. He led Black Pot in closer to the short stone wall and allowed the stallion to draw water. "Where's all your men?" he asked. "I don't hear any work going on." He casually drew his Winchester from its boot as he spoke.

Beside him, Lang and Adele watered their horses and themselves. They listened closely as the nervous man spoke to the Ranger.

"They're all in New Delmar, celebrating," Hilton said.

"The guards too?" the Ranger asked, sipping more water, gazing toward the second shack as he spoke.

"The guards too," Hilton said. "I've sold out to the John Bulls. There's no ore to guard right now, and there won't be until next week when the new owners take over." He paused, then said, "Say . . . Ranger, you don't seem awfully concerned, these men wanting to kill you."

"*Wanting to* is never the problem," Sam said, still looking off toward the shack. "Somebody is always *wanting to*, I expect."

"These are bad ones," Hilton cautioned.

Sam watched the shack, hearing the door start to squeak from forty yards away.

"They always are *bad ones*," he said wryly. "Else I'd be greatly disappointed."

"Oh dear!" Hilton said, seeing the door to the shack open slowly.

"Ranger . . . ?" Lang said, standing beside his horse, cuffed to his saddle horn. His voice sounded muffled behind his swollen purple jaw. His broken nose stood large between two eyes still black from his previous move against the Ranger.

"I see them. Keep watering, Cisco," Sam replied quietly. "This would not be a good time for you to try another getaway plan," he added, cautioning him.

"I'm not trying nothing else," Lang said. "I'm running out of places for you to hit."

"That's a good attitude," Sam said, not believing a word of it. He watched the three men step down from the porch and start walking slowly toward him, spreading apart on their way.

The tallest of the three approaching gunmen called out to Sam as he walked forward.

"Did he tell you what we said last night?" he asked.

"Some," Sam replied.

"Obliged for you shooting your mouth off, Hilton," he said, staring hard at the mine manager as they drew nearer. "We'll talk more about it later on," he threatened.

"Stop where you are," Sam called out, "or *later on* won't matter to you." He held a hand up sideways, his thumb up, and deftly compared its length to the height of the gunman.

The three continued defiantly another step, but stopped short as the Ranger levered the rifle and put it to his shoulder.

"Whoa, hang on, Ranger," said the tallest gunman of the three. "I saw you pull the rule of thumb on us." He tried a sly grin. "We're not even in pistol distance yet."

"I know that," Sam said. "I like it that way." He lowered his left hand back to his Winchester and raised the rifle, pointed and cocked at the tallest man.

"Ranger," Lang said from beside his horse. "That's Toy Johnson, one of the gunmen I told you about. The one on his right is Randall Carnes. They're both wicked good with a pistol."

The Ranger only nodded in reply.

"I don't know the third one," Lang said.

"I do," said Adele. "It's Dan Stubach. Watch him," she warned.

Sam nodded again, staring out at the three gunmen, wondering if they would all three make their play, in range or not.

"Ranger," Toy Johnson called out. "It's true that last night we got a little drunk and got our bark on. But all we want to do now is talk, okay?" He got set to take a step, testing the Ranger.

"No talking," Sam said. "One step will get you killed. If you want to play three on one, play it from there, or else crawfish out of here like the poltroons you are."

The Ranger's words were harsh and goading, but that was all right; he'd meant them to be. If there was going to be a fight here, it was going to be his way, not theirs—not with three of them facing him.

"Nobody calls me a coward! I've never crawfished from a gunfight in my life," said Dan Stubach, a stocky young gunman with a ruddy whiskey-blotched face, partially hidden by a stringy beard.

"Today will be a good day to start," the Ranger said, moving his aim away from Toy Johnson and leveling it on Stubach's chest, the hammer cocked, his finger on the trigger.

"Come on, Ranger Burrack, be reasonable," said Toy Johnson, sounding like a man who knew he'd made a big mistake and only wanted to correct it. "We only wanted to talk. That's not against the law, is it?"

"Today it is," Sam said. "I know about the bounty." He nodded sidelong toward Lang. "Cisco here told me the other day you and Carnes were interested in collecting."

"Thanks a hell of a lot, Cisco," Johnson said, recognizing Lang for the first time. Looking back at the Ranger, he said, "That was just more whiskey talk. Hell, look at us, we didn't even bring our rifles."

"Poor planning," Sam said, unrelenting. "Now back away and get out of here."

"Ha," said Stubach. "He ain't going to shoot a man out of range and I know it." He took a step forward as he spoke. "He's a lawman. He won't do nothing that—"

His words stopped; the Ranger's first bullet ripped through his chest. As Stubach flipped backward, leaving a boot spinning in the air, Sam levered a fresh round and brought his rifle back to Johnson, aimed at his chest.

Johnson and Carnes had both drawn their revolvers and commenced firing when the Ranger made his move on Stubach. Their bullets struck the hard ground fifteen feet in front of Sam.

Seeing their pistol shots fall short, Johnson was suddenly wide-eyed in fright.

"*Run!*" he shouted at Randall Carnes.

The two turned, still firing, and tried to sprint back to the safety of the shack.

Sam's next shot hit Johnson low in his back, a little to the left. The bullet sliced through Johnson's gun belt and bored down into his hip. The severed gun belt fell and tangled at Johnson's knees as the impact of the bullet in his hip spun him around like some lopsided top.

Before Johnson even hit the ground, Sam turned the rifle toward the other fleeing gunman, knowing that once Carnes made it into the shack, it could take all day to get him out.

Sam took aim as Carnes raced away, having enough savvy to zigzag across the dirt. Still, the Ranger's shot hammered him in his left shoulder and hurled him forward, facedown on the ground.

With one man dead and two struggling in the dirt, Sam lowered the smoking rifle and stepped sidelong over to Lang. As he kept watch on the two downed gunmen, he reached for the key to the handcuffs and unlocked Lang from his saddle horn.

"I want you to help Adele and Mr. Hilton round these two up and get them bandaged," he said. "Think you can do that without getting yourself killed?"

Lang looked at the body on the ground, and at the other two badly wounded gunmen knocked off their feet by rifle shots.

"Yes, I can do that," he said in a somber tone. He started to turn and hurry toward the first wounded gunman, but Sam grabbed the third dangling cuff and jerked him back.

"Not so fast, Cisco," he said. "Don't get to one of them ahead of me. I wouldn't want a gun jumping into your hand."

Lang slowed down and walked beside the Ranger to where Toy Johnson lay pulling himself along in the dirt, hand over hand.

"Slow down, Johnson, let's patch you up. It's all part of the service," Sam said dryly, placing a boot down firmly on the wounded outlaw's shoulder. Johnson grunted and came to a halt.

Johnson rasped, "You dirty son of a—"

But Sam jostled him under his boot.

"Don't start with the name calling," Sam said. "I might decide it's easier to leave you lying here with buzzards waltzing on your belly."

Sam looked over and saw Adele and the mine manager roll Carnes onto his back and help him sit up.

"This one's got a big hole punched in him, but it looks like he'll live," the mine manager called out to Sam.

Sam nodded and stooped down with Lang and rolled the groaning outlaw onto his back. His severed gun belt lay in the dirt a few feet away.

Seeing Cisco Lang bent over him, Johnson growled, "You rotten bastard. Did you tell your pard here it was you who first told us about the reward on his head?"

Sam looked at Cisco.

"Is that so?" he said.

Cisco averted his eyes and gave an embarrassed shrug.

"I might have mentioned it to them. I don't recall," he said.

Sam shook his head and appeared to dismiss the matter.

"Let's get them patched up and get into town, before Dankett starts wondering what's happened to us."

The usual heavy traffic on the streets of New Delmar parted for the Ranger and his party of five as he rode Black Pot forward at a walk. Adele Simpson was riding beside him, leading the roan carrying her belongings. Ahead of Sam on a long lead rope rode Cisco Lang, his eyes black, his jaw purple and swollen. Ahead of Cisco, the dead man was strapped across his saddle. And ahead of the dead man rode the two wounded men, both patched and bloodstained.

"Uh-oh. Here's the Ranger who's taking charge for a while," one miner said to another, the two standing in an alley drinking from a bottle of rye. "It looks like a good time to get headed back up the gully."

Pedestrians stopped instinctively along the walk planks. Riders veered their buggies and wagons to the side of the street and stopped there, staring at the approach of Sam's ragged, bloody, dirt-streaked assortment of dead and wounded. The rattling twang of the piano resounding from inside the Number Five Saloon fell silent as the Ranger followed the dejected prisoners forward to the hitch rail out in front of the new jail.

From the batwing doors of the saloon, Henry Teague and Sonny Rudabough stepped onto the boardwalk and stared toward the jail as Deputy Dankett walked out to meet the Ranger, his long-barreled shotgun in hand.

"Well, well, Sonny," said Teague. "There's our Ranger, coming to watch over New Delmar just like I predicted he would." He blew a stream of smoke he'd drawn from a thick black cigar.

"Yep, you called it right, saying that he'd come here once Sheriff Rattler was dead," Sonny said. "But don't forget, I'm the one did the shooting."

"Damn it, Sonny, keep your voice down," said Teague in a lowered tone. He looked all around quickly, then back to Sonny. "You know the spot outside town where Coyle said him and his men will make camp?"

Sonny stood watching the Ranger, Adele and the prisoners step down from their saddles. Sam climbed down first to assist the woman.

"Yeah, I know where it's at," Sonny said without taking his eyes off the Ranger and his prisoners, seeing Dankett line the men up and file them inside the jail.

"I want you to ride out and tell Coyle the Ranger's here," Teague said. He grinned. "It's time we start getting under the Ranger's skin a little. Soften him up some, make sure he'll step out on the street with Coyle when the time comes."

"I'm on my way," said Sonny, making his way to where his horse stood at a hitch rail.

Inside the jail, a town councilman turned from the front window toward the Ranger as Dankett stopped the line of prisoners and closed the door behind them.

"Councilman Childers," said Dankett, "here's Ranger Burrack, just like he said he would be." He turned to Sam and said, "Ranger, meet Town Councilman Felix Childers."

"Ranger, we are glad you could make it," said Childers, extending a hand to the Ranger.

Shaking hands, Sam nodded and looked around as Dankett motioned the prisoners over behind the chalk line on the floor.

"Ranger, as you can see, we're in the process of building a dandy jail and sheriff's office here. We hope to have it finished in due time." He smiled with an air of patience toward the project.

"By tomorrow morning," Sam said quietly but firmly.

"Pardon me?" said Childers. He looked taken aback.

"You heard me right, Councilman," Sam said. "Get a carpenter crew over here *now* and have a holding wall finished and in use by morning."

"But, Ranger," said the stunned councilman, "we can't possibly have it completed that soon. These things take time. Sheriff Rattler was a patient man. We're all hoping that you would be the same—"

"By morning," Sam repeated. "That gives them today and tonight if they need it. If it's not finished by morning I'll give these men their guns back and set them loose on your streets. I'll take *my* deputy and ride out of here."

Childers looked at Dankett, then back at Sam.

"Dankett is going to be your deputy?" he said, still sounding shocked.

"Yes, he is," Sam said. "If that's a problem, you and him walk out back and discuss it between yourselves. Otherwise, let my deputy and me get to work while you rustle us up some carpenters and make this place a jail instead of a *joke*." He saw a slight grin show on Dankett's pale face. He continued, saying, "If the jail was finished the way it should have been, Dankett could have handled this town by himself instead of sitting here warming a chair bottom, waiting for some prisoner to make a move on him."

"Ranger, I—" Childers managed to say before Sam cut him short.

"If you want the law to work, Councilman," Sam said, "you've got to give the lawmen what they need to *make* it work." He looked at Dankett. "Do you agree, Deputy?"

"Chapter and verse," Dankett said. He took a step toward the councilman and said, "Or are we going to talk out back about me staying on as deputy?"

"No! No indeed, Deputy," said Childers. "If the Ranger wants you, it's fine with me. I mean with *the council*. I mean with the *town*, that is," he corrected himself nervously. He backed toward the front door, his derby hat in hand. "I best get going if I'm to get this holding cell completed by morning." He started to leave, then caught himself and said in afterthought, "Oh, and I'll have them bring lanterns, in case they have to work throughout the night."

"Good thinking, Councilman," Sam said as the man hurried on out the door.

"What do you want me to do, Ranger?" Dankett

asked, looking excited at the prospect of getting a real and complete jail.

"For now, string everybody together with handcuffs and cuff them to the iron ball, Deputy," Sam said. "Then get us a doctor or whoever you've got here to take a look at their wounds."

"You've got it, Ranger," Dankett said. He turned to the prisoners and said, "All right, everybody close together. Let's get you cuffed until the doctor gets here."

Toy Johnson struggled to his feet and called out to Sam, "You've got no reason to hold me and Carnes. What's your charge? We didn't shoot you. You shot us."

"Believe it or not, Johnson, some call it a crime, trying to kill a lawman," Sam said. "But that aside, I am setting you both free as soon as the doctor says you can ride."

Johnson and Carnes looked at the Ranger in disbelief.

"With our guns?" Carnes asked.

The Ranger just stared at him.

"Shut up, Randall. That's pushing our luck," Johnson said.

"You're letting them go?" Dankett asked just between him and the Ranger.

"Don't worry, Deputy," Sam replied. "They're not leaving before we get this jail finished."

Chapter 13

At a campsite outside New Delmar, Little Deak Holder and Blind Simon Goss had managed to scavenge a large, ragged canvas and make an overhead lean-to of it to shield them from the harsh sun. Between the lean-to and a large line of wind-sculpted sandstone rock, Sieg had built a campfire and set a pot of coffee to boil. Beside the coffeepot, he'd stood a kettle of water to boil for evening stew.

As Sieg fed more broken-up brush into the fire, he looked up and saw Dave Coyle riding the trail back from town with a one-horse buggy rolling along beside him.

"It looks like your brother found us a doctor, Oldham," Sieg called out to where Oldham Coyle sat on a blanket beneath the overhang, cleaning his big Colt.

Oldham looked up from his broken-down Colt and out along the trail. But it was Chic Reye who replied from his seat atop a low rock.

"About damn time," he said in a weak, strained voice. "I wouldn't have made it another hour, bad as I'm shot."

Oldham gave him a dubious look and blew through his gun barrel. He looked through the clean, shining barrel and snapped it back to the frame of the Colt.

"Stop your bellyaching, Chic," he said.

"*Bellyaching?* Jesus, Oldham, I'm shot! Look at me here," said Reye in a thick, pained voice. A bloody bandana circled his face, a knot tied atop his head holding it in place. His left hand clutched a large circle of blood on his navel.

"Yeah, we all saw it," said Oldham, sounding unconcerned. "If we hadn't seen it, we all would have heard about it a hundred times since this morning."

"Not shot just once . . . but *twice*," Reye went on, "by that sneaking, murdering little son of a bitch."

"It's hard for us to draw up much sympathy when we've all watched you bully and gripe so much about Little Deak that he finally had to shoot you to shut you up."

Reye looked over to where Little Deak and Blind Simon stood picking through some cookware and eating utensils left by some former campsite inhabitants. The two turned toward Dave and the arriving buggy, then started walking to the lean-to.

"I'll shut up for now," Reye said as Dave and the buggy drew closer to camp. "But soon as I'm able to draw and cock a hammer, I'm going to set things straight—"

"Listen to you," said Oldham. "You're still bleeding from the last time the little fellow had to clean your clock. You're already getting set for him to do it again."

"I'll clean *his* clock next time," Reye grumbled. "Not only clean it, I'll stop it altogether—"

"Shut up, Chic," Oldham said in a dark warning tone punctuated by the sound of his newly assembled Colt being cocked in his hand. "I just cleaned this gun. Don't make me dirty it on you."

Reye took the warning seriously and sat in silence as Dave Coyle and the one-horse buggy reined in close to the lean-to overhang and stopped. Dust bellowed in their wake. Finally Reye managed to take a deep breath as Dave stepped down from his saddle. A thin, short man wearing an eye patch hopped off the buggy carrying a black leather doctor's bag.

"I don't know what gets me so upset like this," Reye said, his fingers getting bloody pressed to his navel.

"Are you apologizing?" Oldham asked.

"Yeah, more or less," Reye said humbly.

"Then save it for Deak and Simon," Oldham said dryly, standing up as Dave and the doctor walked under the overhang.

"I take it this is my patient?" the doctor said, his patched eye slightly cocked to one side to give him a better view. He stooped beside Reye as he spoke and set the bag in the dirt.

Reye gave him a sour look up and down. The doctor snapped the bag open.

"Are you going to be able to *see* how to patch me up?" Reye said gruffly. "I've had my fill of blind fools and sawed-off little sons a' bitches."

The doctor snapped the bag shut.

"Well . . . all through here," he said, standing. He started to turn toward his buggy, but Dave stepped in and blocked his way.

"Whoa, Doctor, hold on," Dave said. "We know he's a damn fool. But if you won't treat him, we'll prop him against a rock and leave him for the night feeders."

"Suits me," the doctor said. "Night feeders have to eat too. I have too many sick people to have to waste time being insulted." He started to step around Dave, but the big gunman continued to block him.

"Dr. Starr, we're paying cash," he said, but it was the sinister look on Dave's face that stopped him more so than the promise of money.

"All right, then," said the thin doctor, turning back to Reye. "But he'll keep his mouth shut unless spoken to. *Agreed?*" he asked Reye pointedly.

"Agreed . . . ," Reye said. He bowed his head a little. "I don't know what makes me say things like that."

"*You* don't know, and *I* don't care," Dr. Starr said curtly. He set the bag back on the ground, pulled Reye's hand away from his bleeding belly and peeled off the blood-sodden bandana. "This is most rare," he murmured. "A perfectly centered hole in the navel—has to hurt like the dickens, I'll wager." He glanced around. "But well aimed nevertheless."

"Wait until you see his face," Little Deak said with a slight smile. He stood watching from the edge of an overhang, Simon standing right beside him.

The doctor looked at the dwarf, who stood not a lot shorter than he did, and at the blind man, who had only one less eye than himself. He nodded, connecting these two to Reye's prickly attitude.

"I dread looking . . . ," he said almost under his breath, spreading Reye's bloody shirt open. "But first things first. Whoever shot you here most fully intended to kill you, fellow," he said to Reye.

"Don't I know it?" Reye said, staring past the doctor's shoulder at Little Deak, who gave him a thin smile and clicked his short thumb up and down toward the wounded disgruntled gunman.

Dave stepped around the doctor and his patient and stooped down beside Oldham's blanket.

"I expect I might just as well tell you, I saw the Ranger heading into town while the doc and I were leaving," he said.

Oldham looked surprised that Dave had shared the information with him, yet he nodded and let it go, glad that his brother was starting to accept his idea, if not warm to it.

"Did he see you?" he asked.

"Would it matter if he did?" Dave asked.

"No," said Oldham. "Just wondering."

"I doubt he saw me," Dave replied anyway. "We were well out one end of town. I looked back and saw him guiding a string of riders in off the desert floor. He had one strapped over his saddle. Two more looked shot up some." He paused, then added, "The two upright looked like Toy Johnson and Randall Carnes."

"Johnson and Carnes . . . ," Oldham mused. "He does stay busy, that Ranger."

"Yes, he does," said Dave somberly. "And he's not a man to treat lightly."

"I know that, brother Dave," Oldham said more seriously. "That's why I need you and Deak, both with your bark on, watching my back until I get this thing done."

Dave shook his head and let out a tense breath.

"I'm there," he said. "Let's just get it done quick and get it over with."

"We will, brother," Oldham said. He gave him

a grin. "But not so quick that we can't have some fun with it."

"Fun . . . ? Damn the fun," Dave said angrily. "There's nothing going to be fun about it."

"We'll see, brother Dave," Oldham said. He was still grinning, hefting the shiny, clean Colt he still held in his hand.

Sam sat watching the prisoners when Deputy Dankett returned from Dr. Starr's office alone and closed the front door behind him. Adele Simpson had left earlier, leading her black barb and the roan and all of her belongings to a weathered half-pine-board, half-adobe hotel named the Desert Rose at the end of the block.

"Dr. Starr's gone on a visit, Ranger," Dankett said, his long-barreled shotgun cradled in his left arm. "He left a note on his door. Didn't say when he'd be back. I stopped by the Number Five and asked a dove named Lila to come give a hand. She's good at birthing, cutting hair, treating fever and whatnot. Said she'd be right along, soon as she finishes trimming a miner."

Sam stood and took a breath, staring at the three sweaty, wounded prisoners who gazed back at him. They sat leaning against the plank wall, the big iron ball on one end of the chain, the men strung wrist to wrist by handcuffs on the other end.

"There you have it, men," Sam said to the three prisoners. "Help is coming, soon as a miner gets his hair trimmed."

The three groaned as one. Johnson sat with his leg stiff and covered with dark dried blood beneath the wound in his hip.

"Damn it," he said. He struggled to his feet,

jerking Lang's cuffed hand up with him. "Can I at least get out back to the jakes before I spring a leak here?"

Dankett and the Ranger looked at each other.

"What about you two? I suppose you both have to go also," he said to Cisco Lang and Randall Carnes.

"I've been needing to," Carnes said. "I just didn't want to say so, especially while the lady was here."

"That's well mannered of you, Carnes," Lang said with a bitter tone. "But that woman couldn't care less if you'd pissed on the wall."

"That's enough of that, Cisco," Sam said, glancing around as if to make sure Adele wasn't still there. He looked at Dankett. "Let's lead them out back before the dove gets here."

Dankett turned toward the three prisoners quickly enough to startle them.

"All right, you heard the Ranger!" he shouted. "On your feet. We're going to the jakes. Anybody makes a false move, it'll be their last." He looked back at the Ranger as the three hurriedly stood up along the wall. "There they are, Ranger, ready and waiting for orders."

"Good work, Deputy," Sam said, liking the way Dankett's fiery unsettled nature kept the prisoners a little off balance.

He watched as Dankett loosened the chain from the large ball and marched the three in a tight line to the side door—Johnson limping badly—that led outside to a new pine-plank privy.

Walking a few feet behind, his Winchester in hand, Sam noted that the privy was wide enough to accommodate two patrons at a time, but for safety's sake, he wouldn't allow that.

"Loosen them one at a time, Deputy," he said to Dankett.

"You heard the Ranger," Dankett said, "one at a time."

As Sam stood watching, he heard a faint cry in the distance, like the soft meowing of a weak or injured cat. He waited, listening, as the first prisoner entered the privy and came back out. As the second man entered, he heard the sound again, and this time it piqued his interest enough to cause him to stare off in its direction.

"What is it, Ranger Burrack?" Dankett asked, seeing Sam look toward a stretch of rocky ground lying behind the main street of New Delmar.

"What's over there?" Sam asked, gesturing a nod, without taking his eyes off the direction of the faint sound.

"Nothing," said the deputy. "Just the makings of a new town dump. It was the town public ditch before these jakes got built and stuck here and there. Now nobody goes there except to dump garbage and the like. Why?"

"I heard something," Sam said. "Couldn't tell if it's a cat or a person. But I heard it from back behind the Number Five."

"Yep, that'd be the public ditch all right," Dankett said. "You'd best hope it's a cat. If it's a person, he's neck deep in stuff back there too ugly to mention by name."

"Shhh—there it is again," Sam said. He listened intently as Johnson limped out the door of the jakes and stepped back into line. Dankett snapped a cuff on his wrist and turned Lang loose. Lang stepped into the privy and closed the door.

Sam stood listening closely, staring toward

the rocky ground behind the saloon until Lang walked out of the privy buttoning his fly and got in line. Sam watched Dankett snap Lang's cuff back around his wrist.

As the three prisoners walked to the side door and stepped inside the jail, Sam stood to the side and waited until Dankett got them seated along the wall. When the three were secured once again to the large iron ball, he motioned Dankett over to him.

"Get them settled," Sam said. "I'm going to see where that sound is coming from."

"You got it, Ranger," said Dankett. "Fire a shot if you need help."

"Don't leave these prisoners alone, Deputy," Sam told him pointedly. "Shot or no shot."

"I won't," said Dankett. "If I hear you shooting, I'll bring them with me."

"All right, just bring Lang," Sam said. "Leave the other two cuffed to the ball. I just want them here to get the jail cell finished. If they break out before they get medical treatment, that'll be their problem."

Chapter 14

On his way to the rocky stretch of ground behind the Number Five Saloon, Sam heard the faint whimpering one more time. This time he heard it clear enough that it sent a dark chill up his spine, knowing that the sound was not that of a cat, or of any other kind of small animal. It was human, it was female and it was the sound of someone in trouble. *Yes, bad trouble,* he told himself, hastening his steps, his Winchester hanging in his hand.

Fifty feet from the back door of the saloon, he walked along the edge of the recently abandoned public ditch. Since the coming of the newly constructed public outhouses, townsfolk had begun discarding garbage and other worthless items into the ditch in order to fill the wretched twenty-yard cesspool of human waste as quickly as possible. Still the open ditch lay splayed like a violent ax wound welling infection in the belly of the earth.

At a point along the edge—a spot most frequented by patrons of the Number Five Saloon—the Ranger stopped and gazed down into the public ditch, his eyes searching across unsavory streaks of dark waste that had built up over time and spilled into the blackish sludge deepening in the ditch's bottom.

At first he saw nothing, save for a few greasy-coated rats perched on the rock incline, picking at something of a rat's interest. Yet as he started to turn his eyes away, he heard the sound again. He swung to his left, where he saw scratching and scrapings in the dirt just above the pool of dark sludge. He made out a tremor of movement, something that rose and fell weakly in the pool of excrement.

An arm? he thought, already stepping down over the edge into the suffocating stench. The terrible smell rose around him, a rancid vapory steam engulfing him. But searching the ditch intently in spite of the smell, the fetidness of humanity's leavings, he saw the movement again.

My God, yes, it is an arm, he told himself, *down there, in all that . . .*

Even as he hurried down the stained, soiled wall of the ditch toward what he now more clearly saw was the outline of a body struggling beneath a layer of waste, he raised his rifle. One-handed, he fired a signal shot in the air, then levered and repeated the action twice for good measure on his way farther down into that terrible trench.

At the edge of the blackish sludge, he set his smoking rifle aside, stooped and reached out for a small, pale wrist coated over in a substance too vile to consider, lest his mind and his hand refuse to engage. Without thought or hesitation, he grabbed the wrist and pulled, feeling the woman come unstuck from the sludge's grasp. She slid upward on her belly onto the rocky ground.

When she was out of the sludge, Sam kept her on her stomach as he reached under her face and wiped it as best he could with his gloved hand. The woman coughed weakly, but otherwise lay limp and still, remnants of her dress pressed to her.

"Who's down there?" a voice called out from atop the edge behind him. Sam looked around over his shoulder and saw three townsmen looking down at him.

"It's the Ranger!" another voice replied. "Ranger Burrack, is that you?" the same voice asked as if doubting itself.

"It's me," Sam shouted up to the townsmen as he loosened his bandana from around his neck. "I need some hands, and some rope. Get down here and help me."

The townsmen looked at each other.

"Good Lord," one said under his breath.

With no time to concern himself with what manner of substance he was handling, Sam turned the woman onto her back and propped her onto his knee. He wiped the bandana across her mouth and eyes. Beneath the slime and feces, he saw the bruised and battered condition of her swollen face.

"Ma'am, can you hear me?" he asked. "We're going to get you out of here. You hold on, you hear?"

The woman's breath wheezed and rattled faintly in her chest.

The Ranger looked back up and saw the same three men, still in the same spot, staring down at him.

"Did you hear me?" he shouted at them. "Get a rope, get down here!"

The three townsmen looked back and forth at one another.

"I can't do it," said one, shaking his head. "I would, but so help me, I can't."

Looking up, Sam saw Deputy Dankett appear, shoving the other men aside.

"Out of the way, flatheads!" Dankett said to the townsmen. "You'll get him a rope if you don't want to carry your teeth in a jar," he threatened. Beside Dankett, the Ranger saw Cisco Lang peer down and shake his head in disgust.

"Come on, prisoner," Dankett said gruffly to Lang. "You're going with me."

Sam watched the deputy and Lang step over the edge and start making their way down to him.

"And some water, Deputy," he said. "We need some water bad."

Dankett looked up over his shoulder as he and Lang continued to make their way down.

"I better see canteens and rope fly over that edge," he warned the townsmen. "I'm making a heads-to-bust list here."

"It's coming, Clow!" a townsman called down to him.

Within a second, a coiled rope flew out over the edge and landed almost at Dankett's feet. Behind it came a canteen, then another. Lang caught the first one with his cuffed hands and snagged the strap of the second midair before it slammed onto the rocks or rolled into the dark soft mire.

"What have we got here, Ranger?" Dankett asked, stooping right down beside the Ranger, appearing mindless of the smell, and of the substance surrounding them.

"I don't know," Sam said, still wiping the woman's face with the bandana. "We've got to get her up out of here. Does she look familiar to you?"

Dankett wiped his bare thumb across the woman's lips and across her eyes, one at a time.

"Yep," he said. "I can't swear to it, but she looks like one of the doves from the Number Five."

"Here you go, Ranger," said Lang, stooping down with them. He reached out with an open canteen and poured a trickle of water onto the woman's face. Sam wiped her face some more.

"Obliged, Cisco," Sam said. He looked at Lang as if to question him being there. Although the prisoner had no choice, he might have balked and put up resistance to coming down in the trench with Dankett.

As if reading the Ranger's mind, Lang glanced around the rancid ditch and shrugged.

"Can't say I've ever been in worse," he said.

Sam washed the woman's face with canteen water. While he did so, Dankett and Lang fashioned a rope sling to carry her in.

"Where are we taking her until the doctor gets back?" Dankett asked.

"You said she works at the saloon?" Sam replied.

"I'm pretty sure," Dankett said.

"That's where we're taking her," Sam said, watching Lang reach the rope under the woman. With no regard for the odor and the waste matter clinging to her, he drew the rope snug enough to lift the woman among the three of them without harming her.

"Ready, Ranger," Lang said.

The three lifted the woman in the rope sling and ascended the steep side of the ditch with her. When they reached the top and hoisted her over the edge, they laid her down on the ground. The townsmen hurried forward with bucket upon bucket of water and poured it over her while the Ranger covered her face with a towel someone brought to him.

Picking her up, rope sling and all, out of the mess the water washed off around her, Sam carried her across the fifty feet of ground and into the saloon through the rear door.

Inside the open rear door, the doves, bartenders and patrons had gathered in anticipation, having heard about the Ranger's find in their waste ditch.

"Oh no!" said the dove named Lila, a pair of barber scissors sticking up from the bodice of her dress. "It's Anna Rose, God help her." She looked at the battered face of the unconscious woman in Sam's arms.

"Get out of my way. Let me see her," said Wesley Fluge. The wide, stocky saloon owner pushed the others aside and stepped forward for a look. "I'll be damned, it is Anna Rose," he said. He looked up from the battered dove's face at Sam. "Found her in the shit ditch, huh?"

Sam gave him a hard look.

"She's one of yours, then?" he said.

"Was," said Fluge, shaking his head. "But not anymore. She robbed a customer and made her getaway a few days back."

"Some getaway," Lang put in, soiled up and down his front, his cuffed hands wet and grimy. Beside Lang, Dankett looked around and saw a billiard stick leaning against a table where a game had been going on.

"Where can I lay her?" Sam asked the owner.

"Anywhere, except in *my saloon*," Fluge said with a dark chuckle and a half grin. No sooner had he spoken than he let out a pain-filled grunt as the tip of the billiard stick Dankett had grabbed was jammed into his belly.

"What was that, Mr. Fluge?" Dankett asked the owner in a mock voice. "Oh, I see . . . on the faro table, you said. My, but that's kind of you!" He held the stick in both hands, ready to jam it again.

Fluge staggered a step back, one hand clutching his belly.

"Please," he rasped, his other hand gesturing the Ranger and the wet and battered dove toward a closed gaming table in a corner.

The doves crowded around as Sam laid the battered woman down.

"You and your deputy take your prisoner upstairs, Ranger. Get yourselves cleaned up," said Lila. She reached out to pat the Ranger's shoulder, but stopped herself. "We'll see to Anna Rose until the doctor gets here."

"Obliged," Sam said, looking down at himself for the first time. He winced and turned to Dankett. "Deputy, take the prisoner upstairs. Both of you get scrubbed. I'll watch about the jail until you get done."

Lila said to Sam, "I was headed to the jail to see about your prisoners, but that will have to wait. We'll send all your clothes over to the laundry and get somebody to scrub your boots too." Lila shooed her hands at the three of them. "Now get out of here. You're stinking up the place."

As the Ranger left through the rear door and Lang and Dankett walked up the stairs to one of the rooms that offered a bathing tub, Henry Teague gave Sonny Rudabough a knowing look. They sat at a table in the corner of the saloon.

"Jesus, Sonny, you told me you took care of her," Teague whispered. "Said she'd never be seen again. Now Coyle is going to know she didn't steal his money."

"So what if he does? Anyway, I did take care of her," Sonny whispered, staring toward the crowd of doves round the faro table with a troubled look on his face.

"You didn't take care of her," Teague said. "You just dunked her like a plug of bread into brown gravy." He frowned. "Did she see you?"

"I don't think so," Sonny said.

"*Don't think so* won't dry your leg when you see a noose swing over a limb," Teague said. "If Hugh Fenderson calls me down over this, what are you going to do to keep me from flying ugly and blowing your head off?"

"Don't threaten me, Henry," Sonny cautioned the older gunman. "I took care of her once, damn it. I'll take care of her again."

Inside the unfinished jail, the Ranger sat in silence in Dankett's wooden chair, wearing nothing but a thin ragged towel tied around his middle. Before coming in through the side door, he'd shed his soiled clothing and left it in a pile on the dirt, boots, sombrero and all, to be picked up by someone from the town laundry. He'd wiped himself down with water and a washcloth, then thrown the washcloth away. He'd dried himself,

stepped inside the door naked, rifle in hand, and
tied the towel around his waist.

Toy Johnson and Randall Carnes had given
each other looks of stunned disbelief, then turned
stiffly back to the Ranger as he sat down with his
Winchester across his lap and stared at them.
After a long, tense silence, Toy Johnson cleared
his throat and ventured to speak.

"So, Ranger Burrack," he said, "is it being too
forward of me to ask what's going on here?"

"Nothing's going on here, Johnson," Sam said
flatly. "The dove's not coming. We're just waiting
for the doctor to get back and patch you two up.
Come morning you're out of here."

"You're not going to charge us for trying to
kill you?" Carnes asked in a suspicious tone.

"That stays between us," Sam said. "If either
of you ever comes at me again, I'll make sure
you're dead before I even reload."

The two looked at each other as if suspecting
a trick.

"You and the deputy took Harvey Lang out
and shot him, didn't you?" Carnes asked in an
accusing voice.

"No," Sam said, witnessing their fear and
dark misconceptions at work on them.

"Why are you sitting there naked, Ranger?"
Johnson asked.

The Ranger didn't answer.

Johnson stood up defiantly and steadied himself, wincing from the pain in his hip. "Just so
you know, I'll die before I'll be put upon to par-
ticipate in anything contrary to my nature."

"Sit down and shut up, Johnson," the Ranger
said. He stared at the two in silence until at length

a knock resounded on the front door. "Come in," the Ranger called out.

Adele Simpson stepped inside carrying an armload of neatly folded clothing and a pair of boots she'd picked up at the mercantile store. She averted her eyes at the sight of the Ranger as he stood wrapped in the towel.

"Sam, I came from the hotel as soon as I heard what happened to that poor woman and what you three did to save her," she said. "I brought you these clothes, compliments of the store owner. I hope they fit."

"Obliged, Adele," Sam said eagerly. He leaned his rifle against the wooden chair. "They'll fit, I promise, leastwise until mine are washed and dry. Stepping in, taking the clothes she held out for him, he walked around behind a freestanding gun cabinet waiting to be installed and dressed himself.

"Ranger, can I ask you something?" Adele called out to him after a moment of contemplation.

"Yes," Sam said, pulling on the black miner boots.

"Did Cisco help you?" Adele asked. "I mean did he do his part getting her out of that waste ditch without you threatening him, or forcing him to?"

Listening from their seat against the wall, Carnes and Johnson looked at each other.

"*Waste ditch?*" Johnson whispered with a wincing expression.

"Adele," Sam answered, straightening his shirt collar as he stepped around the gun cabinet, "I have to say, Cisco surprised me, the way he pitched in when none of the townsmen would help—none except Deputy Dankett, that is." He paused, then added, "Sometimes it takes the worst situation to bring out the best in a man."

"Then you would admit that maybe there is some *good* in Harvey Lang?" Adele asked.

"I would not have thought it, but yes, maybe so," Sam replied.

Adele smiled. "That's all I wanted to know." She sounded satisfied with the Ranger's answer. As she turned to leave, she stopped and said, "They say the girl had stolen a man's money . . . ?"

"So they say," Sam replied. He watched Adele shake her head, open the front door and close it behind herself.

From the wall, Toy Johnson, appearing relieved to see the Ranger fully dressed, called out, "Am I to take it you found a woman stuck in the public ditch out back of town? She robbed somebody?"

Sam picked up his rifle from against the chair and sat down, again placing it across his lap.

"So they say," he repeated.

"She made one hell of a getaway," Carnes threw in.

"A young dove named Anna Rose," Sam said, ignoring Carnes' joke. "She's beat up awfully bad. My hunch is someone thought they'd killed her, threw her in the public ditch to get rid of her."

"In the public ditch. . . ." Johnson pondered the thought with a look of disgust on his face. "They could have had the decency to make sure she was dead first."

"Yeah," Carnes said. "That's as low as anything I've ever heard. I've been the worst, rottenest, meanest no-good bastard on three legs," he continued. "I've done every terrible thing a man can do, robbed, killed, looted, burned down barns—" He caught himself and looked at the Ranger. "Not really, although I have *imagined* myself doing all that at one time or another," he said. "But I would never even have *thought* of doing something that low down."

"Neither would I," Johnson said. He rubbed his jaw, considering the matter. "Although you have to admit, if you didn't want to drag somebody out of town and leave them for the critters . . ." He let his words trail.

The Ranger only watched and listened as the two discussed the matter. He was grateful for another knock on the front door. Dr. Starr opened the door a crack and looked in with his good eye.

"Coming in, Ranger," Starr said. "There's some workers coming along behind me, carrying some iron bars for the jail cell."

"That's good news, Doctor. Come on in," Sam said. He stood and looked past the doctor at a wagon rolling slowly up the street, three men in leather aprons sitting in the bed atop a load of wood and iron bars.

"I would have been here sooner," the doctor said, leather bag in hand, a bottle of rye under his arm, "but I took care of the young woman first."

"I understand," Sam said. He gestured a hand toward the two prisoners seated against the wall. "Here they are, Doctor, one with a shoulder wound, one with a bullet stuck in his hip."

Carnes and Johnson leered at the bottle under the doctor's arm.

"All right, then, Ranger, may I have some clean water?" the short, one-eyed doctor said, setting his bag down, his sleeves still rolled up from caring for Anna Rose. "Who wants to be first?" he said to the two wounded gunman.

"Here you go," said Carnes, standing attentively.

"Right here, Doctor, I'm hurt worst," said Johnson, struggling onto his feet.

They watched the doctor take the bottle from under his arm, take a long drink from it, cork it and set it aside in a manner that suggested he wasn't going to share it.

"Go ahead, then," Carnes said to Johnson, sitting back down against the wall.

Chapter 15

When the doctor had cleaned and prepared and finally probed deep into the bleeding flesh to remove the half of a bullet lodged deep into Toy Johnson's hip, he set down his tongs and wiped his bloody hands on a towel. Then he picked up the bottle of rye and pulled the cork from it again.

While Dr. Starr had worked on the wound, the Ranger stood by at one end of the desk where the gunman lay sleeping under the influence of chloroform the doctor had administered to him. Should the chloroform wear off, Sam's job would be to hold the gunman down and press the cloth over his nose and mouth to put him back to sleep.

Setting the bottle of rye aside, Starr spoke to the Ranger as he picked up the tongs again and bent over Johnson's wound.

"You might be interested to know, this is not the first bullet I've cut out of some knot-head today, Ranger," he said. His one good eye slid away from Johnson to the Ranger, but only for a second.

"You don't say," Sam replied.

"I sure do," said Starr, probing back into the wound with his pointed tongs. "This was a bunch camped outside town. They had a fight between two of their own. One of them came and got me. A dwarf put two bullets into a big ol' scrappy fellow named Reye—leastwise he *said* his name is Reye. You never know with discards like these. They looked like they'd steal the coins off a dead man's eyes."

"Reye, huh?" Sam said. He ran the name through his mind. "Chic Reye, was it?"

"Yep, I believe it was Chic Reye," Starr said. "The one who came and got me was Dave Coyle."

The Ranger looked at him more intently. The doctor continued probing into the open wound with a pair of long, slim tongs. Carnes watched beside the iron ball with a sick look on his face.

"He had a brother, this Dave fellow," the doctor said. "But his name is different—stepbrothers, I suspect. Said his name is Joe North . . . or was it Jonas? I can't recall."

"Either one will do," Sam said. He looked at Randall Carnes. "You know anything about the Coyle brothers being around here?"

"No," said Carnes. "But I expect it stands to reason if we heard about the bounty, so did they."

"Bounty?" the doctor asked.

"It's nothing, Doctor," Sam said. "Just a reward some railroad man put on my head."

"*Nothing*, huh?" The doctor glanced up at him. "Just a reward on your head, men wanting to kill you? All right, then . . ." He gave a dismissing shrug. But before Sam could reply, he said, "Peculiar thing about that name *Joe North*. It's the name the dove from the ditch kept saying over and over while I treated her . . . unconscious, of course."

Sam just stared at him, connecting the name Joe North to Oldham Coyle. From what he knew about Oldham Coyle, he was not the kind of man to harm a woman. *But things change*, he told himself.

"Where are they camped?" he asked the doctor.

"North is south of here," the doctor said. He gave a grin for his witticism. "Pardon me, Ranger. This is a long day for me, plucking out bullets." He nodded southerly. "They're not more than three miles out."

The clanking of heavy boots walking on the boardwalk resounded from out front. One of the men from the wagon in a leather apron stood in the open doorway.

"We've got jail bars to hang here," the man said. "Anybody object to us doing that?"

"No, not at all," Sam said. "Come on in and go to work."

"Thank you, Ranger," said the carpenter. "We'll be in and out of here before you know it."

As the carpenters went to work, the Ranger watched Dr. Starr finish with Toy Johnson and bandage his hip. As the doctor reached for his bottle of rye, Sam helped the staggering, half-conscious gunman off the desk, back to the iron ball, and cuffed him. Johnson slid down the wall with the Ranger's help and sprawled back against it as Carnes stood up to be uncuffed and led to the desk for treatment.

"Doctor," Carnes said, seeing the doctor lower the rye bottle from his lips, "wouldn't a good stiff drink benefit me right now, before you give me that knockout water?" He gestured to the small bottle of chloroform sticking up from the leather bag.

"Not as much as it might *benefit* the rest of the world," Starr said dryly.

"Huh?" said Carnes.

"It would likely kill you, is what I'm saying," Starr replied.

"*Likely . . . ?*" said Carnes. "Meaning, there's always a chance it wouldn't?"

"Forget it," said Starr, reaching for the bottle of chloroform.

From the street, Cisco Lang walked in, handcuffed, bathed and wearing his own clean but damp clothing. His boots were still noticeably wet from a good scrubbing. Behind him Deputy Clow Dankett walked in wearing his own clean but damp clothes as well, carrying his long-barreled shotgun at his side.

"Sorry we took so long, Ranger," Dankett said. A smell of lilac water permeated the air around him. "You just can't rush clothes drying, especially when the wind's down."

"I understand," the Ranger said.

The two walked Lang over to the iron ball while a carpenter measured out a line on the plank floor.

"The injured dove woke up a little before we left," Dankett said as he reached out to cuff Cisco Lang back to the heavy ball. "But nobody made any sense out of her before she fell back asleep."

"I want the man who did this," Sam said. He reached out and stopped the deputy from snapping Lang's cuff to the chain on the ball.

"No more than I do, Ranger Burrack," Dankett said. "I want to thump upon his head over and over 'til his brains bleed out his ears." As he revealed his violet fantasy, he stared coldly into Lang's eyes. Lang stepped back uncomfortably against the plank wall and swallowed hard.

"Ranger, I was with you the whole time," he said.

"He knows that, Cisco," Sam said, seeing Lang's fear of the deputy. To Dankett he said, "When the doctor's through, we're going to leave Carnes and Johnson cuffed to the ball. I want you and Lang to ride outside town with me. I'm going to talk to a man named Oldham Coyle." As he spoke, he slid Lang a look, recalling what Lang had said at the Desert Rose about how fast Coyle was with a gun—how he would bet a hundred dollars on Coyle should he and the Ranger ever meet.

"Oldham Coyle, here?" Lang ventured.

"Yep, I believe so," said Sam. He gave Lang a harsh stare. "Don't you wish you had a hundred dollars?"

"Ranger, I shouldn't have said that," Lang said, shame-faced.

"Said what?" Dankett wanted to know, a harsh look coming to his eyes, staring at Lang.

"Nothing to it, Deputy," Sam said, defusing Dankett. "Lang here was warning me a while back, how fast Coyle is with gun. But if he was with this Anna Rose, I want to talk to him first thing."

Lang looked relieved that the Ranger withheld the whole story from Dankett.

"Can I say something, Ranger?" he asked.

Sam looked at him.

"From what I know of Oldham Coyle, he's not the kind of man who would do something like this. Being honest, I don't know many men who would."

"I'll keep that in mind, Cisco," Sam said. He

looked Lang up and down and said almost grudgingly, "I'm obliged for your help out there."

"I had no choice," Lang said, rattling his cuffs.

"You know what I mean, Cisco," Sam said. "I took note. You could have made it harder on us. Instead you helped out. It appeared you might even have cared what happened to the poor young woman."

"Did it?" He gave a thin grin and shrugged. "Well . . . it wasn't like we were being shot at," Lang offered. "I figure I could always—"

"Keep it up," Sam said, cutting him short. "You'll convince me I was wrong thinking you might have the slimmest thread of decency."

"Yeah," said Dankett, not reading Lang's actions the way Sam read them, "and I bet I can wipe that grin from under your nose, take part of your chin with it." He gripped his shotgun, ready to swing the butt of it into Lang's face.

"Easy, Deputy," Sam said. "Why did you do it, Cisco?" he asked Lang.

"All right, I'll come clean," Lang said, seeing cruel craziness in Dankett's eyes. He let out a breath. "I helped because I have a sister who become a dove—or *had* a sister by now . . . far as I know." He looked away.

"It was looking for her that brought me west. I searched and searched for her, never found her. Never knew what become of her." He paused and chuffed, looking down at his cuffed hands. "All I know is what become of me." He took a deep breath, let it out, raised his face and looked at Sam. "Anyway, that's my sad story, Ranger. Think the judge would listen to it?"

"You never know," Sam replied. "It all depends

on who your judge is. Some judges listen better than others."

"I never had much luck drawing judges," Lang said.

"Then you are gored deep," Dankett said in a black tone. He gave him a sharp, menacing grin, grabbed the short chain to Lang's cuffs and jerked him forward. "Come on, Sad Story, let's go get the horses."

Sam watched the two walk out the front door and around toward the livery barn.

"Deputy Dankett is loco top to bottom, Ranger, in case you haven't noticed," the doctor said as soon as Dankett and Lang were outside, out of hearing.

"He takes some getting used to," Sam said, repeating what Sheriff Rattler had told him about the deputy.

On the desert floor, seated beside a stand of rock fifteen yards from a ragged canvas lean-to, Blind Simon Goss stood in the waning afternoon sunlight and lifted his head toward the trail leading out to New Delmar. Karl Sieg, Deak Holder and Dave Coyle watched from beside the campfire as he cocked his head slightly, sunlight glittering sharply on his black spectacle lenses. Oldham Coyle saw him as he stepped from under the canvas, a plate of beans in one hand, a spoon in the other.

"What's this?" Oldham asked no one in particular. Behind Oldham beneath the overhang, Chic Reye sat up on his blanket with a hand pressed to his bandaged stomach and stared out with everyone else.

"Riders coming," Simon called out. "Three riders, moving at a gallop."

The three men at the fire stood and stared in the direction of New Delmar until a rise of dust drifted up along the trail. Without a word, they instinctively spread out in a half circle and stepped toward the trail.

"Good work, Simon," Oldham said. He took a large mouthful of beans and chewed them as he set the tin plate and spoon down and picked up his gun belt.

While his brother swung the gun belt around his waist and buckled it, Dave Coyle turned to Karl Sieg, who stood holding his rifle.

"Get up in the rocks, Karl," he said. "Let us know what we've got as soon as they ride into sight. It could be travelers passing by."

Outside the overhang, Oldham straightened from tying down his holster. He'd drawn his bone-handled Colt, checked it and slipped it loosely back into his holster when he heard Reye call out.

"Boss," the wounded gunman said in a pained voice, his face swollen from the bullet through his cheek. "Come look at this. My navel is turning black."

"*Jesus . . . ,*" Oldham said under his breath. Raising his lowered voice, he said to Reye, "Not now, Chic, we got riders coming."

"Boss, I'm not lying," Reye said, sounding even more in pain. "I'm turning black all around my belly."

Oldham heard the first rumble of distant hooves on the hard, rocky ground. He walked back under the overhang and stooped down beside Reye. He looked at the sore, swollen wound in Reye's navel as Reye pulled the bandage aside.

"Damn it, Chic," he said. "The doctor said leave the bandage alone. "You're not doing like he told you."

"I loosened it because my belly's turning black," said Reye. "I'm telling you this is not right. Is my face turning black too?"

Oldham looked closely at Reye's wounded cheek, around the edge of the bandage covering it. It was turning a sickly greenish black, but Oldham didn't want to tell him while the sound of hooves drew nearer.

"No, your face is all right," he said. Looking down at Reye's navel, he frowned and looked back up. "But your belly don't look so good."

"I've got the infection," Reye said. "That little bastard pisses on his bullets, makes them poison."

"That's crazy talk, Reye," said Oldham. He saw the heavy sheen of sweat on Reye's forehead, beads of it running down his face like tears.

"No, they do that, these dwarves! I've heard of it," he said, enraged. "Help me to my feet, boss," he groaned, struggling to stand up. "If I'm going to die, I'm taking the little murdering son of a—"

"Stay still and shut up, Reye," said Oldham, pressing him back down onto his blanket. Both Reye and his blanket were soaking wet. Oldham felt the burning fever through the gunman's wet shirt. "We'll get you taken care of as soon as we see who's coming from the main trail." As he spoke, he slipped Reye's gun from its holster and stood up. "I'll hold this until you're feeling better."

"You're taking my gun?" Reye said, almost sobbing. He began to tremble all over.

"You'll get it back, Reye," said Oldham. "Take it easy."

From atop a sandstone rock, Sieg watched the three riders gallop into sight.

"Simon's right," he called down to the others, "three of them. One is that crazy-looking deputy." He paused for a second. "Damn, one of them's Harvey Lang."

"Cisco Lang?" said Oldham. "What the hell . . . ?" On his way to the rock, he passed his horse and jerked his rifle from his saddle boot. He pulled a telescope from his saddlebags.

"Stay up there, brother," said Dave, watching Oldham start to climb up to join Sieg on the rock. But Oldham didn't seem to hear him.

Up beside Sieg, he stretched out the telescope and held it to his eye as the three riders drew closer.

"The deputy, Cisco Lang . . ." He paused for a moment staring at the third rider in the circle of the lens, the silver-gray sombrero, the big bear-paw Appaloosa. "I'm *betting* that's the man Dave's been talking about all day." As he spoke he watched the badge come into sight behind the lapel of the Ranger's riding duster. "Yep, I won *that* bet," he said to himself. "Stay up here, Karl. But when the Ranger and I throw down, keep out of it."

"Come on, boss," said Sieg. "You know I can't do that."

"Yes, you can, Karl," said Oldham. "There's wagering involved between this man and me. Don't you cross me on this."

"All right, boss, you've got it," Sieg said, catching the threat in Oldham's voice.

"What's the deal up there?" Dave called up to Oldham. He stood staring up at the two.

Oldham grinned and said, "They're not passing by, brother Dave." He handed Sieg the telescope and climbed down to the ground.

"Well?" Dave said expectantly as Oldham dusted his knees and the front of his shirt, his rifle cradled in his arm.

"One's the deputy from town. The other is Harvey Lang," he said.

"Cisco Lang, riding with the law?" said Dave. Oldham looked closely at his brother.

"The Ranger is riding with them," he said.

"The Ranger . . . ," Dave said. He didn't appear surprised. "All right, stay up there with Sieg. We'll take care of this."

"Whoa, hang on, brother," said Oldham. "How do we know it's not a social call? We're not wanted for anything around here. He might be coming for coffee."

"Quit it, Oldham," said Dave. "We can cut this thing off right here. You cut out. We'll come meet you down the trail."

Oldham called out to the others, "Anybody wanted for anything in Arizona Territory?"

"You asked us that before we went into New Delmar the other day, boss," Sieg said from atop the rock.

"Now I'm asking you again," said Oldham. "Because I want to make sure we've got no trouble coming at us until I'm ready to make my move on Burrack."

Sieg shook his head and said, "I'm clean."

"What about you, Deak?"

"I'm clean in Arizona," Deak said. He gave a

faint smile. "Unless the doctor reported me for shooting Reye all to hell."

"Simon?" said Oldham.

"I'm good everywhere I go," the blind man said, still facing the trail.

"I knew you would be," Oldham said. He smiled. "Now everybody get spread out. Let's see what the Ranger has on his mind." He looked at Dave and said, "If him and I throw down, I want everybody to stay out of it. You got that, brother Dave?"

"I've got it," Dave said grudgingly. "I don't like it, but I got it."

Chapter 16

The Ranger saw the figures standing off the trail, four men spread out in a half circle facing him as he and the others rounded a stand of rock and came upon them all at once. As Sam reined his stallion down, Lang sidled in close. Dankett reined his horse down too, but he pulled away from the Ranger, taking a position for himself with his long shotgun.

"There's the Coyle brothers," Lang said to Sam under his breath, gazing away from the two as he spoke. "That's Oldham on the left."

"That's what I would have guessed," Sam said, also under his breath. He stared straight at the two brothers from twenty yards away. He looked to the Coyle brothers' right and saw a man seemingly staring at him through blacked-out spectacles. Yet he also saw the tapping stick leaning against Simon's leg and made the connection. Looking to the Coyles' left, he saw the dwarf, his small fingers tapping on the handle of the big belly gun strapped across his middle.

"Oldham Coyle," he called out from his saddle, his Winchester propped up in his right hand. He sat silent, his eyes locked on to Oldham's until the gunman felt he had to take a step forward and speak.

"Well, well, Ranger Samuel Burrack." He stepped forward. His right hand fell deftly beside his clean and holstered Colt. "I was wondering when we'd meet up. I suppose you heard all about the reward? About the odds being set in my favor?"

"I heard about it," Sam said flatly. "But I'm not here to kill you right now, unless it comes to that."

Oldham stopped moving forward. He smiled at the Ranger's bluntness, liking his brassy, confident tone.

"That's gracious of you, Ranger," Oldham said. "What are you doing here? None of us are wanted in your territory."

"I could probably come up with some paper on a couple of you if I scratched hard enough," Sam said, letting his eyes shift across from one man to the next. "But I come to talk to you about a woman."

"Sorry, Ranger Burrack," said Oldham, relaxed, enjoying the confrontation. "But I've got none to spare. When it comes to women, we all have to do the best we—"

"Anna Rose," Sam said flatly, cutting through his nonsense.

"Anna Rose?" said Oldham. The name appeared to have a sobering effect on him. "What about her?" His smile fell away; his shoulders stiffened. The Ranger took note of the change.

"So you do know her?" he said.

"Know her? Yeah, I know her, Ranger," said Oldham with a darkness coming to his face. "You might say we got *well acquainted* in New Delmar."

Reading something more in the Ranger's question than Oldham appeared to, Dave cut in.

"She robbed him, Ranger. What about her?" he asked.

"Robbed you, huh?" Sam said to Oldham, without answering his suspicious brother.

"Picked me to the bone," said Oldham, his hand still hanging ready near his gun butt. "I never had won so much money or lost it so quick in my life." He paused, then added, "Why are you asking me about her, Ranger?"

"I understand she was being friendly with a *Joe North*, a name I know you've shown a fondness for."

Oldham glared at Lang, who sat with his hands cuffed to his saddle horn.

"Cisco didn't have to tell me anything," Sam said. "I work these badlands something fierce."

"All right, so what? She and I played around some before she disappeared with all my chips," said Oldham.

"Somebody beat her up real bad. Left her for dead in the public ditch," Sam said. "I don't suppose you know anything about that, though?"

"The public ditch? Jesus. . . ." A look of repulsion spread across Oldham's face. "You supposed right, I don't know nothing about it," he said. "How bad off is she? Is she going to be all right?"

"I don't know yet," Sam said, not giving up any more than he had to. "When is the last you saw her?"

"Hold it right there, Ranger," Dave cut in. "If you're accusing my brother of hurting that dove, come out and say it."

"Make no mistake, if I was accusing any of you, I already would have come out and said it," Sam replied, making his answer to Oldham instead of Dave Coyle. "I'm searching for whoever done it.

Far as I'm concerned, everybody is guilty until proven innocent."

"Are you sure you don't have that backward, Ranger?" Dave asked, not liking the way the Ranger ignored him.

"No, I don't think so," Sam said. He looked from one face to the next, even up toward the rock where Sieg stood out of sight ready to pull an ambush.

"You're peering down the wrong well, Ranger," Oldham said. "If one of these men did something like that to Anna Rose, I'd kill him myself, straight up."

From the side, Deak Holder stepped forward, his fingers on the butt of the big revolver.

"And I don't like being accused of something—" Deak stopped short at the sound of Dankett's long shotgun cocking and swinging toward him.

"Keep your short ass in line, Mr. *Bite-size*," Dankett warned sharply. "I'll turn you into a spot of grease." Seeing Deak freeze, he added, "And don't think you're going to yank some iron out of your sleeve or any place else. We heard about you shooting one of your own pards with a hideaway."

Deak looked surprised, but settled himself into place. Seeing things start to take an ugly turn, Sam looked at Oldham.

"Is this the direction you want things to go?" he asked. "I was halfway thinking you sounded concerned over this dove."

"Settle down, Deak," said Oldham. To Sam he said, "I am concerned about her. I'm also wondering about my money. Maybe she didn't steal it after all, or maybe she was working with a partner. Maybe they double-crossed her."

Sam saw Oldham working things over in his mind.

"I want to see Anna Rose as soon as she's able. Any problem with me riding into town?" he asked Sam.

"So long as you start no trouble," Sam said, "I've got no reason to tell you to stay out."

"What about that reward, Ranger?" Oldham asked. "I'm still out to collect it."

"That'll be your mistake," Sam said. "I'll kill any man who sticks a gun at me or breaks the law. But I won't fight because somebody is wagering money on it. The law is not a sporting event." He looked around at Dankett, who stepped his horse back and lowered his shotgun an inch. "You're welcome in New Delmar, unless you go wrong," he concluded to Oldham.

Oldham glanced around at the others.

"Hear that, men? The Ranger has invited us all to town," said Oldham. "So I'm telling everybody here and now, *be on your best behavior.*"

The Ranger backed his Appaloosa and turned it, Lang right beside him.

"You didn't ask him much, Ranger," Lang said in a whisper.

"I didn't need to," Sam replied, looking around as Dankett turned his horse and fell in alongside him. "I was stirring the brew. I told him enough to get him interested. He'll come to town either to see about getting his money back from the dove or to find out who took the money from her. Either way, we'll benefit from him being there."

"All right," said Lang, "I guess I can see that."

"Ranger, how did I do backing you up?" Dankett asked.

"A little harsh, Deputy," Sam said, "but good."

"I'll work on it . . . ," Dankett said thoughtfully. He stared over his shoulder at Deak Holder as he turned to ride away.

"Let it go, Deak," Oldham cautioned the small gunman who stood staring coldly at the three riders.

Deak released a tight breath and shook himself out. Simon Goss stood with his face toward the Ranger, Lang and Dankett as they rode away along the trail.

"Tell me we're not going to ride into New Delmar, brother," said Dave Coyle.

"I can't tell you that, brother Dave," said Oldham, "because we are riding in. We're riding in tonight, as soon as we get our horses and break camp."

"Damn it, no!" said Dave. "This is crazy. Do you believe this lawman won't set you up and kill you, before you get a chance to kill him? You're favored to win, Oldham. He'd be a fool not to kill you from behind if the opportunity comes up."

"It doesn't matter, brother Dave," Oldham said. "We've got to ride in tonight anyway. We've got no choice."

"What are you talking about, we've got no choice?" Dave demanded. "We've got a choice. All we have to do is ride away, forget the dove, the money, the whole damn deal."

"Reye's burning up with fever and turning black on us," said Oldham. "If we don't get him to town, he'll likely be dead by morning." Seeing the look on Dave's face, Oldham shrugged and said, "Like I said, brother Dave, some things are meant to play themselves out. We've no choice but to roll with them."

"Damn it," Dave said, looking toward the lean-to, his fists clenched in anger at his sides.

"Go see for yourself," Oldham said confidently. "While you do, we'll be getting your horse ready."

On their ride back into New Delmar, Lang stopped his horse suddenly. So suddenly, in fact, that Deputy Dankett swung the big shotgun around toward him, ready to fire. But Sam slowed and circled his stallion, coming to a halt facing Lang, who sat with his cuffed hands held chest high. He was ducking slightly, as if that alone would stave off a shotgun blast.

"That was a stupid move, Lang," the Ranger said. He raised a hand toward Dankett and had him lower the shotgun.

"I'm sorry, Ranger. I wasn't thinking," said Lang. "It just came to me all of a sudden. There were two of Hugh Fenderson's men in the Number Five when we took the dove in there."

"What?" Sam stared at him. "You're just now mentioning it?"

"It just came to me," said Lang. "It's been eating at me all along. I recognized them but I couldn't figure from where. Now I know. One of them is Henry Teague. The other is a young gunman named Sonny Rudabough. Some say he's kin to Dirty Dave Rudabough."

Listening, Dankett stepped his horse in closer.

"Are you talking about the two men sitting at the table by the wall?" he asked.

"Yep, that's the two," said Lang. "Teague is said to be Fenderson's right-hand man."

Sam looked back and forth between them.

"I've noticed them myself, Ranger Burrack," said Dankett. "It struck me that they've been hogging that table like they own it the past few days and nights. I would have mentioned it, except they haven't done nothing out of the ordinary—haven't caused any trouble."

"That's all right, Deputy," Sam said. "You had no reason to mention it." He looked at Lang. "What are you saying, that they have a hand in what happened to the dove?"

"I'm saying . . ." His words trailed off and he looked confused. "I'm not sure what I'm saying. There's just something about them being there that strikes me as more than a coincidence."

Sam considered it.

"Obliged you told me," he said. "I see no connection, but the fact that they work for a man who has a bounty on my head makes me want to talk to them."

Dankett put in, "I can walk into the Number Five and butt-smack them up from their table," jiggling his big shotgun in his hand. "Soften them up for a more constructive conversation?"

"You can go with me for backup, Deputy," Sam said. "But no butt-smacking, unless you have to."

"Butt-smack . . ." Lang gave the deputy a look of fear and disbelief until Sam took Lang's horse by its bridle, turning it and his own stallion back to the trail.

As they rode, Lang said to the Ranger, "I'm going to be getting some harsh treatment from other prisoners once word gets out I'm riding with you."

"You're not riding with me by your choice, Cisco," Sam said. "Once the jail's finished, you'll be in it."

"I understand that, Ranger," said Lang. "But you saw the look on the Coyle brothers' faces.

They've got it in their minds that I'm cooperating, telling you everything I know about them."

Sam looked him up and down.

"Aren't you?" he said. "I hope you're not holding anything back from me."

Lang let out a breath.

"All right, I suppose I am cooperating," he said. "But it's not like I'm telling you places they've robbed—"

"That's because you don't know what places they've robbed, unless you were riding with them, Cisco," Sam said, stopping him.

"That's true," Lang said, considering it. "Looking at it that way, I haven't told you anything except about somebody putting a reward on your head."

Sam gave him a sidelong gaze.

"The truth is, Cisco, you haven't rode on any robberies except that mercantile store."

"Oh, I've rode on some," Lang said in defense of his bad reputation. "Plenty, in fact—"

"You *want to be* a bad man, Cisco," Sam said before Lang could go on any further about any alleged criminal exploits. "I've watched and listened, and I've figured you out," he said as if in conclusion. "What puzzles me is *why* you want to be a bad man."

Lang grew sullen and silent, anger boiling inside him. Dankett drew in closer on the Ranger's other side to better hear them both.

"I figure maybe you came searching for your sister and because you never found her, you figured you failed her."

"Leave my sister out of this, Ranger," Lang said, but Sam heard no threat, no conviction in his words, just a weak defense against a truth.

"But you didn't fail her," Sam went on. "You failed yourself. The West showed you that you weren't the tough young man you thought yourself to be. You tried to prove you are by mistaking toughness for meanness. You picked the wrong people to look up to, and now here you are, on your way to prison for what I figure was you holding the horses while some real bad men did the robbing."

"You're wrong, Ranger, dead wrong!" said Lang. He settled himself when he saw Dankett's shotgun rise an inch.

Sam shook his head and said, "Wherever your sister is, Cisco, I wonder how she would feel, knowing that searching for her played a part in bringing you to where you are."

Dankett chuffed under his breath and laid his shotgun back across his lap.

"Well said, Ranger," he murmured.

The three fell silent. They rode onto the main street of New Delmar, and followed it through long slices of evening shadows to the hitch rail out in front of the jail.

"I don't hear any hammers," Dankett said, stepping down from his saddle.

Yet upon walking through the front door, the three found a straight and sturdy wall of shiny new bars crossing the floor where only the chalk line had been before.

"With two whole cells," Dankett whispered as if in awe. At the desk, they heard Dr. Starr snoring, his head down, the nearly empty rye bottle standing at his elbow. Bedside the desk lay the heavy iron ball. Inside one of the two cells sat Carnes and Johnson on two short stools, smoking freshly rolled cigarettes.

"We didn't do nothing to him," said Johnson. "He just drank until he fell over."

Sam looked beside the bottle of rye and saw a large metal key on a brass ring. Picking up the key, he gestured Lang toward the cell door. When he started to unlock the door, he found it already standing an inch ajar.

"If it's all the same, Ranger, you said we could stay until morning," Carnes said.

"That is what I said," Sam replied. He opened the door, took off Lang's handcuffs and motioned him inside the other cell.

Lang walked into the cell without protest and turned and faced Sam through the bars.

"I'm thinking about what you said, Ranger. Maybe there's some truth in it," he offered quietly. Then he turned away.

Sam only nodded and shut the door. Locking it, he walked back to the desk and dropped the key on it.

Dankett stood in the middle of the floor still looking in wonderment at the new wall of shiny black bars.

"I don't think I'll know how to sleep tonight, not sitting in a wooden chair," he said.

"Good," said Sam. "You can go with me to Number Five, help me make some new friends. How does that sound?"

"It sounds like more fun than sleeping," Dankett said, grinning beneath the wide brim of his Montana-crowned hat.

Chapter 17

Looking in the dusty window of the busy Number Five Saloon, the Ranger and Deputy Dankett picked through the crowd until the deputy spotted the two railroad gunmen. Henry Teague and Sonny Rudabough sat at the table they had staked out for themselves along a side wall. A tall bottle of whiskey stood on the tabletop between them.

"That's them?" Sam asked, his face close to the glass.

Just to be certain, Dankett huffed his breath on the wavy windowpane and rubbed his coat sleeve around on it, making a large circle on the thick glass.

"Yep, that's them, Ranger," he said sidelong to Sam. "The same men, the same table." He hiked the shotgun cradled in his arm. "Want me to walk Big Lucy in, have her bat their heads around some?"

Sam looked at Dankett for a moment until he decided he was serious.

"No, Deputy," Sam said. "In a crowded place like this, it's best we keep down any trouble if we can."

"Too bad," Dankett said, glancing down at his shotgun.

"First thing, I want to see if the dove is able to

tell me anything. Then I need you to stand to the side, watch my back for me while I talk to these birds."

"All right," Dankett said, sounding a little disappointed. "Where do you want me and Lucy?"

"Keep between me and their table when we go upstairs," Sam said, drawing his big Colt, checking it, and lowering it back into its holster. "Stay to my left when we come down and I go talk to them."

"You've got it, Ranger," Dankett said. He turned and followed Sam inside and across the crowded floor, the player piano rattling, jumping and bouncing wildly, like some lunatic on visiting day.

Having seen the Ranger eyeing the piano, Wesley Fluge, the stocky saloon owner, grinned behind the bar and stood with his stubby hands spread along the bar's edge, his shirtsleeves rolled up to his elbows.

"She a beauty, eh, Ranger?" he said to Sam, raising his voice above the loud twangy music. Before Sam could reply, he said, "Had her made and shipped here from Philadelphia—fellow by the name of McTammany built her. A *genius*, that man." He slapped a hand down and said, "I know Deputy Clow here doesn't drink, but what can I get for you?"

"I want to see Anna Rose," Sam said, keeping an occasional glance toward the wall table.

"Ranger, you might want to pick somebody else tonight," said Fluge. "Anna Rose is not what I'd call back to working at her *usual quality*?" He gave him a wink.

"He wants to talk to her, you fool," said Dankett. "About what happened." The deputy leaned against the edge of the bar top. Sam saw that at any moment he might reach over and grab the saloon owner by his throat.

Fluge jumped back a step; his face lost its color.

"I—I know that, Deputy Clow," he stammered. "I was being humorous, trying to get a laugh, is all."

"You want to get a laugh, pour kerosene over your head and stick a match to it," Dankett said.

"Easy, Deputy," Sam said in a calm tone.

"Right up there, Ranger," said Fluge, gesturing a nod up the stairs, "second room on the left. Lila's with her. Tell her I said let you in."

"The Ranger is our sheriff, *fool*," said Dankett. "He gets let in, no matter what."

"Obliged," Sam said to Fluge. He gave Dankett a look as he turned to the stairs.

"What?" said Dankett. "Was I still a little harsh?"

"A little, maybe," Sam said, "but not bad." He turned and walked through the crowd and up the stairs, Dankett right behind him.

At the door to Anna Rose's room, Lila answered Dankett's knock and gave him a wary look. Seeing the Ranger beside him, she stepped back and said, "Come in, Ranger—or *Sheriff*, whichever one you want to be called."

Sam stepped inside and looked across the darkened room at the bed where the young woman lay under a blanket. He took off his sombrero and held it in front of himself. Seeing the Ranger's display of respect for the injured dove, Dankett took his hat off as well and held it in the same manner.

"How is Anna Rose doing?" Sam asked quietly. He could smell the lilac water and other assorted scents and balms that had been used to help extinguish the terrible odor of the public ditch.

"Not so good, Ranger," Lila said. "She wakes up for a while, but goes back out. I hoped that was the doctor knocking."

"He's at the jail, ma'am," Sam said. "I'll send him over as soon as he finishes up there." He slid a knowing look past Dankett. The deputy only nodded.

"Can I see if she'll wake up and talk to me?" Sam asked.

"Just don't push her, Ranger," Lila said. "She took a bad beating."

Sam and Dankett stepped over to the bedside.

"Anna Rose," Sam said quietly, "can you hear me?"

To everyone's surprise, the young dove partly opened her swollen eyes and turned them to the Ranger.

"Yes . . . I hear you, Joe," she whispered in a painfully weak, dreamlike voice. "I lost . . . your money . . ."

Sam didn't offer to correct her; he leaned in close and took her hand as she tried to raise it from the bed.

"That's all right, Anna Rose," Sam pressed. "Can you tell me who did this to you?"

"No . . . ," she replied, already drifting away again.

"Please, Anna Rose, help me," the Ranger said. "Help me catch the man responsible."

"It's my . . . fault, Ranger . . . ," she said, dropping back into unconsciousness.

"Let her rest, Ranger," Lila said. "She's not making much sense right now."

"Has she been able to tell you anything at all, ma'am?" Sam asked quietly.

"Not much, but some," Lila said. "She rambled about losing the winnings she was holding for a drifter named Joe North."

"Did she say how much?" Sam asked.

"No," said Lila. "But Ozzie White, the poker dealer, can tell you. He was dealing the night the fellow North won it."

"Is Ozzie White working tonight?" Sam asked.

"Ozzie White is always working," Lila said. "What time he's not dealing for the house, he's playing for himself."

"Which table does he work?" Sam asked.

Lila passed a look at Dankett, realizing he already knew most of the answers to the Ranger's questions.

"Ozzie's not hard to find. He always sits on the platform table where the whole place can see his game," she said. She passed Dankett another look and said, "Clow here knows all this, Ranger."

Dankett gave a slight grin.

"I know," Sam said. "But I wanted to hear it from you."

"Oh, I get it," said Lila, "you wanted to see how cooperative I am."

"Lawmen get tired of only hearing each other's voices," Sam replied without admitting his motive. "Sometimes it's good to hear what others have to say."

"I'll cooperate any way I can to help catch whoever done this to Anna Rose," Lila said.

"I'm obliged," Sam said. He looked up at Dankett as he played an idea through his mind. "For Anna Rose's sake, it might be best that no one knew how much or how little she might already have said about what happened to her.

"Deputy, let's go downstairs and talk to Ozzie White. It's time we start turning over some rocks," he said, "see what comes crawling out."

At the poker table on the raised platform in the Number Five Saloon, Ozzie White gathered in the loose cards from the last hand. He worked them into a deck, shuffled them three times and neatly laid the deck on the tabletop for the player next to him to cut. Yet, as the player reached over to cut the deck, the butt of Dankett's shotgun came down with a slight thump and rested there.

Sam gave Dankett a look, not expecting him to make such a move. Then he shot a glance at the dealer, who sat staring up at them.

"Ozzie White," Sam asked, "we need to talk." As soon as the Ranger spoke, he looked around the table at the faces of the three other players. Their chairs scooted back almost as one.

"Have a drink at the bar on me, fellows," Ozzie White said. "This shouldn't take long." He looked up at Sam and asked, "Should it, Ranger?"

Dankett started to make a remark, but a look from Sam stopped him cold.

"Only a minute, White," said the Ranger, realizing the man was busy making his living. He waved Dankett's shotgun butt away from the deck of cards. "Lila says you were dealer the other night when a fellow named Joe North won a few hands," he said.

"More than a few hands," said White. "He was on a streak, at first anyway."

"How much do you say he won?" Sam asked.

"Three thousand, easy enough," White said. "Is this about the money taken from Anna Rose?" he asked.

"It is," Sam said.

"Then I'm glad you're here, Ranger," White said. "North had a healthy pile of chips and cash. Anna Rose cashed in half the chips while North talked to those two men over at the table by the wall." He gestured toward the table with only a nudge of his head. Dankett and the Ranger managed not to look in that direction.

"Go on," Sam said.

"I knew North would be coming back when he didn't have Anna Rose cash in all his chips. He did come back, but it was with a couple stacks of cash—superstitious, I guess."

Sam just looked at him, listening.

White shrugged and said, "Anyway, he ended up falling apart, lost all his cash and went up to get the rest of his winnings from Anna Rose. That's when they found out Anna Rose was gone. So was the rest of North's money—all of it in chips." He gave the trace of a thin, knowing smile.

"Are you beating around the bush, Ozzie?" Dankett said angrily, stepping in close, gripping the shotgun tight in both hands. "Because if you are—"

"Stand down, Deputy," Sam said firmly, stopping Dankett's advance. "Let the man talk." He looked back at White. "Go on," he said.

"Jesus, Clow," White said to Dankett, looking him up and down. He turned his eyes back to the Ranger. "I figured whoever had those chips would show up sooner or later to cash them in. They're not good anywhere but here."

"Good thinking," Sam said. "Has anybody who wasn't in a game cashed in a large amount of chips?" he asked.

"No," said White, "not a large amount." He sat staring up at the Ranger for a moment. "But the younger fellow at that wall table has been pestering me three or four times a night, cashing in just a few now and then."

"You don't say . . . ," said Sam.

"I sure do say so," White said. "The thing is, he hasn't played a hand of poker since he's been in New Delmar. I asked around some of the other dealers about him." White shook his head slowly. " 'No,' they all told me the same. None of them have seen them at their tables." The thin, knowing smile came back to his face. "He had to get those chips somewhere."

"That's interesting," Sam said, deliberately not looking toward the wall table, knowing the two men there would be looking toward him and his deputy. "Now, I'd be obliged if you would turn around and point the deputy and me toward the side door."

"What?" said White.

"It's for your benefit as well as ours," said Sam. "They won't think you've told us anything, and we'll be able to talk to them without upsetting the whole place." As Sam spoke, he raised a coin from his vest pocket and laid it on the table without being seen. "I'll take one of them for myself," he said nodding at the tray full of house chips.

White nodded. Without another word, he slid a chip onto the tabletop. Sam picked up the chip and put it away. Dankett watched curiously as Ozzie turned in his chair and pointed toward the side door.

"I like how you did this," Dankett said, turning toward the side door with the Ranger, "giving the wrong signal to those two watching us." They walked on across the crowded saloon toward the side door leading out to an alley.

"When you know you're being watched," the Ranger said, reaching for the door, "you take the advantage by showing them only what you want them to see."

"I'll remember that," said Dankett, hurrying to keep up with the Ranger. Once they were in the alley, Sam hurried around to the front door and went back inside the busy saloon. Dankett followed and moved away slightly to his left where Sam wanted him to be.

Henry Teague's and Sonny Rudabough's attention was still focused toward the side door as the Ranger and Dankett crossed the floor. Customers scurried aside and out of their way. Sam's big Colt leveled out at arm's length, the hammer cocked and ready.

By the time Teague caught a glimpse of the two advancing lawmen, it was too late to get an upper hand. He'd seen them as he'd reached down and raised his whiskey glass toward his mouth.

"Damn it!" he murmured, the glass stopping, suspended two inches from his lips.

"What is it, Henry?" Sonny asked as he turned his eyes away from the side door, back to Teague. Even as he asked, he saw the big shotgun moving forward from the side; he saw the black open bore of the Ranger's Colt staring him in the face from fifteen feet away, moving ever closer.

"We just got ourselves jackpotted, Sonny," said Teague with disgust and anger, "that's what *it is. . . .*" He set his glass down without taking a drink and placed both hands on the table in front of him.

"I like a man who knows what to do without being told," Sam said, seeing both of Teague's hands in clear view. He stopped close enough to swat Sonny across the nose with the barrel of his Colt if it came to that. "Now table your hands the same way," he said to Rudabough.

"Oh? What if I don't?" Rudabough said defiantly.

Teague winced, knowing what was coming almost before his younger partner had gotten the words out of his mouth.

Dankett blinked in surprise, but he grinned crookedly, having seen and heard the Ranger's Colt streak across the side of Rudabough's head and send it bobbing on his right shoulder. The deputy watched Sam reach out and take Rudabough's gun from its holster as the knocked-out gunman slid, liquidlike from his chair, onto the dirty floor.

"Damn, Ranger!" said Teague. "You didn't have to hit him that hard."

"Probably not," Sam said. "But it never hurts to be thorough." He opened Sonny's Colt and dropped round after round onto the floor beside the unconscious gunman. Then he pitched the empty gun onto the tabletop. A crowd of customers had drawn in around them.

"Move them back, Deputy Dankett," Sam said to his deputy, gesturing a nod toward the customers.

Upon hearing Clow Dankett's name, the customers who knew him pulled back quickly and instinctively before Dankett even stepped over in front of them.

Sam nodded down at the knocked-out Sonny Rudabough and said to Teague, "While we're waiting for him to get back to us, let me ask you, how are things coming along with Fenderson's bounty situation?"

"You tell me," Teague said. "I keep hearing another one bit the dust every place I go."

Sam looked back down at Rudabough and said, "Looks like he's going to be a while. Let's talk some." He lowered his Colt to his side but kept it cocked, and stayed close enough to Teague to reach out with the big barrel if need be.

Dankett smiled a little to himself. He liked working with this Ranger. He believed there were things he could learn here.

"All right, everybody stay back, and *shut up!*" he shouted over his shoulder. "I want to hear what our *sheriff* is saying here."

Chapter 18

Pulling Sonny Rudabough up by the nape of his neck, Sam and Teague propped the gunman up into his chair. Sam dragged a chair out with the toe of his boot and sat down across the table from the veteran gunman. While Sonny mumbled and spluttered and struggled to get a grip on consciousness, Sam set his big Colt on the table near his hand and began asking questions.

"So, this whole issue with Fenderson is over family pride, about me shooting his nephew, Mitchell Fenderson?"

"Is that what you believe?" Teague said, tight-lipped on the matter.

"What I believe, Henry Teague," Sam said, "is that if you're going to answer a question with a question, I might just as well change your place with this one." He nodded at Rudabough. "Maybe he'll be more sociable, and you can rest your head on the floor awhile."

"Is that your answer to everything, Ranger? Crack a man's head if he doesn't cooperate with you?"

See? There he goes, doing it again, Sam reminded himself.

"Yes, it is," Sam said, "today anyway. I've got a sheriff killed, a dove beat half to death, a prisoner

I need to get to Yuma and a rich man wanting to pay to have me put underground. What's a busted head here and there?" He gave a wry thin smile. "Now, I'm going to ask you another *question*, about something else, and I dare you to *answer me* with a question of your own." He placed his hand on the butt of the big Colt. "All set?"

Teague looked across the table and saw a string of reddish drool bob down from Sonny's parted lips.

"All right," Teague said, giving in. "I'll answer what I can. Keep in mind I work for Hugh Fenderson. I'm not giving that up."

"Fair enough," Sam said. "Then let's talk about Oldham Coyle, about the dove losing the winnings he had her holding for him."

"He turned his money over to a saloon dove," Teague said with a tilt of his chin. "He might have gotten what he deserved, doing something that stupid. We came here looking for him, but he was too busy gambling, swilling rye and taking dope to want to deal with us."

"You brought him the news about the bounty on my head," Sam said firmly. "Even offered a little extra for him killing me, since he's got such a reputation with a gun."

"I won't admit that we talked to him about killing you, Ranger. That would be against the law," said Teague. "But if you wanted to think it, well, that would be okay too—it's a free country."

"A free country. . . ." Sam only nodded.

"I'll be honest," said Teague. "I figured the way he was going, he'd lose his winnings and end up wanting to take my proposition after all. And he did," he added. "I rode out and talked to him. He seemed ready and eager to take on any deal Fenderson had to offer. That's all I'm saying on that."

Sam studied his face for a moment, seeing no way for him to stop anybody as powerful as Hugh Fenderson. Even Fenderson's men had been schooled on what to say and what not to say. This was paid killing at a higher level than he was used to.

All right. . . He still had to figure it out and stop it, he reminded himself.

"How will Fenderson know when it's over?" he asked.

"He'll know it's over when I telegraph him and let him know it's over," Teague said. "My job is to stick right here and wait until it's done." He couldn't resist giving a smug grin as he spoke. Both of them knew that *when it's over* meant when the Ranger was dead.

Sam shook his head at the thought of what they were discussing. But he had to play it this way, for now, he told himself.

"Telegraph him where?" he asked.

"Oh," said Teague, "I suppose you didn't realize. Hugh Fenderson has his own rail car. It has a telegraph set up in it. He stops anywhere along this rail spur and has his men throw a jumper rod over the lines—runs messages in and out of his car window." His smug grin widened a little. "It's slicker than striped socks on a rooster."

"I see," said Sam. He took a deep breath and let it out, as if overwhelmed at the power he found himself up against. "That's why folks are still waiting for the train to arrive? Fenderson is holding up, waiting to hear I'm dead before he rides up here?"

"Yep, that's it in a thimble," said Teague with a dark chuckle. "Sort of makes you wish you'd stayed home, eh, Ranger?" he added. "Of course it can all be settled easy enough. Get two big guns on the street, you and Oldham Coyle—see who comes out standing."

Without answering, Sam looked over at Rudabough, who had come around some, enough to raise a hand to the side of his head and groan. Dankett stood back, watching, listening to as much as he could but not catching all of it. Behind him the crowd had dispersed, losing interest now that the potential for bloodshed had died down.

"It looks like you fellows have it all figured out," he said.

"I'd say so," said Teague with haughty satisfaction.

Henry Teague had shown him his whole hand. Now it was his turn, Sam thought. He fished the chip he'd purchased from his vest pocket.

"Here's something else we need to talk about," he said. He flipped the poker chip out onto the tabletop.

"What's this?" asked Teague.

"A poker chip," said Sam. He raised a hand and motioned Dankett in closer.

"I can see it's a poker chip. So what?" Teague said, sounding a little impatient.

Sam leaned forward and said, "What if I told you my deputy and I both saw this fall from your pard's pocket a while ago?"

Teague tried a carefree smile, but it wasn't working.

"I'd say *thank you* both for returning it," he said. "Sonny will be happy—"

"What if I told you we already checked? That

your pard hasn't played a hand of poker since the two of you have been here?"

Teague's face tightened a little.

"So what? He might have found it on the floor," he said. "In fact, I remember him saying he found a chip."

Sam leaned in closer, his hand resting atop the Colt.

"Search him, Deputy," he said.

Dankett pulled his left hand away from his leveled shotgun long enough to reach inside Rudabough's coat and rip down on the inside lapel pocket. A stream of poker chips spilled down to the floor all around the half-conscious gunman's boots.

Teague clenched his jaws and his fists. From all corners of the saloon, eyes turned toward the sound of the chips falling. Dankett stepped away and gave the onlookers a warning stare.

"He's been cashing in chips steadily every night," Sam said to Teague. "So many that he's got all the dealers wondering where they come from. I say these chips came from Anna Rose, and whoever has them is the person who beat her and left her for dead—"

"This stupid son of a bitch!" said Teague, exploding before he could stop himself. He reached over and shook Sonny. "Wake up, damn you to hell. This is your doing! Explain all this!"

Sonny gurgled, swooned and swung his head, awakening enough to hear what was going on.

"Look at me, Henry Teague. There's more," Sam said, drawing Teague's attention back to him. "I can prove that whoever beat up the dove also ambushed Sheriff Rattler out back of his new jail."

"You can? How?" Teague asked, staring coldly at him.

Sam relaxed and sat back in his chair, his hand still on the Colt. Things were turning, starting to go his way.

"I don't want to tell you too much at once," he said. "If I do that, I'll have no surprise left for you when the judge gets up here from Yuma."

"You're bluffing, Ranger," Teague said. "You've got nothing to show that either one of us killed the sheriff. At the best maybe you can say this idiot beat up a dove. So what? Some doves like getting knocked around. Some only charge a little bit extra for you beating them up."

Ignoring his remark, Sam said, "You do not want to make the mistake of thinking I'm *bluffing*, Teague. What you want to do is decide who you'd best like to see hang for this, you or your pard here. If I ask him that same question, I bet I can guess what his answer will be."

Teague gave Sonny Rudabough a look up and down, realizing the Ranger was right. Sam saw his confidence overtaken by a dark, troubled look.

"Here's another way we can settle this thing easy enough," he said, giving Teague a sharp stare. "Forget me and Coyle. We can get some *bigger guns*, get out on the street, like you and Hugh Fenderson, me and the law—let the court say who *comes out standing*." He pushed his chair back from the table. He had run a bluff; now it was time to see where it took him.

"Wait, Ranger," Teague said, seeing Sam had finished talking and was ready to make a move. "I'm not to blame for anything this fool has done! If he beat the dove and robbed her, it's on his head."

"And Sheriff Rattler?" Sam asked, stone-faced.

"For killing him too," Teague said. "I don't know what proof you've got, but whatever it is, you can't prove I had anything to do with it."

"You think you kept yourself clear of it, Teague," Sam said, "but you didn't. You made a mistake trusting a fool. Now you'll have to share that fool's reward." Instead of standing, he raised the Colt and cocked it in Teague's face.

A strange, puzzled look came to Teague's eyes.

"You're arresting us, taking us to jail?" he said, seeing Dankett step back in closer to Rudabough and shake him by his shoulder.

"You're half right," Sam said. "I'm arresting you. But we'll never make it to jail. You'll both make a run for it, and I'll drop you in the dirt. Deputy Dankett here will see the whole thing, right, Deputy?" he said quietly to Dankett.

"You've got it," Dankett said, the big shotgun aimed down at Teague. He scraped the chips into a pile with his boot, then stooped and loaded them into his corduroy coat pocket. He reached down to pull Rudabough to his feet.

"Ranger, wait!" said Teague, his hands chest high. "We can work something out here." But Sam didn't wait, instead he reached down and lifted a big Remington from Teague's holster. "I'll give you Rudabough for everything," Teague continued. "I can even call off the fight with Coyle, at least tell him that Fenderson has dropped the reward."

Sam lowered the Colt an inch and took a deep breath.

"Yeah, I can do that," Teague said, seeing the Ranger consider his words. "Believe me, you don't want to go up against this fellow Coyle. I know your reputation. But this man is faster than you. He's faster than anybody I've ever seen."

"All right," said Sam. "We'll talk about it at the jail."

"Am I going to get shot in the back on my way there?" Teague asked.

"Not unless I change my mind," Sam said, pulling him to his feet.

"Here, help your pal," said Dankett, shoving the wobbling Rudabough to him. Teague grabbed Sonny's flailing arm and looped it across his shoulders.

"Where . . . we going?" Sonny said thickly, his head cocked sideways, his swirling eyes staring into Teague's ear.

Dankett walked them past the bar and stopped long enough to empty the chips from his coat pocket onto the bar top.

Beside him, Sam said to the bartender, "Bag these and mark them for Oldham Coyle when he gets here."

"Oldham Coyle, you've got it, Ranger," said the bartender. He raked the chips into a cloth sack and tagged it as the Ranger, his deputy and their unsavory consorts filed out the door.

On the way to the jail, Sam spotted Adele Simpson leading the roan away from a hitch rail out in front of a small restaurant, her belongings still loaded on its back. Seeing the Ranger, his deputy, and the prisoners, their arms encircling each other like two drunkards, she stopped and stared as they drew nearer.

"Ranger?" she said. "Is everything all right?"

"It's getting there," Sam replied, touching the

brim of his sombrero toward her. He slowed almost to a halt as Dankett continued walking with the two prisoners.

"As you see, the train still has not arrived," she said, spreading her arms slightly. "I still wait."

"Be patient, Miss Adele. I've got a feeling it won't be much longer," Sam said.

"I will," said Adele. Knowing the Ranger would turn and walk away any second, she asked, "How is Harvey doing?"

"He's doing as well as might be expected, ma'am," Sam said. "Did he ever tell you what brought him west?"

"No," Adele said. "The law chasing him would be my guess, once I realized the kind of man he is."

"That would be my first guess too," Sam said. "But that's not it at all. He was just a young man who came out here . . ." He paused and let his words trail. He shook his head a little. "It's something you'd have to have him tell you, I suppose. It's not my way to pass along things told to me in confidence."

"In confidence?" Adele said. Sam could tell he'd piqued her interest.

"Not that I'm anybody's confessor, ma'am." He smiled. "After all, I'm a lawman, not a priest." He watched her curiosity rise. "We got our jail finished. It looks good. If you get a chance, stop and see it before you leave."

"Yes, thank you, Ranger. I just may do that," Adele said.

Sam looked at the roan and said, "Come see it right now, if you've a mind to," he said. "I'll hitch the roan out front. I'll escort you to the hotel afterward."

"I suppose I could," Adele said, looking around.

"Good," Sam said, taking the lead to the roan. "I know Cisco will be pleased to see you."

They walked on behind Dankett and the prisoners, and stepped onto the boardwalk as the deputy reached around Teague and Rudabough and opened the door to the sheriff's office.

Walking inside, they saw Dr. Starr looking at them through bloodshot eyes, drying his freshly washed face on a clean towel.

"Is that fellow all right?" he asked, seeing the welt alongside Sonny's head, Sonny swaying as if in a strong breeze.

"I believe he is," Sam said.

"Very good, then, if you'll excuse me, Ranger," Starr said, "it's time I get out of here and go see about my patient." He picked up his leather bag and left, rolling down his shirtsleeves, his coat draped over an arm.

From his cell, Lang stood up at the sight of the woman.

"Adele?" he said in a gentle voice. "You haven't left?" His voice had a ring of hope in it.

"No, Harvey, I'm still here," Adele said, almost in the same tone. She looked to the Ranger, who gave her a wave forward.

As the two met at the bars, Sam and Dankett walked Teague and Rudabough over to the cell where Carnes and Johnson sat staring beneath a gray cloud of cigarette smoke.

"I bet I know where he got that," Carnes said, eyeing the print of the Ranger's gun barrel on Sonny Rudabough's head. Rudabough gave Carnes a starry-eyed look as Teague walked him inside the cell and slid him down against the plank wall, beneath the window now covered with bars. Johnson held up a bag of tobacco and some rolling papers to Henry Teague as Teague stepped over closer.

"Build a smoke for yourself, mister," Johnson said. "It'll help take your mind off things."

"Get it rolled and get out here, Teague," Sam said from the other side of the bars. "You and I are going to take a walk to the telegraph station."

"Teague . . . ? Henry Teague?" said Johnson, looking at Teague with a lowered brow. "You're the one who works for Hugh Fenderson—who damn near got us killed going after the Ranger?" He reached out and jerked the tobacco from Teague's hand.

Sam watched. Johnson gave Teague a hard stare for a moment. Finally he handed the tobacco bag back to him and shrugged.

"What the hell?" he said. "It wasn't your fault we didn't kill him."

Teague walked away from the extended tobacco bag and stood in front of the Ranger, looking at him through the corner bars of the cell.

"What are you talking about, going to the telegraph station?" he asked, feeling bolder now that he hadn't been killed on his way to jail.

"You're going to wire your boss for me," Sam said. "I want you to get Hugh Fenderson up here where he can see for himself what his money's buying."

"I can't do that, Ranger," Teague said. "Fenderson won't come up until he hears that you're dead."

"Good, that's what you'll tell him," Sam said.

"Huh-uh," Teague said. "I'm not pulling any shenanigans on Fenderson."

Ignoring his refusal, Sam said, "I figure you've got private words or numbers you use when you wire him so he'll know it's you. You give me those words or numbers and I'll wire him myself."

"It's code words. But how will you know I gave you the right words?" Teague said shrewdly.

"I'll trust you the first time," Sam said. "If you give me the wrong words and he doesn't show up, I'll have my deputy get the right words from you." He paused, then said, "Or I can have him walk you out back, make sure you give it right the first time."

Teague just stared at him, deciding whether or not he wanted to test him on the matter.

Without hesitation, the Ranger called over his shoulder to Dankett, "Deputy, I've got a man needs to go to the jakes. I need you to talk to him some on the way."

"All right, Ranger, call him off," Teague said. "I'll go with you to the telegraph station."

"Obliged, Teague," Sam said flatly. He called out to Dankett as the deputy walked over with his long-barreled shotgun, "Hold up, Deputy. He's changed his mind. But I need you and Big Lucy to watch about the jail for a few minutes."

"We'd be pleased to the core," Dankett said, patting the shotgun on its walnut stock.

Lang and Adele looked around from talking quietly at the next cell.

"Are things getting better between you and the deputy?" Adele asked.

"Yes, maybe . . . I mean, I don't know," said Lang. He sounded remorseful. "Adele, I have had to think about so many things." He shook his lowered head. "I've been nothing but a fool. I used you, and I'm sorry," he said. "I have to tell you that before I leave here. I only hope someday you can forgive me."

Adele said under her breath, "Harvey, I forgive you right now, this minute, if you're sincere."

"I've never been more sincere about anything in my life, Adele," he said. He gripped the bars with both hands. Adele reached up and cupped her hand over his.

"Then yes, Harvey, I forgive you," she said. She paused, then said just as quietly, "The Ranger said you told him what brought you out west?"

"Yes, I told him," said Lang. "But you don't want to hear about it . . . do you?" he asked, almost longingly.

"Harvey, I'd like to hear anything you want to tell me about yourself," she said. "As long as the Ranger will allow me to stay, I've got nothing but time."

They looked toward the door where the Ranger stood snapping the same cuffs he'd used on Lang onto Teague's wrists. They heard Sam say to him, "Let's go get this done, Teague."

When the door closed behind the Ranger and his prisoner, the two looked back at each other through the bars, their hands entwined around the cold black iron.

PART 3

Chapter 19

Outside the Sand Hill Depot, the big engine and its five-car train sat off to itself on a siding in the purple starlit darkness. The first car coupled to the engine, an ornate custom-made Pullman Plainsman, rested with a single lamp glowing behind its drawn curtains. Coupled behind the Pullman sat a mail car that had been converted to an office and operations center for the Fenderson-Gaines Frontier Investments Company. A lamp burned brightly through the half-drawn curtains of the operations car as a telegraph clerk stepped down from its open door and looked back at the man still on the metal steps.

"I don't like waking him, Serg," the clerk said under his breath as the large man stepped down behind him.

Sergio Oboe grinned at him through a thick dark beard. He held a glowing rail lantern up for the two of them to see by.

"*Sleeping . . . ?* If you think he's sleeping right now, you must be as dumb as you look, Harkens," said Oboe.

"You know what I mean," said the clerk, Chester Harkens. "I know he's not asleep. But if I was doing what he's doing right now, I wouldn't care if my dog had a wild ape by its ass—tell me about it later."

"Yeah . . . well," Oboe replied in a somber tone. "That's why he is who he is, and we are who we are. Mr. Fenderson sticks to business. If this was about his dog sinking its teeth in a wild ape's ass, he probably wouldn't care either."

"I was saying that about the dog and ape just to prove a point," Harkens said. "I find it odd that you might consider that a plausible situation."

"I don't," said Oboe. "But I find it equally odd that in a conversation about *sticking to business*, your mind jumped first thing to a dog biting a monkey on its ass." He gave a dark chuckle. "See? That's what I mean about Fenderson sticking to business."

"I never said *monkey*," Harkens offered sullenly. Then he let it go and raised the folded sheet of paper in his hand. "Think this is true?"

"I've never known Henry Teague's word to be in doubt," Oboe said. "I wish I could have gotten ahead of everybody and collected that reward myself."

"Me too," said Harkens as they walked on. "Can you imagine five thousand dollars to kill just one man?"

"I know," said Oboe. "I'd kill a whole roomful of folks for half that."

As the two men walked forward in the bobbing circle of lantern light, Harkens looked back at the train's black silhouette against the purple desert sky. Next in line behind the operations car sat a stock car housing the needed horses for Hugh Fenderson himself and the six personal guards accompanying him.

Behind the stock car sat a car that the guards

shared. Behind it, at the rear of the train, sat a red caboose where the train's oiler, fireman and brakemen resided. Turning his eyes forward again, Harkens said, "How can one man be smart enough to acquire all this?"

"I can tell you," said Oboe. "I worked for his pa. His pa gave him a bank full of money and said, 'Here, take this and make some more with it.'" He chuckled. "How smart does that make him?"

"He could have lost it," said Harkens.

"He did lose some of it," said Oboe. "Some deals he lost on. Some he won on. The same can be said by any of us, only in his case he had more money to begin with."

"I was born wrong," Harkens speculated.

"Yep, most of us were," said Oboe. "Mr. Fenderson thinks he made it, but all he did was buy people smart enough to keep making it for him. I know damned well I could have done that much."

They stopped at the dark platform of the Pullman car, where the red glow of a burning cigarette met their eyes.

"I could hear you two halfway down the train," said a voice behind the red fiery glow. The glow rose and fell as the man took a draw and let out a swirl of gray smoke. "What's going on anyway?" he asked.

"We just now got word from New Delmar, Singleton," said Oboe to Tom Singleton, the man behind the cigarette glow. "The Ranger is dead."

"Yeah?" Singleton said, stepping forward out of the deeper blackness of the platform overhang. "Who got him?"

"Keep your voice down," Oboe cautioned

him. "Nobody is supposed to know until Mr. Fenderson gives the news. Anyway, that's all the telegram says. 'The Ranger is dead.'"

"Damn," said Singleton.

Oboe and Harkens looked over at a fancy buggy sitting with its top up, hitched on the other side of the Pullman car.

"Let's get it done, then," Singleton added. "I've been wanting to take a peep inside this car all night."

He grinned and rapped a big brass knocker on the Pullman car door. Oboe and Harkens stepped up close, the lantern held up, lighting the platform.

"What is it, Smiley?" said a winded voice on the other side of the door. "This better be good."

"We got a telegram from Henry Teague, sir," Singleton replied. The three looked at an unlit lantern fixture on the upper side of the car door. The fixture made a half turn and disappeared inside the car. A moment passed. The fixture reappeared in a half turn, this time glowing with candlelight. Oboe lowered his lantern, no longer needing it, as the door opened.

Hugh Fenderson stood in the doorway in a nightshirt and robe he had hastily thrown on. He eagerly grabbed the folded telegram that Harkens held out to him. Behind him, the men watched two women stand up naked from the bed and walk away behind a dressing screen, their arms around each other's waist.

Reading the telegram quickly, Fenderson jerked a fresh cigar from the robe's breast pocket and shoved it into his mouth with a broad grin. At the end Fenderson checked for and found Teague's three code words: *High Wild Desert*. He read it again to make sure his eyes were not playing tricks on him. Then he drew a deep, calming breath.

"Men, the Ranger is dead," he chuckled. "D-e-a-d! Dead."

The three men nodded in unison.

"Congratulations, Mr. Fenderson," said Oboe. "May we ask who killed him?"

"Oldham Coyle, I'm certain," Fenderson said. He gave Oboe a look of disbelief. "We'll find out more when we arrive in New Delmar. I would not have Henry Teague mention names on a telegraph line."

"Of course not, sir," said Oboe. "Shall I have the fireman stoke us up and make ready to roll out of here?"

"Yes, do that, Serg," said Fenderson. "Have everyone assemble in the operations car. I'll get dressed straightaway and join you there."

As the three backed out the door and left, Fenderson turned toward the dressing screen and met the two women who stepped out, hitching, hiking, buttoning and straightening their clothes.

"Ladies, I only wish we had more time to spend together this evening, but I'm afraid business calls."

As he spoke, Fenderson pulled up two rolls of cash held round by thick rubber bands. He dropped a roll into each outreached hand, turned and swung the door open for them. Stepping out onto the platform behind them, he stood and waved as they walked down to the fancy buggy. Tom Singleton appeared and assisted each of them up into the buggy.

From the opposite side of the Pullman car,

Sergio Oboe stepped back up beside Fenderson. He pulled out a long match, struck it and held the fire to the tip of Fenderson's cigar.

Fenderson puffed the cigar to life and blew out a long gray stream of smoke.

"Thank you, Serg," he said. He looked the big, burly gunman up and down. "I take it you are ready to help me carry out this little sporting matter I'm involved in?"

"I'm ready, sir," said Oboe. "I've wanted to kill this Coyle bastard ever since he left us all chasing our tails in Kansas." He paused, then said, "Can I say something?"

"Of course, feel free," said Fenderson, waving again as the buggy rolled away into the darkness.

"Sir, the thing is, I can't understand why you didn't let me kill this Ranger and Coyle both for you."

"I said you could *say something*, Oboe," Fenderson replied in a stiff tone. "I didn't say you could question my decisions, did I?"

"No, sir, you did not. Sorry, sir," Oboe offered quickly.

The two stood in silence for a moment in the glow of flickering lantern light from the doorway fixture.

At length Fenderson said in a more affable tone, "Although I suppose explaining why I'm doing things this way may help you carry out my orders in a more confident manner."

"Yes, sir—I mean, if that suits you, sir," said Oboe.

"It does," Fenderson said. "When I learned that an oddsmaker like Silas Horn would set odds on two notable gunfighters facing off on each other, I devised a way to clean up my problem in one swift, easy stroke and make myself a tidy sum of money in the process."

Oboe listened intently.

"When Horn speculated the odds three to one in Coyle's favor against the Ranger, I decided why not turn Coyle's gun skills into something profitable and at the same time have him take my vengeance out on the Ranger for shooting my nephew, Mitchell?" He drew on his cigar and blew out a steam of smoke.

"Being the gambler Coyle is," he said, "I knew he couldn't resist the challenge of taking on the Ranger, not when the sporting world had him favored so highly to win."

"So," Oboe reasoned, "instead of us still chasing him all over Kansas, you come up here where he's not wanted, wave reward money at him for killing the Ranger and he comes right to you." He grinned. "Not bad, sir."

"Thank you, Serg," Fenderson said coolly. "Now that the Ranger is dead, we go and meet with Coyle to give him his reward, and you and the men chop him to pieces. Him and anybody riding with him."

"And you even save yourself the reward money," said Oboe.

"Indeed." Fenderson grinned. "Not to mention the *enormous* amount I wagered on Coyle with Silas Horn."

"Sir!" said Oboe, impressed. "If I might say so, that right there is why this country needs you to run for president. We need a man like you who can think on his feet, and doesn't mind shedding a little blood if it gets things done."

"Nice of you to say so, Oboe," said Fenderson, again blowing smoke. "Now go hurry those men along. I want to get under way. I'm excited by what awaits me in New Delmar."

Leaving the telegraph office, the Ranger and Henry Teague walked back toward the jail along the dusty street lit by rows of torchlight on either side. Teague stared down at the cuffs on his wrists, noting the third cuff hanging from a short chain between the two. For a moment he thought of how easy it would be to swing around all at once and launch the chain, cuff and all, into the Ranger's eye. But as if reading his thoughts, the Ranger touched the tip of the rifle barrel to the center of his back.

They walked on.

"Whatever you've got up your sleeve, Ranger, you won't get away with it," Teague said over his shoulder as they drew nearer to the jail. "Fenderson will see you're alive and sic his whole guard force on you."

"I'm doing my job as it comes to me, Teague. Fenderson is too rich and powerful for me to go chasing after him. This will bring him to me."

"That's your whole plan, Ranger?" Teague said, glancing back over his shoulder.

"That's it, more or less," Sam replied.

"In that case, you might just as well cut me and Sonny both loose. We'll be cut loose anyways soon as Fenderson gets here and you're not lying dead in the street."

"After you tell him I'm dead?" Sam said. "You don't think he's going to be just a little put out with you for lying, for setting him up?"

Teague fell silent.

"I've got over a full ten thousand dollars in a bank in Denver City, Ranger," he said finally.

"Why are you telling me, Teague?" Sam said. "You wanting to secure a first-class burial?"

"Come on, Ranger," Teague said in frustration. "You're supposed to be a good lawman. Deal with me here!" He almost came to a stop. The tip of the Ranger's rifle touched his back again.

"I am a good lawman," Sam said, prodding him on. "I am dealing with you."

"Damn it, you know what I mean, Ranger!" said Teague, trying hard to work a deal with the Ranger as they neared the jail, now only fifteen yards away.

Before Sam could reply, Oldham Coyle, his brother, Dave, and Chic Reye stepped their horses out of an alleyway and into sight on the Ranger's left. Reye sat bowed in his saddle, his left arm hugging his lower belly. The bloody bandage on his face had come loose and flopped down his cheek, revealing the ugly open wound.

"Well, now," Oldham Coyle said, staring at the Ranger with his hand on his holstered Colt. "Look what we've got here. It appears you've arrested the man holding the purse strings."

On the Ranger's right, he saw Deak Holder, Karl Sieg and Blind Simon Goss step their horses out of the shadows into the flicker of torchlight.

"Take him down, Coyle!" said Teague. "Take him down and cut me loose!" He raised his cuffed hands. "Kill him now! Fenderson is on his way here with your money!"

"Is that a fact?" said Coyle. He stared at the Ranger with a dark smile. "These Hugh Fenderson people sure want you dead, don't they, Ranger?" he said quietly, his hand still on his gun.

"So it appears," Sam replied. As he spoke, his left hand reached forward and took a grip on

Teague's coat collar, the tip of his rifle barrel at the base of Teague's head. "This one so much he's willing to die with me."

"What did he do, Ranger?" Coyle asked.

"Public drunkenness," Sam said flatly. He wasn't about to tell Coyle right here and now how Teague and Rudabough had jackpotted him.

"He doesn't look drunk to me," said Coyle.

"Drunks can fool you," Sam replied, dismissing the matter.

"Would you rather die than set him free?" Coyle asked.

Sam only stared coldly without answering.

"This is what we call a conundrum of sorts, Ranger," Oldham said. "I kill you, but you kill him. Who will I get my reward from? There'll be no witness to speak on my behalf." He ended his words staring at Teague. "This doesn't sound like such a good deal for me."

"We can take him, boss," Deak Holder put in confidently. "Kill them both. Take the Ranger with us—just his head if we have to. Fenderson has to believe us when we throw his head down at his feet."

"Ouch!" Oldham said to Sam with a wince. "Hear that, Ranger? This tough *hombre* wants to hack your melon off, carry it to Fenderson on a stick, I suspect."

"Let it go, Oldham," Dave Coyle said quietly beside him. "We need to get this one to the doctor—you said you wanted to talk to that dove. Forget the Ranger."

"I need that doctor, something awful," Chic Reye moaned beside Dave.

Oldham sat staring at the Ranger, his hand ready. Sam could see him weighing things out in his mind. Any second he could make his play. Sam knew he was in a bad spot. He could kill Teague with the squeeze of the trigger, but then he had to either lever the rifle or drop it and go for his Colt. Reaching for the Colt would be faster, but either move would cost him time . . . *precious time*, he warned himself.

"We can take him, boss," Deak put in. "Just say the word."

"And point me where to shoot," said Simon, a sawed-off shotgun in his hand.

"You can't take him, Little Dick." Dankett's voice resounded from the darkness of the alley as Big Lucy's hammers made a hard, slow cocking sound. "Try it, they'll pick you up with a bucket and a sponge."

Deak's head turned to the dark alley behind him, where Dankett stood back out of sight.

"Now your deputy wants to get into the mix of things, Ranger," said Oldham.

"There ain't no *wants* to get," said Dankett. "I *am* in the mix of things."

"Somebody get me pointed," said Simon. "If you don't, I'll be spraying brains everywhere."

"Settle down, Simon," said Oldham. To Sam he said, "See how game my men are, Ranger? They're always this way."

Sam just stared without replying.

"Like my brother just said, we're here to see the doctor and Anna Rose. Maybe I'll kill you later on." His hand finally slipped away from his gun butt.

"Don't come after me, Coyle," Sam said. "That's all the warning you're apt to get."

"Coyle, damn it—" said Teague. Sam jostled him by his collar.

"Shut up, Teague," he said. To Oldham he said, "Get your man looked after, see the dove." He paused, then said, "Tell the bartender I sent you there. Then get out of New Delmar."

"See the bartender?" said Coyle. "Why, Ranger, are you buying me a drink?"

The Ranger only stared coldly without reply. Oldham returned the stare as he backed his horse and reined it toward the doctor's office, just past the Number Five Saloon where the twangy piano rattled loudly from two blocks away. As his men started turning their horses behind him, Deak Holder jerked his horse around toward Dankett still standing back in the darkness.

"Get this straight, Deputy," he warned Dankett. "My name is not *Little Dick*. Don't ever call me that again." He spun his horse and rode away, bobbing in his short stirrups.

"Sure thing, *Little Dick*," Dankett said coolly.

As the six riders moved out of sight toward the doctor's office in a rise of dust, Dankett stepped out of the darkness and walked closer to the Ranger and Teague.

" 'Take him down, Coyle'?" he said, staring hard at Teague as he mimicked him. " 'Kill him now . . . '?" He raised the big shotgun. "You ought to be ashamed of yourself."

"Don't do it, Deputy. Let it go," Sam said, seeing what was coming.

"Aw, Ranger, just one or two good ones in the nose?" Dankett said, almost pleading. "It won't kill him."

"No, Deputy, that's not my style of law," Sam said. "When you get to be sheriff someday, you'll understand why."

"Get to be sheriff?" Dankett said, lowering his shotgun, much to Teague's relief.

"Why not?" said Sam. "You sure came through well enough to get my endorsement."

"I was just doing my job," Dankett said.

"I know, Deputy," Sam said. "That's what sets the quality of it."

Dankett grinned under his lowered hat brim.

"Obliged, Ranger," he said.

"Let's get this one to jail now, Deputy," Sam said. "We've got company coming."

Chapter 20

When the Coyle brothers and their men reached the doctor's office, Dr. Starr had only recently returned from checking on Anna Rose. He had taken off his shoes, dropped his suspenders from his shoulders and settled down with a new bottle of rye he'd picked up at the Number Five Saloon. He'd sunk down into an overstuffed chair by the fireplace and raised the bottle to his lips, but no sooner had he downed a long drink than the front door knocker resounded loudly.

"Holy Moses!" he said aloud. "Does anybody ever sleep in this town?"

He stepped into a pair of soft house slippers and plodded to the front door, opening it.

"You fellows," he said, almost taking a step back from the six men crowded onto his front porch. In front of the others, Chic Reye staggered in weakly and grabbed the doctor's shoulder for support.

"Doctor, help me, I'm hurting . . . something awful," Reye said in a halting, pain-racked voice. Sweat poured freely down his face, some of it mixed pink with blood from the uncovered bullet wound in his cheek. "My guts are all on fire."

"Get his arms and follow me," the doctor said to his companions.

Oldman Coyle and his gunmen stepped in. Dave Coyle and Karl Sieg took Reye by his arms and followed the doctor as he gestured them toward his treatment room. Inside the room, they laid Reye down on a gurney. The gunmen gathered around as the doctor leaned over Reye and peeled back the bandage from his greenish blackened stomach.

"Tell me straight, Doctor," Reye said. "Has that little sawed-off sumbitch killed me?" He stared down at Deak Holder standing amid the gunmen. Deak gave a short grin.

Dr. Starr winced at the sight of his infected navel wound, as did the onlooking gunmen.

"That would be my first prognosis," Starr said. "But let's see what we can do to keep you from dying." He turned to the men. "All of you out of here."

"Except me," Oldham said firmly as the others backed out into the other room. "I want to know about Anna Rose, Doc. Is she going to be all right?"

"Damn, Oldham," said Reye. "What about *me* here? Look at this belly wound."

"You're going to be all right, Chic," Oldham said, dismissing the moaning gunman.

"I think she will make it," Starr said. "She's beat all to hell, her ribs are broken—most of them anyway. She needs to wake up, but I'm optimistic she will before long. She's just coming around more slowly than I would prefer. Whoever beat her had no intention of her ever living through it." He shook his head, feeling the surge from the long drink of whiskey loosening his tongue. "Thank God the Ranger caught him. If they hang him, I'll declare him dead whether he is

or not. Bury him alive—send him to hell still
breathing."

"What?" said Oldham. "Did you say the Ranger
caught the man who did it?"

"Yes, he did," said Starr. "He's in the jail right
now, him and his pal both."

"Henry Teague?" said Oldham.

"No, the other one," said Starr. "Rudabough, I
believe his name is."

"I'll be damned," Oldham said, feeling anger
welling up inside him as the reality of it sank
into his mind. "The Ranger didn't tell me this."

"From the look on your face, I think I can
understand why," Starr said as he gathered in-
struments and fresh bandages for Reye's treatment. "I suppose he failed to tell you about the
money as well?"

"He didn't say anything about money," said
Oldham. "You mean the money of mine that
Anna Rose was holding for me?"

"Yes," said Starr. "Rudabough had the money
on him, all of it in chips from the Number Five
Saloon. The Ranger and Clow Dankett took it
off him."

Oldham's jaw tightened, but he forced himself
to remain calm. He thought about how he'd
asked the Ranger why Teague was in cuffs.

Public drunkenness, he thought angrily. The
Ranger knew what would have happened had
he told him everything.

"Can I see her, Doctor?" he asked Starr. Before
any killing got under way, he wanted to hear
from Anna Rose's own lips what had happened
to her and who was responsible for it.

"Her? What about me here?" Reye said again.
"I'm the one with my liver on fire."

"Shut up, Chic," Oldham snarled. He drew back a hand, tempted to reach out and thump the moaning gunman on his rosy swollen navel, but he stopped himself.

Seeing what Coyle had almost done, Starr stepped in between the two, protecting his patient.

"Tell Lila I said you can see her—but mind you, only for a minute or two," Starr said, raising a finger for emphasis. "If Anna Rose is awake, don't wear her out talking. If she's still asleep, leave her alone."

Without another word, Oldham turned and walked out of the room. As the men watched, he walked across the room to the front door.

"Wait up, Oldham," said Dave Coyle, seeing his brother swing open the door. "Where are you going?"

"To see Anna Rose," Oldham said with determination.

"Not by yourself you're not," Dave said. "We said we'll all stick together here, remember? We don't know what that Ranger is apt to do."

"I remember," Oldham said, yet he continued on out the door anyway.

"Damn it!" Dave cursed, headed for the front door as it shut behind Oldham. "Sieg, you and Deak come with me. Simon, stay here with Reye."

At the door to Anna Rose's room, Lila stepped aside as Oldham walked in and took his hat off. Behind him at the bottom of the stairs, Dave, Deak and Sieg slowed to a halt after trying to catch up to him. They had stood looking up the stairs as Oldham entered the room.

Oldham stopped and looked over at the bed

where the battered sleeping dove lay, her head propped up on a thick pillow. Lila watched him stare across the room at Anna Rose for a moment. At length, he spoke to Lila without taking his eyes from Anna Rose.

"I've got to see her," he said bluntly, not asking the big blond dove's permission. But he turned to Lila and awaited her nod of approval all the same.

"Sure," Lila said softly.

Oldham walked quietly across the room and kneeled beside the dove's bed as if in prayer.

"Oh, Jesus, Anna," he said under his breath, seeing the condition of her face, running a hand ever so gently over her bruised and battered brow.

To his surprise, Anna Rose's eyes sought him from beneath blackened, swollen lids.

"Joe . . . ? Is that . . . you?" she said, her words trailing weakly.

"It's me, Anna," said Oldham. "Only I'm not Joe North," he said, ashamed of himself for having lied to her. "My name is Coyle . . . Oldham Coyle."

"I . . . knew that, Oldham," Anna murmured. "I thought you . . . wanted me to call you . . . Joe North."

"I suppose I did," Oldham said, hanging his head. He reached over and cupped his hand over hers. She summoned enough strength to turn her hand palm up and let him hold it.

"It's okay . . . Oldham," she said. "I'm sorry I . . . lost your money. I fought him hard. That's why . . . this." She tried her best to smile, but her lips were too swollen and cracked to allow it.

Anger glowed white hot inside Coyle. He

fought it down and swallowed hard, settling himself.

"The money wasn't important, Anna Rose," he said softly, consoling her.

"Now you . . . tell me," she said, with a short faint laugh that quickly turned to a deep, painful cough.

"Shhh, take it easy, Anna Rose," Oldham said, seeing she was weakening and in pain from talking so much. "I'm going to be around New Delmar for a while. We'll have time to talk." He paused, then said quietly, "Was it Henry Teague and Sonny Rudabough who did this to you?"

"Not Teague . . . just Rudabough," she said, summoning strength in her voice. She squeezed his hand. "He said . . . you sent him, so I let him in. Said you told me to go with him . . . take care of him."

That son of a bitch! Oldham clenched his teeth in anger.

"He—he liked . . . beating on me," she continued. "I should have thought and . . . charged him." Again she tried a brave smile; again her battered lips wouldn't permit it. She coughed and cringed from the pain of it.

"Please, stop talking, Anna Rose," Oldham whispered. "You need to lie still, let your ribs mend."

"All right, Oldham . . . I will," she whispered, already dropping off to sleep.

Oldham stood and slipped his hand from hers. Lila stepped in beside him and guided him away from the bed toward the door.

"I should have waited longer before coming here," he said, his hat in hand.

"No, I think it was good for her, you being here," Lila said, at the door. "This is the first she's been awake. It was hearing your voice that brought her around."

"You really think so?" Oldham asked. He gazed back toward Anna Rose's bed.

"Yes, I do think so," said Lila. "Now you need to go and let her sleep." She turned him and ushered him out the door, into the hallway.

"I'll be back," Coyle said. "I mean it, I will." He turned and watched the door start to close.

"She'll be glad to see you," Lila said, nodding. Her face narrowed with the closing door until she disappeared and the door stood closed in his face.

"I mean it," Oldham repeated to himself.

Twenty feet away at the top of the stairs, his brother, Dave, stood watching him. Oldham spotted him when he turned, putting his hat back on.

"How's the dove?" Dave asked.

"She's doing okay, brother Dave," Oldham said.

"You could've waited for us to catch up to you," Dave said in a flat, harsh tone.

"I could have, but I didn't," said Oldham. "Sorry, brother, I was in a hurry."

"I get a feeling we're walking deeper and deeper into trouble here," Dave said as they made their way down the stairs and crossed the floor toward the bar. Deak and Karl Sieg followed them.

At the crowded bar, Oldham ordered a bottle of rye and four shot glasses. The bartender stood the bottle on the bar and spread the glasses out in front of the men, waiting for Oldham to pay him. Oldham took out a gold coin but held it for a moment.

"Ranger Burrack said to tell you he sent me," he said.

"Oldham Coyle?" the bartender said.

"You know who I am," Oldham said. "You've seen me here before."

"Right you are, sir," said the bartender. "But I'm supposed to always ask when there's a pickup."

"A pickup?" Oldham looked at him curiously.

The bartender stooped down and came up from under the bar with the cloth bag. He checked the name tag as he set the bag on the bar.

"There you are, Oldham Coyle," he said. "The Ranger instructed me to give this to you upon request."

Coyle looked at the bag, then at his brother, Dave, standing beside him, then back at the bag. The bartender picked up the fresh bottle and uncorked it.

"I'll be damned," Oldham said quietly, already having a good idea what was inside the bag.

Sieg and Deak drew closer for a look as Oldham reached out and loosened the bag's drawstring.

Oldham dug a hand into the bag, grabbed some chips and let them spill from his fingertips.

"Burrack must be a straight shooter after all," he said to Dave, seeming a little surprised to ever see his money again.

"Yeah," said Dave. "Maybe in more ways than one." He watched the bartender finish pouring their glasses full, set the bottle aside and walk away. "I say let's drink up, gather Reye and Simon and ride out of here."

"We just got here, Dave," Oldham said as he hefted the bag of chips, then looked around at

the gaming tables, centering his gaze more
intently on the raised-platform table, noticing
onlookers gathered around a poker game in
progress.

"Oh no, brother Oldham," Dave said in disbelief. "Don't tell me you're even thinking about
gambling!"

Oldham continued staring at the game with
a sheepish grin and spoke to Dave over his
shoulder.

"It's my nature to think about it," he said. His
stare lingered a moment longer, as if the game
begged him to come sit in. Then he sighed, shook
his head a little as if to clear it and looked back at
Dave. "But no, I'm not going to do it."

"Good," Dave said with relief in his voice.
"Now we drink up and—"

"I've got a bigger game in play right now,"
said Oldham.

"What are you talking about, Oldham?" Dave
said. "We're through here. You even got your
money back. If that's not beating the odds, I don't
know what is. Let's call it a night, get out of here
while the getting's good."

"I'm not leaving yet," Oldham said firmly.
"I've got unfinished business."

Deak and Sieg gave each other a guarded look.

"No, you don't, brother," Dave argued. "This
thing with Hugh Fenderson has smelled like a
setup all along. Now he's on his way here, according to Teague. I've never considered you crazy
enough to sit still and wait for a killing party."

"I've got killing of my own to do, Dave," Oldham said. He raised the shot glass to his lips,
threw back its fiery contents in one drink, set the
glass down and refilled it.

"What!" said Dave in surprise.

"You heard me, brother," said Oldham, setting the bottle down, pushing it aside. He stared straight ahead.

"The Ranger?" said Dave. "After him treating you square, you'd still kill him . . . for money?"

"It's not about Burrack anymore, and it never was all about the money," he said. He picked the cloth bag up an inch and let it plop back down. "I owe for the woman."

"No, you don't," said Dave. "She took a hit of bad luck, but it wasn't your fault. She was doing what doves do. Leave some money for her if you want to. But put her out of your mind."

"Out of my mind?" Oldham chuffed darkly. "You didn't see her face, brother Dave. I did. He used my name to get her guard down. Told her I said *take care* of him." He turned and stared at his brother. "He used her, robbed her, beat her, threw her in a public ditch like emptying a chamber pot."

"I can understand how you feel," Dave said gravely. "But when Fenderson's train rolls in, there could be a dozen men with him—hell, a *hundred*, far as that goes. Think about the odds."

"I don't give a damn about the odds tonight, brother," said Oldham. He raised his glass, threw back another shot and slammed it back on the bar, gripping it tight in his fist. "Sonny Rudabough is going to die. So is Henry Teague, just for being with him."

Chapter 21

———

Well before dawn, Deputy Clow Dankett stuck Big Lucy's barrel against the Ranger's shoulder and nudged him just enough to cause him to open his eyes. He smiled to himself, noting that the Ranger did not awaken with a start. Instead he'd simply opened his eyes and slid them back and forth across the dim-lit jail without moving his head until he'd scrutinized what the world had laid before him.

"What is it?" Sam asked in a whisper.

"You said to wake you if I hear a train?" Dankett said.

"Yes," Sam replied.

"I hear one," Dankett affirmed.

Sam listened intently until he heard the distant roar of a steam engine beneath the sound of snoring from the cell Cisco Lang shared with Toy Johnson and Randall Carnes.

"Right, obliged, Deputy," Sam said, raising the Colt from his lap, straightening in the chair tipped slightly behind the desk.

"You wake up the way my pa always did," Dankett said quietly as the Ranger stretched and slipped the Colt back into its holster. "He was a scout for a privateer expedition into Mexico.

Said he could sleep in a cyclone but wake up if a feather touched the ground."

"He must've been a good scout, your father," Sam said. He looked at Dankett as he picked up his sombrero and put it on.

"Yes, he was," Dankett said. But before he could elaborate, a knock on the front door drew their attention.

Stepping over to the door, Dankett placed his hand on the bolt and looked around at the Ranger.

"Who is it?" he asked.

"It's me, Deputy," came a woman's voice on the other side of the door, "Adele Simpson. May I please come in? I have some breakfast for Harvey."

"Let her in, Deputy," said the Ranger.

Dankett slipped the bolt back and opened the door. He looked around over Adele's shoulder as she stepped inside carrying a tray of food, a red-checkered cloth napkin spread over it.

"Thank you, Deputy," she said, holding the tray in front of her. She looked at Sam as he lit an oil lamp standing on the desk. He adjusted the wick until light fell in a bright flickering circle around the darkened room.

"May I give this to Harvey, Ranger Burrack?" she asked.

Sam and Clow Dankett gave each other a look.

"I'm sorry I didn't bring enough for everyone," Adele said. "Polly Corn, from the restaurant, allowed me to cook this. She is preparing something for the rest of you. It's just that I'm leaving this morning and I wanted to—"

"We understand, ma'am," Sam said, stepping over to her. "Feel free to take it over to the corner there and serve it to Cisco." He glanced over and saw Lang already up and hanging on the bars with both hands, staring at Adele.

As Sam spoke, he raised a corner of the checkered napkin and looked the food over—eggs, hotcakes, gravy, salt pork.

"My, my, Miss Adele," Sam said, catching the wafting aroma of the food as he dropped the napkin back in place. "Losing you was the worst thing that ever happened to Cisco." He glanced over at Lang and looked him up and down. "I suspect he realizes that by now."

Sam stepped aside and let Adele take the food to a feed slot and slip it through to Lang. The prisoner took the tray and walked to the far front corner of the cell, Adele walking alongside him on the other side of the bars.

While Lang sat down on a stool at the bars, the tray on his lap, Sam walked to the other end of the cell, reached through the bars and shook Johnson by his shoulder.

"Wake up, Toy, wake up, Randall," he said. "It's time to get you both up and out of here." In the other cell, Teague and Rudabough sat up from their blankets on the plank floor. They stared at the Ranger in silence.

"Huh, what's that?" said Johnson.

"Wake up, both of you," said Sam. "I'm letting you go, like I said I would."

The two stirred and stood up, Johnson using a crutch Dankett had rummaged up from somewhere and given to him. They looked at each other.

"The things is, Ranger," said Carnes, bleary-eyed, "we don't know where to go."

"Your horses are at the livery barn," Sam said. "Get them and get going before I change my mind. There's big trouble coming. I want you out of here."

"Is it trouble we can help with?" Johnson asked, leaning on the crutch under his arm.

Sam just looked at him.

"All right, let's go," Johnson said to Carnes. "We've lost our spot here."

As Sam opened the cell door for the two to leave, a knock on the front door prompted Dankett to open it for the cook, Polly Corn, from the restaurant. She walked in carrying a large tray full of food and a steaming pot of coffee.

"Oh, good Lord, Ranger," said Toy Johnson. "Me and Randall can't remember when we last et. Can we, Randall?"

"It's been a long stretch," Randall said, his eyes on the heavy tray as Polly set it on the desk.

"All right," Sam said, locking the cell door behind the two. "Get yourself some coffee and food first. Then get going. I don't want to see either one of you again for at least a month."

"What about us in here?" Teague said from the bars of the other cell. Sonny Rudabough sat up holding his sore head with both hands.

"It's coming to you, Teague," Sam said.

"God bless you, Ranger," said Carnes, already swooping down on a warm biscuit while Polly poured coffee for him. Through a mouthful of biscuit, he said, "I don't suppose we could impose on you to return our firearms?"

"Not a chance," said the Ranger, stepping

over to get himself a cup of coffee. When Polly
had poured a cup for him, Sam carried it over to
where Adele sat at the bars and watched Lang
eat his breakfast, the checkered napkin stuck
down in his open shirt collar, serving as a bib.

"Your train will be arriving at the depot in a
few minutes, Miss Adele," he said.

"Oh. So soon?" She paused, looking regret-
fully at Lang through the bars. "Then must I
leave now, Ranger?"

"No hurry on my part, ma'am," Sam said. "I
just wanted to let you know."

"Then it's all right if I stay here a little longer?"
she said. "The train will have to take on water
and wood."

"Suit yourself, ma'am," Sam said. "Deputy
Dankett and I are going to take a little walk in a
few minutes. I'm sure I can trust you here with
the prisoner."

Adele only looked at Lang through the bars.

In the other cell, Teague and Rudabough took
tin plates of food that Dankett had passed
through the food slot in the bars.

"There's still time for you to let us go, Ranger,"
Teague said. "I might be able to save your life."

"You'd be lucky to save your own, once Fenderson finds out I'm not dead," said Sam.

"I knew we should have killed you the first
time we laid eyes on you, Ranger," Rudabough
said.

"Trying to make friends, are you, Rudabough?"
Sam asked dryly.

"I'm saying, if I get my hands on a gun—"

"Shut up, idiot," Teague growled at Sonny.
"When you're sitting in a jail cell, don't be threatening your jailer!"

The Ranger and Dankett gave the men time to eat. As soon as Carnes and Johnson had finished their breakfast and coffee and limped out the front door, Dankett led the remaining prisoners one at a time out the side door to the jakes. When he had locked Lang in his cell and watched him join Adele back in the front corner, Sam picked his Winchester up from against the desk and cradled it in his arm.

"Everybody's fed and had their coffee," he said to the two cells. "Deputy Dankett and I have business to take care of this morning, but one of us will be around to check on you every few minutes."

"Sit tight and don't do something stupid," Dankett put in, swinging a bandolier of shotgun loads over his shoulder. "Or I'll save a couple of these loads for you."

The Ranger gave him a look.

"Sorry, Ranger, I'm trying," Dankett said under his breath.

Adele had started to stand up from her short wooden chair.

"Ma'am, you're welcome to stay," Sam said. "Be careful you don't miss your train."

Adele sat back down. She and Lang looked at each other through the bars.

Inside his Pullman car, off on a short length of private rails beside the New Delmar Depot, Hugh Fenderson stood putting on a long swallow-tailed coat as Oboe, Singleton and Harkens stepped inside the car door and stood waiting for him. Beneath his long coat, Fenderson wore a new hand-tooled holster housing a custom-engraved, bone-handled Colt. As the men watched, the well-dressed businessman raised the fancy Colt and turned it in his hand, letting them get a look at it.

"I'm sure there'd be a few folks upset that I've had the Ranger killed," he said. "I may have to promise them something—a new hay barn for the town livery perhaps. So, until I get these desert rats soothed down, everybody watch for trouble." He spun the ornate Colt as he spoke.

"Sir, begging your pardon," said Chester Harkens. "But won't you be carrying a shotgun, or a rifle at least?"

"He means in case some of these people ain't interested in a new hay barn," Oboe put in.

"Ha!" said Fenderson. "I know these people. A new hay barn never fails. Besides, I may be only carrying a handgun, but let none of you forget that I was the best pistol marksman at Harvard three years in a row." He grinned, spun the Colt and slipped it back down in his holster.

"Yes, sir," said Oboe. "The rest of the men are gathered behind the operations car. Your horse is saddled and ready."

"Then let's be gone, men," said Fenderson. He placed a well-brushed Stetson hat on his head and walked forward with deliberation. The men parted and fell in behind him as he walked straight through them, out onto the platform and down to the rocky ground. He stopped and stared back along the train to where four more men sat atop their horses, holding reins to other horses in their hands.

A signal from Oboe brought the four riders forward and to a halt, a tall chestnut bay swinging around sideways to Fenderson, ready for him to mount.

"Since Teague did not say where he and Rudabough would be," he said, stepping up into his saddle, "we will start at Polly Corn's restaurant this time of morning." He looked at the others. "I don't know about you, but I could use some of Polly Corn's fresh-made coffee." Without waiting for a reply, he turned the bay and nudged it in the direction of the town sitting three hundred yards away. The men, nodding in agreement, fell in behind him and followed in a loose column of twos.

"By all rights, it should have been me who killed that Ranger," a gunman named Red Mike Sylvane said under his breath to the man riding beside him, a gunman named Dade Burke.

Burke looked at him.

"Why's that, Red Mike?" Burke said in the same lowered tone. "Are you somebody special that the world just hasn't heard of yet?"

Red Mike gave him a snarl.

"It just happens that I could have taken the Ranger cold. He'd have been lucky to get his gun out."

"Yeah, well, I guess we'll never know now, will we?" Dade Burke said, sounding sarcastic.

They rode on in silence through the silvery morning air until they reached a long iron hitch rail out in front of the restaurant, stepped down and tied their horses in line. As Hugh Fenderson started to turn and step onto the boardwalk toward the restaurant door, Sergio Oboe stopped him suddenly, drawing his attention toward the street.

"Mr. Fenderson, sir!" Oboe said in a stunned voice. "Is that who I think it is?"

Fenderson and all his men turned and stared

as the Ranger and Clow Dankett walked toward them up the middle of the nearly empty street, a swirl of silver still lingering, adrift on the early morning air.

Fenderson stared for a moment, his eyes widened in disbelief. Then his eyes narrowed; his face flushed with anger.

"Teague, you lying poltroon *son of a bitch*!" he growled as if Henry Teague were right beside him, his fists clenched tight at his sides. He stood staring fiercely at the Ranger, as if he'd ordered him to die and the Ranger had disobeyed him.

Seeing that his boss appeared to be frozen in place, Sergio Oboe took a sidelong step and stood poised with his rifle in both hands.

"Spread out, men," he said to the others. "It looks like Burrack wasn't none too happy being in the grave."

Widening the gap between them, Dade Burke looked Red Mike up and down with a thin, smug grin.

"Well, Red Mike, it looks like God does answer prayers. You get the chance to kill this lawman after all."

"You think I'm worried, Dade?" said Red Mike, taking a stand, his feet shoulder-length apart. He pitched his rifle to Burke. "Hold on to this for a minute, big-mouth. I won't be needing it."

Burke caught the rifle and gave a chuff.

"I could take your meaning a couple different ways, Red Mike," he said.

"Take it however you want it. I've got killing to do," said Red Mike. He adjusted the front of his gun belt with the inside of his wrists.

"Kill them both," Fenderson said to Oboe under his breath. He looked at Tom Singleton.

"You stay with me, Tom . . . lead the way," he said, gesturing a nod toward the restaurant's door.

"That's as close as you get, Ranger," Oboe called out to Sam and Dankett.

Sam said sidelong to Dankett, "Keep walking, Deputy."

"That's what I intended," Dankett said, sounding as fearless and determined as the Ranger had decided him to be these past few days. He carried Big Lucy at port arms, cocked and ready, the shoulder strap drooping from its walnut stock, two fresh reloads stuck between three fingers of his left hand.

"I said stop, Ranger!" Oboe demanded.

But the Ranger and Dankett continued walking, drawing a few feet closer until Sam knew they were in pistol and shotgun range.

"Right here," he said to Dankett; both of them stopped and stood ten feet apart.

Oboe looked relieved that the two stopped, but he knew that was only part of it. Now he saw the Ranger lower the Winchester and let it hang in his left hand. He watched Sam raise the big Colt from its holster in such an easy, natural manner, as if to merely check it and holster it again before the fight started. But instead of holstering it, the Ranger held it down at his side and cocked it, ready to bring it up into play.

Son of a bitch! Oboe cursed to himself, realizing the Ranger had just drawn first and taken the upper hand.

Red Mike looked at Oboe in disbelief for letting the Ranger get by with drawing his Colt like that.

"What the hell, Sergio?" he said. "Whose side are you on?"

"Shut up, Mike! I wasn't expecting it!" Sergio shouted.

On the boardwalk behind them, Fenderson and Tom Singleton had just disappeared inside the restaurant. It didn't surprise the Ranger at all.

Chapter 22

———

Seeing the Ranger and his deputy face off with the gunmen out in front of the restaurant, the early morning townsfolk along the boardwalks ducked inside stores and open doorways. Signs in windows turned from OPEN to CLOSED with a flick of a wrist. Wagon and horse traffic veered off the street into open lots and alleyways. A gangly hound loping along the side of the dirt street slowed and changed his direction at the sound of the Ranger's voice in the middle of the street.

"None of you have to die here today. Except *Hugh Fenderson*," Sam called out, almost matter-of-factly, yet making sure Fenderson heard him from the other side of the restaurant door. "Pitch him out to me and you can all go home." He knew they weren't going to give up Fenderson. He called out to the closed restaurant door, "Hugh Fenderson, come out, do your own dirty work. Don't make these men die trying to do it for you." He wanted Fenderson to know the penalty for trying to bring about the death of a lawman.

What? Is this Ranger crazy? Oboe asked himself.

"You best learn to count, Ranger," he said. "There's six of us here."

"Yeah, but there are two of us," Dankett put in. He swung the big shotgun down level to the gunmen's midsections. "Three, counting Big Lucy." The deputy appeared exuberant at the prospect of a bloody gun battle.

"To hell with this. I'm claiming the reward," said Red Mike, stepping forward, his hand poised near his holstered black-handled Colt. "Ranger, leave the rest of them out of this. It's just you and me, here and now. We'll settle this thing—"

Without hesitation, the Ranger's big Colt rose and leveled in a glint of gunmetal. The first shot cut Red Mike off as the bullet bored through his chest. A crimson mist appeared to hang for a second in the air behind him. Then a long string of blood ejected out his back, following the bullet, and splattered on over the front of the restaurant. Red Mike Sylvane flew backward and landed dead on the ground.

"Kill them!" shouted Segio Oboe, sidestepping toward the cover of wooden shipping crates stacked in front of a store next door to the restaurant. Even as he shouted, rifles and handguns had already lifted into play. Gunfire erupted; bullets flew from both directions.

The Ranger fired the big Colt, hearing bullets zip past him. He swung the smoking barrel toward Sergio Oboe and fired. Yet Oboe, moving away, took only a deep graze on his upper right shoulder as he retaliated wildly.

All of the gunmen returned fire, in the open, moving only grudgingly, ducking as the Ranger's bullets whizzed at them. But when the cannonlike roar of Dankett's Big Lucy picked up two gunmen and hurled them away in a tangle of bloody limbs and torn flesh, the gunmen broke ranks and dived for any cover they could find before the shotgun exploded again.

In an alley alongside the Number Five Saloon where the Coyles and their men had spread blankets for the night, the group had sat up bleary-eyed and listened intently at the first sounds of gunfire from up the street. But the double blasts from Big Lucy had drawn them quickly to their feet.

"Good Lord!" said Sieg, the shotgun blasts resounding along the street above all other gunfire.

"Dankett," Oldham said flatly to his brother, Dave, standing beside him.

"Yes," said Dave. "Fenderson must've got here without us hearing his train." As they spoke, they grabbed their rifles and ran back along the alleyway and behind the row of buildings in the direction of the gun battle. Sieg and Deak ran along behind them, Deak's short legs pumping like steam pistons, yet still unable to keep up.

At the alley nearest to the restaurant, Oldham and Dave turned and ventured forward until they could see the street around the corner of a building.

"Whoa, look at this!" Oldham said, seeing Clow Dankett go down onto one knee, reloading for the third time as a bullet sought him out. Around the Ranger and Dankett a cloud of gun smoke loomed thickly.

The Coyles watched Dankett almost fall over as the bullet slammed into his side. They watched Sam run to his deputy and help him to his feet. They saw Sam looping Dankett's arm across his shoulder and hurrying away. Sam still fired and levered his Winchester one-handed as they fell in behind a thick stack of nail kegs standing on the boardwalk of the town mercantile store.

"This is just the kind of break I was hoping for," Oldham said almost to himself.

"What are you talking about, brother?" Dave said. "I was hoping after a night's sleep you'd put all this craziness out of your mind, we'd ride out of here."

"I have one thing to do, brother Dave," said Oldham. "I'll do it now while everybody's painting the streets with each other's brains."

"I don't like the sound of it," Dave said. "But I'll go along with it, if it'll get us out of here and back to robbing something."

"You and Sieg go get Simon and Reye," said Oldham. "Meet Deak and me at the livery barn with our horses saddled, ready to ride."

"You got it, brother Oldham. Now you're making sense," Dave said with a look of relief.

Inside the jail, Lang and the woman sat huddled at the front corner of his cell, listening to the sound of the gun battle raging three blocks up the street. In the neighboring cell, Teague and Sonny Rudabough sat listening too, passing a look of awe and trepidation between them each time Dankett's big shotgun let out another earth-shaking blast.

"I've got to get myself one of them," Rudabough remarked quietly after the shotgun fell silent for a reloading.

Outside, they heard big boots run along the boardwalk in a long stride, followed by a rapid, lighter sound a few yards behind. They saw Oldham Coyle swing the front door open, rush inside and keep the door open for Deak Holder. Deak ran in a second behind Oldham, panting, struggling to catch his breath.

"Jesus!" said the dwarf, gasping, bowed at the waist on his short legs. "I didn't know we were racing."

Oldham glanced at Lang and the woman in passing, then looked at Teague and Rudabough, who stood staring in return.

"All right! Coyle, amigo! Get us out of here!" Henry Teague said right quickly. "There's still time for me to straighten all this out and make things right."

"Amigo? Huh-uh," said Oldham, his rifle hanging in his left hand. "I'm here to make things right, Teague." He held his Colt down at his right side, cocked and ready.

Behind Coyle, Deak leaned against the desk, still panting, watching the door. He kept his short fingers lying on the butt of his big belly pistol.

"Make things right? What are you talking about, Coyle?" Teague said, appearing not to see Oldham's Colt. He stepped over to the cell door and rattled it with both hands. "Hurry up, let's get going," he said. "I'll be damned if I'm going to Yuma over this mess."

"You're right about that," Oldham said. He raised the Colt level to Teague's chest through the bars.

Rudabough hugged back against the plank wall as shot after shot walked Teague backward haltingly to the rear wall. Teague slid down the wall and settled onto the floor beneath a long smear of blood.

"Okay, I have no qualms with you doing that," Rudabough said wide-eyed, flattened back against the wall. "Whatever he did to you, he deserved to die for it, far as I'm concerned. I don't know why you did it. *I don't even want to know.* Lots of folks thought him and I were friends, but we never were—"

"It was over what happened to the dove, Rudabough," Oldham said, cutting him off. In the other cell, Lang had shoved his arms through the bars and held Adele pressed as close as he could.

"The *dove*?" said Rudabough, as if having to probe his memory for anything on the subject.

"Yes, the dove. The one you beat nearly to death and threw in the public ditch," said Oldham. "I killed him just for knowing you did it. Imagine what I'm going to do to *you*." He dropped the two remaining bullets from his Colt and pitched it through the bars onto the plank floor.

"Oh, what? Give me an empty gun?" Rudabough said wryly. As the two spoke, Deak rummaged in the desk for the cell key, standing slightly on his toes to see into the open top drawer.

"There's plenty of bullets for it inside a saddlebag," said Oldham, "on a black-and-white paint horse . . . waiting for you behind the Number Five Saloon. All you've got to do is get there and load up before I can kill you graveyard dead." Speaking over his shoulder he said, "Deak, how about that key?"

"Coming up, boss," Deak said, bent over at the

waist, his short arm searching back in the open bottom drawer. He stood up, the key raised in his hand and a smile of satisfaction on his face, and walked it quickly over to Oldham Coyle.

At the front corner of the other cell, Lang and Adele looked at each other in surprise at the sight of the cell key in Deak Holder's small hand.

Oldham looked down at the two as he unlocked the door to Rudabough's cell.

"What about it, Cisco?" he called out. "Here's your chance to ride away." He held the key up.

Lang started to stand up, but then he slumped down and shook his head.

"Obliged, Coyle," he said. "But I'm not Cisco anymore. I'm just Harvey Lang, ready to do my time."

"Are you sure, Cisco?" said Oldham. "You can ride with me and my bunch. Stop being the man holding the horses. Make yourself a real long rider, eh?"

Lang looked at Adele, then at Oldham. Without saying anything, he shook his head, as if words might fail him.

"Suit yourself," said Coyle. He swung the cell door open and pitched the key over atop the desk.

But Rudabough didn't move from the wall; instead he hugged back tighter against it.

"I'm not playing this game, Coyle," he said. "How do I know that paint horse is there? How do I know what you say is true?"

"First off, I have never lied to you. Second, did I say you had a choice?" Coyle said through jaws clenched tight with anger, stepping inside the cell. The rifle bucked in his right hand; the bullet ripped splinters from the plank wall an inch from Rudabough's side.

Deak jumped up and down laughing, waving his short arms, as Rudabough bolted from his cell and headed out the front door. Oldham Coyle stopped at the front door long enough to lever a fresh round into his smoking rifle.

"If you change your mind, Cisco, have her get the key. Get yourself out of here. The Ranger and his deputy are pinned down. Like as not, they're going to die out there. This town won't pay your fare to Yuma. They'll shorten your trip on the end of a rope."

"Oh my God!" said Adele, clasping a hand to her mouth.

"Wait!" said Lang as Oldham Coyle disappeared out the door behind Deak, in hot pursuit of Sonny Rudabough.

"My God, Harvey," said Adele. "Would they do that? Hang you, I mean?"

Lang looked at her long and hard, thoughts racing through his mind. Finally he said, "Adele, get the key, let me out of here."

"But, Harvey, what about us?" she said. "What about you making amends and straightening your life out—?"

"Adele," he said, cutting her short. "You heard him. You heard what he said! I can't just sit here and do nothing. Get the key, let me out!" He stood and gripped the bars with both hands.

She hurried to the desk, picked up the key and ran back and unlocked the cell door.

"What if they're not going to come hang you afterward?" she said, stalling, the key half turned in the lock. Gunfire still exploded three blocks away.

"Adele, look at me. Listen to me!" he said, reaching through the bars and turning her hand along with the key. "I'm not talking about what Coyle said about me hanging. I'm talking about the Ranger and his deputy being pinned down!"

The gunfire grew more intense, as if to emphasize Lang's words.

"What are you saying, Harvey?" Adele said as he ran past her to the gun cabinet, grabbing a Winchester and a box of ammunition. "That you're going to risk your life trying to save the Ranger and his deputy?"

He looked at her as he feverishly broke open the box, grabbed a handful of bullets and loaded the rifle. He looked at the remaining bullets in the box, knowing it wasn't enough, not if the two lawmen were pinned down.

"Yes, Adele, I have to go. I have no choice," he said. "I told you, I've seen what I am, and I don't like it. I want to make myself right."

"I understand you wanting to do that," said Adele. "And I admire you for it. But not like this! What if it's too late to help them? What if you only manage to get yourself killed?"

"Then I'll die a better man, in a better place than I was a week ago," Lang said. "With no small thanks to you and Sam Burrack." He levered a round up into the rifle chamber.

"Harvey . . . ," Adele said. She stood watching with tears on her cheeks as he walked to the front door and swung it open. He stopped for a moment.

"I can't be *half right*, Adele. It's all or none. I won't sit here feeling new and righteous while two good men die in the dirt. Neither you nor I either one could live with that." He gave her a thin smile of regret and said, "I love you, Adele . . . I have all along, I just wish I'd known it sooner, instead of being the no-good stupid son of a bitch I was—if you'll pardon my language," he added. He touched his fingers to his bare forehead in farewell.

Adele stood with her fingertips pressed to her lips and watched him step out and close the door behind himself.

Lang turned on the boardwalk, the sound of gunfire still going strong. Instead of running toward the gun battle, he looked back and forth, then ran in the opposite direction, to where a two-horse buckboard sat out in front of an essaying office. Without a second of hesitation, he jumped into the driver's seat and slapped the reins on the horses' backs.

Ducked down behind a large ore barrel inside the essay office, a miner raised his head and watched his buckboard go racing away, leaving a stream of dust twisting in the air behind it.

"Damn it all! One of them is getting away in my wagon!"

"Stay down, forget your damn wagon!" a voice called out from behind another ore barrel. "They're killing each other out there!"

Chapter 23

———

The gunfire had grown far too hot and heavy for the Ranger and his wounded deputy. During a short lull while Fenderson's gunmen reloaded, Sam had looped Dankett's arm over his shoulder and dragged him from behind the wooden nail kegs to a building still under construction three doors up and across the street. Bullets from the gunmen followed the two lawmen as they fell through the open storefront. Sam guided Dankett through sawdust and discarded nails, until they stopped behind a stack of boards. He stripped the bandolier of ammunition from Dankett's shoulder.

"Don't worry about me, Ranger," Dankett said. "I'm just bleeding a little."

Sam didn't answer. He untied the deputy's bandana from around his neck, wadded it up and stuffed it inside Dankett's shirt against the wound in his side. He planted Dankett's hand on it.

"Keep this in place, Deputy," he said as gunfire began to erupt heavier from the alleyways and cover on either side of the restaurant.

"How am I supposed . . . to shoot Big Lucy?" Dankett said.

"I'll take care of her, Deputy," Sam said. "You

lie still for a minute, try to stop bleeding on us." As he spoke, he noted how few loads were left in Dankett's bandolier.

Seeing the Ranger looking at the low shotgun ammunition, Dankett gave a crooked smile beneath his lowered hat brim.

"I put out a powerful barrage, Ranger," he said weakly.

"Yes, you did, Deputy," said the Ranger. "Now lie still."

Both of them ducked down as a rifle round whined through the empty storefront and thumped into a workman's ladder leaning against a wall. Checking his own ammunition, Sam realized that he too was running out of bullets.

"Listen to that, Deputy," Sam said, taking note that after their reloading, the gunmen were not firing as heavily as before. "It sounds like we're not the only ones running out of bullets." He looked around, then said, "Can you hold out here awhile, Deputy? I need to get to the window and throw some fire back at them, else they'll get bold and try rushing us."

"You go ahead, Ranger, and take Big Lucy with you. I've still got this ol' six-shooter," Dankett said, growing weak from losing blood. He patted his holster, then drew his Colt and laid it across his lap.

"Good man," Sam said. He stood in a crouch, bandolier and shotgun in one hand, his Winchester in his other, and ran to a large open window frame at the front of the store, where he dropped behind a knee wall and took position.

"There he is," said Sergio Oboe to the men huddled beside him inside the restaurant. He had shot a glance through the front window and seen the Ranger drop out of sight in the store-front across the street.

"Where's the other one?" Dade Burke asked, a bandana tied around his upper arm where he'd taken the deep bullet graze.

"Dead, most likely," Oboe said. "I put one in his side, saw him go down with it."

Oboe looked all around the disheveled, bullet-riddled restaurant. The back door stood open, the way fleeing customers had left it. Among the last ones making an escape through the back door had been Tom Singleton and Hugh Fenderson.

"The boss is out of here," he said. "I say we rush him, right now while we can."

"We're awfully low on bullets," said Harkens, huddled beside him, against the restaurant's front wall.

"Right," said Oboe. "And if we are, so are they." He levered a round into his rifle. "I still want that reward money, even if I have to split it with you buzzards."

Burke looked puzzled and asked, "Why is it he wants the Ranger dead? I forgot."

"The Ranger killed his cousin," Harkens said, reloading his six-shooter, the barrel still smoking and hot in his hand.

"No," said Oboe. "It was his *nephew*, damn it. And he didn't kill him, just sent him to Yuma Penitentiary to rethink his future. What's wrong with you men, you can't remember why you're killing a sumbitch?"

"I'm killing him for the bounty on his head," Harkens said. "Plain and simple." He clicked his loaded gun shut and wagged it in his hand. "That's as much reason as I ever need."

"Amen to that," said Sergio Oboe. "Let's rush him, then. Get this done, have Polly Corn boil us up some coffee afterward." No sooner had he spoken than a rifle shot exploded from across the street, sending a bullet slicing through the restaurant's open window, slamming into the far wall. "Damn Ranger!" he cursed, ducking his head, jumping away from the window frame.

"It ain't the Ranger, Oboe. Look at this!" said Harkens, managing a peep over the window ledge.

"Damn!" said Oboe, peeping around the corner of a bullet-riddled window frame. "He's got help coming."

Another bullet sliced through the open window. The gunmen looked out and saw the buckboard racing up the street, fishtailing toward them in a twisting spiral of dust.

"Who the hell's this?" said Oboe. "I thought everybody here knew better than to get involved against Hugh Fenderson."

"I know him," said Harkens, raising his rifle, leveling it out over the edge of the window frame. "It's Cisco Lang—some idiot who thinks he's an outlaw."

"An outlaw?" said Burke in disbelief. "What's he doing helping the Ranger?"

"Beats me," said Harkens, taking aim at Lang, who stood in the buckboard, reins in his left hand, firing and levering a Winchester in his right. A large satchel hung by a strap from Lang's shoulder.

"Beats me too," said Oboe. "Kill the son of a bitch, before he breaks his own neck."

The gunmen laid down a deadly barrage of

gunfire on the approaching buckboard. The two wagon horses, nicked by the bullets slicing past them, veered and made a hard, sharp turn in the street. Lang wasn't able to control them with the reins. As the horses made their turn, the buckboard jackknifed and slid sidelong in the dirt, raising dust. Lang flew from the buckboard and landed hard, the upturned buckboard barely missing him as it sailed over his head and landed tumbling in the street in front of him.

From the open window frame, the Ranger winced at the sight of Lang rolling in the street; he saw the freed wagon horses in flight down an alleyway.

"Cisco, you fool . . . ," he said under his breath. As the gunfire from the restaurant waned, Sam ran from the protection of the storefront to where Lang lay dazed, yet struggling to rise onto his feet.

"Stay down!" Sam shouted. He knocked Lang back to the dirt as two bullets whizzed past them. Big Lucy was strapped down his back and his rifle in hand. "Follow me," he said, crawling, half dragging Lang a few feet until they found shelter behind the buckboard lying on its side in the middle of the street.

"What are you doing out here, Cisco?" the Ranger asked, looking him over for any gunshot wounds. "I left you in a cell."

"Yes, you did," Lang said, getting his breath back after being hurled from the buckboard. "Coyle killed Teague and chased Rudabough out the door. He left the key, said you were pinned down out here. I brought you this." He swung the satchel from around his neck, shoved it out to the Ranger and pulled the flap open. "You'll need to talk to the mercantile owner, tell him I wasn't robbing him."

Sam's eyes brightened at the sight of the ammunition boxes. Then he looked back up at Lang as he grabbed a box and opened it while bullets thumped into the buckboard and whizzed overhead.

"I'm much obliged, Cisco," he said, shoving bullet after bullet into the Winchester. "I'll give you some cover. You get yourself out of here."

"I'm not going anywhere, Ranger," Lang said. "I'm here to help. I brought a rifle with me." He looked all around for the rifle that had flown from his hand.

"Here, Cisco, take Dankett's shotgun and loads," Sam said, pulling the shotgun strap and bandolier from around his back and shoving them to him. "He's over there, wounded." He gestured toward the open storefront. "Don't shoot him by mistake."

"I'll be careful," Lang said, pulling the bandolier around his shoulder and gripping the shotgun in both hands. "Tell me what you want. I'm good for it."

"I'm betting they're just as low on bullets as I was," Sam said. "If I'm right, they're going to break and run when we charge."

"*Charge . . . ?*" said Lang. A sick look came to his face. But he caught himself, swallowed a knot in his throat and said, "Sounds good to me."

Behind the long row of buildings facing the street where the gun battle raged, Sonny Rudabough stopped beside a dusty telegraph pole long enough to look back and see if he'd managed to lose Oldham Coyle. But before his eyes could search the alleyway behind him, a rifle bullet thumped into the pole only inches from his head.

"I'm on you, Rudabough!" Coyle called out. "You're not going to lose me. You better get to that paint horse and get the gun loaded."

"Yeah, you running son of a bitch," Deak shouted. Raising his belly gun with both hands, he let out a yell and fired it three times in the air.

Sonny Rudabough cursed under his breath, turned and kept running, the empty Colt in his hand.

But at the livery barn over a block away, even as the sound of gunfire roared from the street, Blind Simon turned in his saddle and tilted his head slightly.

"Hold it," Simon said to Dave and the others. "I just heard Deak yelling . . . heard his gun too." He held the reins to Chic Reye's horse in his hand, Reye lying low in his saddle, an arm around his stomach wound, which had been freshly bandaged.

"You're crazy as hell, blind man," Reye said in a weak, testy voice. "There's a gun battle going on. Don't act like you . . . can hear through all that."

Karl Sieg looked at Dave, and Blind Simon turned his dark spectacles in Dave's direction, as if looking at him.

"Well?" Sieg said. "Do you suppose Oldham and Deak have gotten tangled up in all this?"

"I don't know," said Dave, giving a troubled look toward the sound of the gun battle. "Oldham said get their horses and meet them here. That's what we've done." He paused, then said, "Damn it! What's keeping them?"

"Deak's my pard," said Simon. "I've got to go find him."

"Nobody moves. We're waiting right here, Simon," said Dave. "Just like I said we would."

"I'm not," said Simon, jerking his big Colt from its holster, the reins to both his horse and Reye's in his other hand. Before anybody could do or say anything, Simon spun his horse and spurred it in the direction of the gunfire, trusting the horse beneath him to see what his own eyes could not.

Behind him, hanging on to his saddle horn, Chic Reye let out a long scream, bouncing, swaying, seeing the corner post of a building coming straight at him until, within a hairbreadth, both horses cut sharply into a narrow alley and pounded away toward the street.

Dave Coyle and Karl Sieg sat stunned atop their horses, hearing Reye's tortured pleading voice move away from them down the dark alleyway.

"Jesus, God in heaven," Karl Sieg said as if in awe. "I have never seen anything like that in my life."

"Neither have I," Dave said, equally stunned. After a second he shook his head as if to clear it. "We better go stop them. There's no telling where they'll end up."

At the far end of the alley, on the street, the Ranger and Lang heard the sound of the two horses' hooves behind them as they advanced, firing fast and furiously on the bullet-chewed front of Polly Corn's restaurant. Shooting the Winchester from his hip, the Ranger had taken them closer, noting the waning intensity of return fire from Fenderson's gunmen. Beside him fifteen feet away, Lang had fired blast upon blast from Big Lucy, each shot lifting chunks of wood from both building and boardwalk. From the rear of Polly Corn's, three gunmen scurried away across the sand like fleeing rats.

"That's it, I'm out of loads," Lang said, blood running down his forearm from a bullet wound.

"What's this?" Sam said, turning with his rifle as the horses rounded into sight out of the alley.

"Yiiii-hiii!" Blind Simon shouted, his Colt blazing away at anything in front of him. Sam started to take aim and fire his Winchester. Yet, upon seeing Simon's shots flying wild, he backed away to the side, Lang following suit.

The two riders raced past them, Reye looking over at them wide-eyed in terror. A loud scream, *"Heeelp meeee!"* resounded from his gaping mouth.

From the front of Polly Corn's restaurant, a shot rang out. The Ranger swung his Winchester around and fired, knocking Sergio Oboe back inside the open front doorway, but not before Oboe's rifle shot lifted Lang and hurled him to the ground. Sam raced the fifteen feet between them and stooped down beside Lang.

"It's my leg," Lang said, gripping his calf just below his knee.

Even with his leg wound, Lang looked back quickly with the Ranger toward the sound of the two sets of pounding hooves. Reye screamed again, this time as both horses veered hard when a rifle shot from a fleeing gunman struck up dirt at their hooves.

Blind Simon managed to straighten his horse, but in doing so the reins to Reye's horse slipped from his hand. Simon's horse pounded on, but

Reye's mount had veered too sharply and, unable to right itself in time, the animal crashed through the large window of an apothecary store and lost its rider to a low ceiling beam. The Ranger and Lang saw the clapboard building tremble and spill dust from its window ledges and framework as Reye met the beam broad-faced. His horse thundered on, plowing along a gantlet of shelves, large earthen herb jars and glass medicine bottles, until the frightened animal crashed out the back door and kept running.

"What do you . . . suppose all that was, Ranger?" Lang asked, gripping his wounded calf.

"I won't try to guess," Sam said, loosening his bandana and tying it around Lang's calf wound. He looked down the street and saw Adele running toward them, the doctor right beside her. "Here comes the doctor, Cisco. You're going to be okay. Tell him to see about Dankett being inside over there."

"No need seeing about me," Dankett called out in a weak and strained voice. He limped forward from the open storefront. "I'm harder to kill than a gallon of turpentine." He held a hand pressed to his bloody, wounded side. "Where's Big Lucy?" he asked. Seeing the shotgun lying beside Lang, he reached down, snatched it up and gave Lang a hard stare, as if Lang had designs on his long-barreled wench. Straightening, he wobbled weakly in place.

As the doctor and Adele ran in, Sam looped Dankett's arm across his shoulders. The woman and Dr. Starr helped Lang to his feet and steadied him between them.

The wounded and the weary began to walk the length of the wide dirt street to Dr. Starr's

office. A few townsfolk ventured out from doorways and stores and began to gather and stare,
until a shot from behind the row of buildings on
the other side of the street sent most of the
onlookers back toward cover.

"You best go check that out, Ranger," Dankett
said beside Sam. He lowered his arm from
around Sam's shoulders and leaned on Big Lucy
for support. "I'll get to the doctor all right by
myself."

Chapter 24

———

Sonny Rudabough had made it thirty yards farther along a walkway behind the buildings lining the dirt street. He'd only slowed down long enough to listen to the gunfire die down and question whether or not to make a run for it, grab a horse from a hitch rail and get out of town. But as he stood contemplating his next move, another rifle shot exploded. This time the bullet struck the ground an inch from his boot.

"The next place you stop is where you'll die, Rudabough," Oldham Coyle called out, unseen, somewhere along the back of the row of buildings. "Get to the horse and get yourself some bullets. That's the only chance you've got."

Okay, you son of a bitch. . . .

If Oldham Coyle wanted a gunfight bad enough to leave him bullets and a horse to ride away on afterward, he'd oblige him, Sonny Rudabough thought—damn right he would. From the sound of the fighting on the street, he figured the Ranger was dead by now anyway. *The Ranger dead, Teague dead . . .* It was all right by him. He smiled a little, turned and ran toward the rear of the Number Five Saloon, keeping close to the backs of the buildings for cover.

When he could see clearly that there was no

paint horse standing in sight behind the saloon, he ventured away from the buildings and stepped out of cover, still looking all around.

Damn it, why did Coyle do this? Anger began boiling inside him. To hell with Coyle, he wasn't playing this stupid game of his.

"There's no damn paint horse back here, Coyle. No damn bullets either!" he shouted.

A shot rang out near Rudabough's feet, forcing him to jump to the side.

"I lied about the paint horse and the bullets, Sonny," Oldham called out. "I just wanted to get you here without dragging you by your boots after I kill you."

"What are you trying to pull here?" Rudabough looked all around, seeing the abandoned public ditch twenty feet away. *Uh-oh . . .*

"I'm not pulling nothing, Sonny," Oldham called out. "Nothing except this trigger."

Another shot exploded, this one almost hitting his foot. Sonny jumped farther away. He bolted a few feet in reflex, then stopped, cursing himself for moving closer to the public ditch. The smell of waste, of putrefaction, already drifted up, surrounding him, pressing him into a dark, rancid vapor.

"I see what you're doing, Coyle," he shouted. "But I'm not going any closer. This is far enough for me. You want to kill me, go ahead. But you'll have to do it right here—"

His words were cut short as another shot exploded; the bullet grazed the edge of his boot's sole. Instinctively he bolted again. He stopped a few feet away and looked at the edge of the ditch only ten feet from him.

"Damn you to hell, Coyle!" he shouted. "I'm

walking away!" He spread his hands, dropped the empty gun to the ground. "You want to kill an unarmed man, go ahead. I'm not going over that edge, you son of a—"

The rifle rang out again; the bullet thumped high into his right shoulder, spun him half around. He stopped himself, staggering in place. He started to shout again, but before he could, the next bullet hit him high in his left shoulder and he spun another half turn, this time in the opposite direction.

His boot soles rocked back and forth on the edge of the black, odorous ditch. *Huh-uh, this isn't going to happen.* Not to him, he told himself. With both shoulders bleeding badly, his arms hanging limp, he started to take a step forward; but the next shot hit him dead center. He fell backward, did a stiff flip, then a bounce, a short slide through something dark and slimy, then another flip and a facedown landing—a scream cut short by a loud wet slap.

Oldham stepped out of the dark shade of a building and levered a fresh round into his rifle chamber. He walked forward and looked down, seeing Rudabough struggling to come unstuck from a large puddle of human waste. Taking his time, he stooped and picked up his empty Colt, which Rudabough had discarded. Oldham watched the wounded man struggle with useless arms while he took bullets from his gun belt, reloaded the Colt and shoved it down in his holster. In the ditch, Sonny finally managed to free his face and swing it back and forth, making some strange, muffled sound. Then he dropped his face again with a splat, as if into some horrible yet irresistible stew.

All right, that'll do.

"Just wanted you to know . . . ," Oldham murmured under his breath, raising his rifle, taking aim as Sonny's boots kicked and dug in the dark waste matter.

The rifle bucked against Oldham's shoulder; Sonny's boots fell limp, as did the rest of him, the shot still echoing out across rock and desert lands.

"Good Lord, brother," Dave Coyle said behind Oldham, startling him for one reflex second. Oldham turned with the smoking rifle still raised. But he lowered it, seeing Dave and Sieg staring down at Rudabough's body lying half buried in waste. "I would not have gone along with this, had I known."

"Then be glad I didn't tell you," Oldham said, letting his rifle hang in his hand. "This meant more to me than killing the Ranger. I suspect that means I show little promise as a hired killer." He looked at Sieg, who was still staring down at Rudabough's body with a sour, twisted look on his face.

"You got something to say about this, Karl?" he asked.

Sieg looked at Oldham, at the rifle in his hand.

"Hell no!" he said quickly. "If I did, I sure as hell wouldn't say so standing here." He stared at Oldham for a second longer, then stifled a laugh until he saw how it would be taken.

Oldham chuckled under his breath, shook his head and looked away.

Finally Dave let out a breath and gave a short laugh himself.

"All right," he said. "Unless you want to stick around and watch Rudabough sink, let's go chase Simon and Reye down if we can find them. I've got a feeling Reye won't be leaving with us. I saw his horse wandering the streets."

Oldham nodded, looking all around. "Deak's around here somewhere. He had a hard time keeping up."

"I'm over here," Deak Holder called out, running from the alleyway leading to the street where their horses were standing. "I just saw Chic Reye lying dead in a drugstore. The poor bastard." He kept himself from grinning. "I saw the Ranger too. He's coming this way. You want to kill him, boss, here's your chance."

Dave gave his brother a look, seeing excitement flash across his eyes. But he waited and watched the excitement finally give way to good sense.

"I don't want to kill the Ranger," Oldham said. "The man has never done anything to me. There's something doesn't seem right about killing a man just for money." He looked embarrassed and said, "I let the oddsmaking and the sport of it get the better of me for a while. But I'm over it now." He looked at the three men, at the expressions on their faces. "Let's get over to Colorado, find ourselves something to rob."

As Oldham and his men turned to walk to the alleyway where their horses stood waiting, the Ranger lowered his Winchester from the corner of a building where he'd been supporting it.

Good decision, Coyle, he thought, hearing Oldham's plans, realizing his death was no longer a part of them. He let out a breath, knowing that from here, his bullet would have lifted the top of the gunman's head off.

He had followed the dwarf closely through

the alleyway and stood with his rifle aimed and ready, listening to what Oldham had to say. Having heard it, he backed away, rifle in hand, and rubbed a gloved hand across a skittish horse's side, keeping it settled until he'd slipped past them and backed away into the black shadow of a side doorway.

It was nearing noon when Tom Singleton and Hugh Fenderson heard the knock on the Pullman car door. Fenderson half rose from behind his desk, a look of fear in his red-rimmed eyes. He jerked the cigar from between his lips.

"Who the hell might this be, Tom?" he said.

"Don't you worry about a thing, sir," Singleton said, lifting his Colt from its holster as he walked to the door. "I've got you covered here."

None of the three men who had run away from Polly Corn's restaurant after the gun battle had returned to the train. Knowing he sat unprotected, down to one gunman, had Hugh Fenderson unnerved. The railroad men it took to run the train were not gunmen, and they made no pretense at being skilled as such. While he waited for the train to get moving, Fenderson sat at his desk with a shiny, engraved Winchester rifle lying to his right, the elaborate Colt to his left.

"Who's there?" Singleton asked, his face close to the edge of the door.

"Arizona Ranger Sam Burrrack," came the reply.

Singleton and Fenderson gave each other a stunned look from across the Pullman car. Neither of them had expected this.

"Stall him!" Fenderson said in a lowered voice

as he rounded the desk, picking up the rifle on his way.

Stall him? Singleton stared at his boss, seeing him become more and more rattled by this Ranger.

"Uh . . . just a minute, Ranger," Singleton said, huddled up next to the edge of the door. Fenderson stood close beside him, both of them staring at the door.

Neither of them saw the Ranger raise a leg over the edge of the open window behind Fenderson's desk and climb inside. He stood for a moment listening, watching the two men, his Colt out, cocked and ready.

Fenderson pointed at the dressing screen, motioning for Singleton to get behind it and wait in ambush. Sam kept his Colt on Singleton just in case, and watched the gunman slip along the other side of the room and step out of sight behind the screen.

At the door, Fenderson took a deep breath and swung the door open, rifle in hand. Expecting the Ranger, he started to say something. But he stopped and stood staring at the empty platform.

"He's not here!" he said, surprised. "The hell is this?"

Swinging the door shut, Fenderson turned back toward his desk and saw the Ranger staring at him from above his aimed Colt. He started to call out and warn Singleton, yet before he could speak, he saw a streak of gunmetal as the Colt turned in the Ranger's hand and fired three shots through the thin dressing screen.

Fenderson stared in shock as Singleton tumbled forward, dressing screen and all, and landed facedown, dead on the floor.

"Well?" Sam said, turning the smoking Colt toward the armed businessman.

"What?" Fenderson managed to say.

Sam gestured his Colt toward the rifle in Fenderson's hands.

"Oh, this?" He tossed the rifle forward onto the floor as if it had suddenly turned too hot to hold. He tried what he considered to be a winning smile, even though it looked worried and tense. "I'm afraid things have gotten way out of hand between us, Ranger Sam—I hope I may call you *Sam*?"

The Ranger didn't reply.

"It got out of hand when you placed a bounty on my head," Sam said.

"It's true, I did do that," he said matter-of-factly. "But you're going to find that impossible to prove in a court of law."

"I hadn't considered that," the Ranger said.

"Well, you should, you know," Fenderson said. As he spoke, he walked around his desk and stood facing the Ranger now from ten feet away. "May I?" he said, gesturing toward his tall leather chair. Sam backed away and stepped around the desk, giving the man back the security and confidence of his lofty perch. "Because, as you may know, it is not easy to prove a man as powerful as myself guilty," he continued, sitting down in his chair and leaning back a little. "It takes a lot of—"

"That's not what I meant," Sam said, stopping him. "I meant I hadn't considered proving anything in court." He stared intently at him. "I thought we'd settle here. Today. *Out of court*."

"I see, then," said Fenderson, getting it, his face turning grim. "No judge, no trial, no jury. Just you taking the law into your own hands?"

"There you have it," Sam said. He wasn't going to justify himself to this man who had tried to kill him.

"And that doesn't bother you in the slightest?" Fenderson said, looking for an opening, a way to wedge logic and reasoning into the matter—a matter that he himself had created based on neither logic nor reasoning.

"Most days it would. But today it doesn't," Sam said.

"I see," Fenderson said, slumping, letting both of his hands fall below the desk into his lap, letting the Ranger see no threat in him going for the engraved Colt. "Then you've decided I must die simply because I sought to avenge your shooting my nephew, and in doing so, dishonoring my family name?"

"Yes, exactly," Sam said firmly.

Fenderson sighed and said, "So, then, there is no rational way to end this to both of our satisfaction? Say . . . a large cash settlement perhaps? Instead of rewarding someone for *killing you*, I reward you, for *staying alive*?"

"No . . . ," Sam said. "Being alive is its own reward." He noted the lavish engraved Colt, lying so close, yet so far away now that Fenderson had dropped his hands beneath the big, polished desk. "The only way to end *this* is to *end* this." He lowered his big Colt to his side.

Seeing a recognizable look come upon Fenderson's face, he instinctively ducked away to the side. As he did so, he heard shots explode under the large desk, saw bullet holes appear in the desktop, kicking up splinters.

"Damn it all!" Fenderson shouted, realizing his trap hadn't worked. He jerked his right hand from under his desk and swung a smoking Colt Thunderer up at the Ranger.

But the Ranger's big Colt bucked once in his hand. Fenderson rocked back in his leather chair and spun a full circle. When he stopped turning and rocking back and forth, facing toward the Ranger, he wore a shocked look on his dead face and a bullet hole through his heart. A large circle of blood gathered around the gaping wound. Sam heard him make a gurgling sound, and watched him fall forward with a loud thump on the bullet-riddled desk.

Rewards . . . Sam shook his head.

Walking back around the desk, leaving the way he'd come in, he raised a leg and slipped out the window. As he touched ground outside, he looked around and was surprised to see a one-horse buggy sitting beside Black Pot, who stood waiting, his reins hanging to the ground. Inside the buggy sat Adele and Lang.

"Ranger!" said Lang with relief, lowering the rifle he held in his hands.

"Yes, Cisco," the Ranger said. He walked over to the stallion, picked up his reins and laid them over his saddle. "Were you expecting someone else?"

Lang slumped in the driver's seat.

"I don't know what I was expecting," Lang said. He passed the rifle over to Adele, who uncocked it for him and put it away.

"I thought you were getting those wounds taken care of," Sam said, noting all of the bloody bullet nicks on Lang's body, bandanas tied around his limbs here and there, a patch of blood on his side.

"I didn't know what you'd find out here,"

Lang said. "I followed you from behind Number Five." He paused, not saying whether or not he'd seen the Ranger let Oldham Coyle ride away. "I thought I'd come out, see this thing through with you." He gestured at the bullet nicks and cuts on the Ranger. "Besides, it looks like you could use some patching up yourself."

"I'll get it," Sam said. "We'll ride back together."

"Good," said Lang. "I don't like being around Clow Dankett alone. I think he's crazy."

"Crazy enough to be sheriff?" Sam asked, stepping up into his saddle. "Because that's what I'm going to recommend to the town, soon as he's able."

Lang seemed to consider it, then said, "Yeah, he's crazy enough for that." Adele had sat beside him quietly, but as they turned the rig and Sam turned his stallion, she and Lang looked at each other cautiously.

"Ranger, Harvey doesn't want me to say this, but I'd like to say it anyway . . . ," she said, as if asking permission.

"Speak your piece, ma'am." Sam smiled slightly to himself and nodded, staring ahead toward New Delmar.

"We—that is *I*," Adele said, "am wondering. Considering what Harvey did, helping you, might you mention something about it to the judge . . . maybe see if it would get him a lighter sentence?"

"Adele," Lang said quietly. "I didn't do what I did to get myself a break. I did it because it was right."

"Why don't you keep quiet, Cisco Lang?" the Ranger said over his shoulder. "The woman's trying to help you here."

Lang fell silent. So did Adele for a moment. But only for a moment.

"Well, would you, Ranger?" she ventured. "Talk to the judge, that is?"

"I don't know," Sam said. "Does this mean no more holding the horses during robberies while your thieving pards rob places?"

"Yes, it does," said Lang. "Besides, I'm through with that life any way it goes. No more thieving pards for me. I've made some promises to Adele, and to myself. I intend to keep them."

After another pause, Adele said to Sam, "So, would you, then?"

"No," Sam said. "I'm not going to talk to a judge about it, take a chance on him saying no." They rode on for a long second, the Ranger feeling the dark cloud of disappointment set in upon them. "Today, I appear to be judge and jury. So I'm setting you free, Harvey Cisco Lang," he said officiously.

Another silence set in.

"You mean . . . ?" Lang said, his words trailing.

"You're free, Cisco," Sam said, still staring ahead. "That's as clear as I can make it. Get yourself patched up and get on out of here."

"Oh my God, oh *my God!*" Adele said tearfully as the realization set in.

"I better never hear you've broken another law," Sam warned.

"You won't hear it," Lang said shakily. Seeing Sam turn and give him a look, he added quickly, "I mean, I *won't break the law,* I swear it."

"Good," said the Ranger. "Now, why don't you two ride on ahead, tell Deputy Dankett I'm on my way? Get the doctor to fix you up."

"Are you all right, Ranger?" Lang asked.

"I'm all right," Sam said. "Get on out of here."

As the buggy rolled away, Sam veered Black Pot to the side out of the dust and patted the stallion's damp withers.

"Did we do right?" he said, as if the big stallion might offer an opinion. Then he straightened in the saddle and rode Black Pot forward at a walk, looking side to side, at an artist's pallet of sandy colors streaking across distant hill lines, broken ledges and high-rising hoodoos, the land a-dance in wild desert sunlight.

"Yes, I believe you're right," he said quietly to the stallion, as if having asked for such sage and silent equestrian advice, he was now obliged to accept it. Black Pot twitched his ears at the sound of the Ranger's voice and lifted his muzzle toward things unseen. And the two rode on.

Arizona Ranger Sam Burrack is back!
Don't miss a page of action from America's
most exciting Western author, Ralph
Cotton.

RED MOON

Badlands, Arizona Territory

Young Ranger Samuel Burrack lay atop a mammoth boulder overlooking a stretch of spiny hills skirting the Mexican border northwest of the Nogales badlands outpost. A storm was hard blowing. Through the lens of an outstretched telescope he studied three watery figures while raindrops crawled sidelong across the circling lens. To his right lightning twisted and curled in a gunmetal mist on the distant curve of the earth.

"Tormenta mala de viento—ciclón!" an old stable hostler had warned him two days earlier when the sky over Nogales had taken on a pallid yellow-gray and the hot desert wind began sucking southward like some terrible demon drawing in its breath. "Here is the stillness before the terrible storm," the man had warned in stiff English, raising a crooked cautioning finger. "The longer the stillness, the more terrible the storm," he'd added, lowering his voice as if such information was privy only between himself and the Ranger.

Sam had simply nodded in reply. Storm or no storm, he had a job to do. Weather was just a factor to acknowledge, but not a factor to concede to.

He'd thought of the old man when the stillness lingered throughout that day and part of the next as he'd pushed on. He'd kept watch on the sky for what good it did him—watched it gather and loom until at last a roiling blackness rose up from the bowels of the earth and robbed the morning of its light, falling upon the earth as if in vengeance.

"Good prediction, *hombre*," Sam reminded himself with no real surprise, reflecting on the old hostler's conversation from two days ago.

Before leaving town he had said, *"Gracias,"* to the old man for his warning as he unrolled his brown rain slicker and put it on. With his big Colt resting on his hip, protected beneath the slicker, he'd tied down his bedroll atop his saddlebags and stepped up into the roan's saddle, spreading the tails of his long rain slicker down the horse's sides. He'd reminded the hostler that *bad* weather did not stop *bad* men, and the old Mexican had shrugged his thin shoulders either in sympathy or resignation and stood watching as the Ranger turned to ride away.

"Go with God . . . ," the old man had whispered in Spanish, seeing the Ranger's headstrong surplus roan balk and sidle and shuffle on its hooves.

"Always . . . ," the Ranger had replied, tipping a gloved hand as he'd gathered the unruly roan beneath himself and chucked the animal forward. The roan snorted and grumbled in protest, but did the Ranger's bidding all the same. And so their journey had gone.

Bad men and *lawmen* . . . Sam thought now in retrospect, holding a tight focus on the three faces beneath their wet wind-bent hat brims. They tugged and tightened their drenched hats down against a hard blow of wind, the loose tails of their rain slickers wagging and flapping wildly, like the tongues of a gaggle of lunatics. He might say that at times like this neither lawman nor outlaw had sense enough to get in out of the rain. But that wasn't being fair to his own profession—his brothers in arms.

Lawmen endured bad weather because their work required it.

Outlaws, murderers and rogues of the kind he pursued played out their hands fast and loose, with no regard for weather or anything else. He suspected that deep down the lawless realized the broad possibility of each day being their last, and he understood their thinking. It gave lawmen like himself little choice but to follow the lead set forth by their miscreant prey, no matter the climate, no matter the trail.

And that's the whole of it . . .

He drew a closer focus and moved from face to face on the subjects in the small round frame of the wet lens. He could see their lips moving. An arm pointed off toward the trail, rising and falling out of sight across a sandy stretch of squat cactus and scarce patches of spindly wild grass standing cowed beneath the gray blowing deluge. The arm belonged to the group's leader, Wilson Orez, and had Sam not known it already, he would have deduced it, seeing how these other two appeared to listen to the man, nodding in agreement, checking the wet rifles in their hands while Orez raised a wadded bandanna and mopped blow-in rain from the side of his neck, his beard stubble.

Wilson Orez . . .

From what the Ranger had learned of the man, Orez was tough, smart and fearless—a former cavalry scout, desert seasoned, a man trained to keeping a cool head while sudden death lurked all around him. Sam ran down a mental list he'd compiled on him. Wilson Orez was part Scots-Irish, part White Mountain Apache. His skill with a rifle was unsurpassed. He was both fast and accurate with a handgun— an expert with a knife. He had faced the feared Apache warrior, TaChima from the Compa clan, brother to the dreaded Apache leader, Juan Compa.

You know your history when it comes to killing, Sam reminded himself grimly.

In a straight up knife fight, toe to toe, *mano a mano*, Orez had killed TaChima graveyard dead. Sam considered it, finding it noteworthy how these sorts of facts sprang so readily to his mind.

Part of the job, he decided, dismissing the matter, going on with his thoughts.

TaChima had earned the alternate calling of Red Sleeve, a title originated years earlier by the famed Mimbreño Apache leader, Mangas Coloradas.

Being a Red Sleeve Warrior put TaChima at a high position of respect among all the Chihenne warriors in the Animas Mountain range. TaChima had not been a man to take lightly, Sam acknowledged. Yet, according to the story generated among

Captain Edmond Shirland's California Volunteers, Wilson Orez tracked TaChima into the heart of Apacheria, the People's stronghold.

Standing alone, naked save for a loincloth and a knife in hand, Wilson Orez had cast a challenge of honor for the sake of blood vengeance—a matter of powerful medicine among the killer elite of the Apacheria alliance. Thereupon he had calmly, methodically gutted and all but quartered the dreaded bladesman as if he were some sacrificial steer.

And that's the man you're after today. . . .

But he's older now, Sam thought in reply. He lowered the lens from his eye in the heavily blowing rain and thought about it as he wiped a wet gloved hand across his face. At the end of this storm there wouldn't be a hoofprint left to follow between here and the border. He raised the telescope back to his eye and honed down onto the three figures. Thunder split the sky high above the low-hanging blackness.

Stay close, he told himself. Whatever moves these men made, he'd have to be prepared to make them with them. *No matter the climate, no matter the trail . . . ,* he repeated to himself. *Stay close and at the same time try to keep a man as trail-savvy as Orez from knowing he was there.* Lightning glittered as he looked closely back and forth at the faces of the other two men. There was something at work between these two—something secretive. He could see it in their eyes. Were he in any way a friend or associate of Wilson Orez, he would have to warn him to watch out for these two. But that was none of his concern.

Another thing: Forget Wilson Orez's reputation, he reminded himself. Having too much respect for a bad man's reputation was as dangerous as having too little. Either would get you killed. Besides, if there was one thing he learned *quick* out here, it was that a man's reputation was almost always larger, more powerful than the man. Leastwise, enough so that the prowess of the man lived on long after the man himself had gone to dust.

But not Wilson Orez, a voice cautioned inside his head.

Stop it, the same voice rebuked. His hands tightened around the lens.

As he grappled with his thoughts, he saw Orez step into view, blocking the face of one of the men. No sooner had Orez stepped into sight than he stepped back out. When the Ranger saw the other man's face again, he saw a red line of gushing blood spewing from the man's sliced open throat.

Whoa . . . ! He hadn't expected that.

Sam tensed, watching through the circling lens as the man's wet gloved hands clamped up over his throat, attempting to stay the flow of arterial blood. But the reflex didn't help. The dark blood jetted from between his gripping fingers as he staggered forward into the mud and blowing rain. His wet hat came loose and flew from his head in a spiraling spray of water.

Sam watched; the surprise of the brutal act was gone now, yet the intensity of it held him captivated until he swung the lens onto Orez to see what was coming next.

Gray rain blew howling across the land between the Ranger's lens and the grizzly scene of silent carnage. Wilson Orez had moved fast.

By the time the sheet of rain had blown on and the Ranger had Orez back in focus, he saw the other man had bowed forward at the waist. Orez gave a hard sidelong jerk on the handle of his big knife, and Sam saw the blade slip out of the man's abdomen where Orez had just then buried it to the hilt. At the man's side, a big Remington revolver fell from his wet hand into the mud at his feet. The man sank to his knees, then flopped forward, face-first with a muddy splash.

Orez stepped back, and red blood washed from his knife blade, turning lighter, thinner in the rain. Sam turned and scanned the telescope to where ten feet away the man with the gaping throat had struggled along as far as he could and appeared to melt down into the ground.

Two down, one to go . . .

Marking the spot in his mind with a close-by stand of rain-whipped juniper, Sam closed the telescope between his wet hands and slipped it inside his slicker. Picking up his Winchester from beside him, he slid back on his belly to the edge of the boulder and down its side to where the surplus roan stood waiting. The horse appeared annoyed and restless, hitched to the spiky remnants of a weathered pinyon. As Sam shoved the wet rifle down into the saddle boot, the roan grumbled and nickered and tossed its head against its tied reins. A forehoof splashed down hard in a puddle of water.

"Hope I haven't kept you from anything pressing," Sam said wryly, unhitching the exasperated animal. The roan was one of three horses making up the Nogales outpost's surplus riding stock he'd had to choose from. His personal stallion, Black Pot, was still recovering from a pulled tendon he'd picked up during their previous venture across the Mexican border.

The roan snorted and raised a threatening rear hoof. Sam ignored the gesture and patted its wet withers.

"I know . . . ," he said quietly. He stepped up into the saddle as if they were longtime friends. Before the roan could organize itself enough to offer resistance, he'd backed it a step, collected it firmly beneath him and nudged it forward through the mud. "I know . . . ," he repeated. "You're a tough fellow. Now let's go."

The roan settled as if satisfied it had made its position clear and rode on, taking up a steady gait, the Ranger riding easy, his hand drawn loosely on the reins. With the horse's head lowered sidelong against the blow of wind, he'd only managed to get halfway across the rolling terraced land before the constant slam of wind and water and the lack of visibility forced him to step down from his saddle, draw his rifle and lead the roan the rest the way.

When he did reach the place where the killings had taken place, he came upon the spot all at once, the powerful thrust of the storm waning for a moment to reveal the juniper bush. The slant of the rain corrected itself and fell straight and steadily. He stood in the silver-gray mist like some supplicant to the dark sky churning above him. Rifle in hand, he stared through a braided stream of water running steadily from the lowered front brim of his sombrero.

Fifteen feet in front of him, the juniper bush was stooped and dripping. Beyond the juniper, pipe organ cactus stood erect like lean apparitions in a low swirling mist. Sam looked around at the sodden ground expecting to find the bodies of the two men. Yet, only mildly surprised, he found no sign of the hapless thieves except for the dropped Remington and two watery pink puddles lying in the indentations where the two had fallen and the rain had not completely washed the blood away.

He looked at the watery hoofprints, barely visible now in the falling rain. Each set showed signs of equal weight on their backs. Stooping, he picked up the black-handled Remington and inspected it. The initials TQ were carved into the right side of the handles.

You loaded the bodies up and sent them off. Sam spoke to himself as if he was speaking to Wilson Orez. "Wise move, Orez." He shoved the Remington behind his slicker into his gun belt. "You're a cautious man," he murmured aloud, still searching the rolling land while the wind rebuilt and groaned and came hurling back across the land in a low, menacing roar.

Even in a storm Orez had raised any pursuer's chance of following him, no matter how briefly, from a sure thing to the slimmer odds of one out of three.

The wind passed and started to build again as he noted the three sets of hoofprints disappearing in three separate directions before being lost to the pounding deluge altogether.

Standing behind him the roan grumbled and sawed its head against its reins, feeling the rain lashing sideways once again. Lightning sprang up anew and writhed in place, followed by another deep rumble of thunder. The roan whinnied and shied.

"Easy, boy, easy . . ." he said to the horse, jerking firmly on the reins, settling the animal. He stood staring out into a distant swirl of silver-gray until the rain slashed in horizontally again and obscured even that.

Still he stood with his slicker tails twisted and flapping sidelong, the brim of his sombrero pressed straight up on one side. He considered Wilson Orez, trying to sketch out a better picture of the man, this man he was sent to stop— *to kill*, he corrected. He'd seen enough to realize *killing* was the only thing that would stop Wilson Orez. He'd watched two men fall in their own blood as the silent scene played itself out beneath the rumble and roar of the storm. Orez was cautious and deadly, a man who killed quick, kept moving and left little behind to follow.

"So, this is how it is with you . . ." he said quietly out to the dark swirling firmament. In reply, lightning and thunder cracked and exploded all along the far curve of the earth.

"All right, then," he said, clearing all slates, settling all accounts past or present in preparation for what lay at hand. He felt the big Remington cold and wet on his belly beneath his slicker as he pushed forward against the wind, pulling the roan behind him. "You best stay up with me, horse," he cautioned over his shoulder, "Orez might just eat you before it's over."

The roan sawed its wet head in protest, but followed, mane and tail wind-whipped, slinging water.